"Time's always been the problem, Willie," Hoke said. "When we get a chance we work on old cases, but a new dead body is found damned near every day in a car trunk, a tomato field, an apartment—"

"I'm not finished, Hoke. Time is what I'm going to give you. The three of you are going to get two full months to do nothing but work on these fifty cold cases I picked out."

"Three months," Henderson said, "would be better."

"I know," Brownley smiled. "And six months would be better than three months, but you've got two."

CHARLES WILLEFORD

"No one writes a better crime novel...."
Elmore Leonard

NEW HOPE
FOR THE
Dead

CHARLES WILLEFORD

BALLANTINE BOOKS • NEW YORK

Library of Congress Catalog Card Number: 85-10067

ISBN 0-345-33839-1

This edition published by arrangement with St. Martin's Press

Manufactured in the United States of America

First Ballantine Books Edition: January 1987
Second Printing: May 1988

To Betsy and the boys

"Man's unhappiness stems from his
inability to sit quietly
in his room."

—Pascal

"CRAP," Sergeant Hoke Moseley told his partner, "is the acronym for finding your way around Miami." He glanced at Ellita Sanchez as he shifted down to second gear, and waited for her to nod.

She should know that much already, having been a police dispatcher for seven years, so there was no need to explain that *C* stood for courts, *R* for roads, *A* for avenues, and *P* for places. It didn't always hold true that courts, roads, avenues, and places all ran north and south. Sometimes they looped in semicircles and wild arabesques, especially the roads.

Hoke's major problem with Ellita was making conversation. He never knew exactly what to tell her or what to take for granted, even though he was the sergeant and she was the new partner. She seemed to know almost every-thing he told her already, and she had only been in the Homicide Division for four months. Some of the things Hoke knew from experience and had tried to explain to her—like the fact that junkies sometimes rubbed Prepara-tion H on their track marks to reduce the swelling—she knew already. CRAP was one of those oddities that very few cops knew about, and he really hadn't expected her to say, "I know."

Perhaps, he thought, her two-year A.S. degree in police science at Miami-Dade Community College was actually worth the time and money she had invested in it. At any rate, she was getting more sensitive to his moods. She just nodded now, instead of saying "I know," and this had begun to irritate him visibly. And something else was both-ering Sanchez. Her pretty golden face was more somber lately, and she no longer smiled as broadly in the mornings as she had at first. Her quiescent moodiness had been going on for more than a week now. At first, Hoke had attributed it to her period—if that's what it was—but a week was a long time. How long did a period last? Well, whatever it was that was bothering her, it hadn't affected her work. Yet.

One thing Hoke knew for sure: He hadn't done anything to offend her. If anything, he had bent over backward to make her an *equal* partner—subject to his directions, of course. He almost always explained why he was doing something. But Sanchez was, first of all, a woman, and she was also a Latin, so perhaps there were some sexual and cultural differences here and he would never really know what was on her mind.

Sometimes, though, when he wanted to make a humor-ous comment, the way he had with his old partner, Bill Henderson, and then took a look at her, with those huge tits looking voluptuous and maternal in the loose silk blouses she always wore, he held his tongue. Having a female partner in the car instead of Bill wasn't the same. Maybe he should let Sanchez drive the car once in a while. But that didn't seem right either. The man always drove, not the woman, although when he and Bill had been together, Bill had driven most of the time because he was a better driver than Hoke, and they both knew it. For all Hoke knew, Ellita Sanchez was a better driver than either Bill or himself.

Tomorrow, then, maybe he'd let her drive—see how it worked out . . .

"The next street," Sanchez said, pointing to the green-and-white sign, "is Poinciana Court."

"Yeah." Hoke laughed. "And it's running east and west."

They were looking for an address in Green Lakes, a Miami subdivision built during the housing boom of the mid-1950s when the developer was looking for young families with small children, for Korean war veterans with $500 saved for a down payment and jobs that paid them enough to afford a $68-a-month house payment. These had all been $10,000 houses then, with thirty-year fixed mortgages at $5^{1}/_{2}$ percent interest. That wasn't expensive, even then, for a three-bedroom, one-bathroom house. Today, however, these same houses in Green Lakes, now thirty years old, were selling for $86,000 and more, and at 14 percent interest rates. Many similar housing areas in Miami, depending upon their locations, were slums now—but not Green Lakes. The wide curving streets and avenues, named as well as numbered, were lined with tall ficus trees and Australian pines. There were "sleeping policemen," painted yellow, every hundred yards or so, road bumps that didn't let a driver get into high gear. Many owners, as they prospered, had added bathrooms, "Florida rooms"—glass-enclosed porches—garages, and carports, and most of the homes, if not all, had their backs and new Florida rooms facing

3

man-made square lakes, with water the color of green milk. The lakes were originally rock and sand quarries, and much too dangerous for swimming (at least a dozen people had drowned before the Green Lakes Homeowners' Association had banned swimming altogether), but the lakes had Dade County pines and jogging paths around their borders, and in the evenings there would usually be a cooling breeze sweeping across the water.

As neighborhoods go, Green Lakes was a nice place to live.

The subdivision was close enough to Hialeah for most shopping purposes, but far enough away to avoid the Latin influx, and still much too expensive for a lot of black families. These conditions would all change with time, of course, but when they did the houses would probably appreciate to $100,000, and variable interest rates would be sitting in the low twenties. The residents who lived in Green Lakes now were lucky, and they knew it. The crime rate was low because of an effective Crime Watch program; there hadn't been a homicide in this subdivision for more than two years.

Hoke spotted the blue-and-white squad car parked in front of the house. The hatless harness officer was leaning against a ficus tree at the curb, smoking a cigarette and talking to two teenage girls. The girls, wearing tank tops, jeans and running shoes, kept their ten-speed bikes between themselves and the cop. As Hoke pulled to a stop behind the police car, the radio in the blue-and-white crackled. Aggressive birds sang back from the trees, and sprinklers whirred on a nearby lawn. A few houses down, a dog barked from behind closed doors.

As Hoke and Sanchez got out of the car, the officer, a Latin with square-cut sideburns down to and even with his dark eyes, moved away from the tree and told the two girls to get moving. They rode away for about a hundred yards, stopped and looked back.

4

"Sergeant Moseley," Hoke said. "Homicide." He glanced at the officer's nameplate. "Where's your hat, Garcia?"

"In the car."

"Put it on. You're under arms, you're supposed to be covered."

Garcia got his hat from the car and put it on. The hat looked two sizes too small resting on his abundance of black curly hair. He looked ridiculous in the small cap with its scuffed visor, and Hoke could see why the man didn't want to wear it. On the other hand, he could also get a decent haircut.

"Where's the decedent?" Hoke asked.

"In the house. Officer Hannigan's inside."

Sanchez started toward the house. Hoke indicated the two girls who were inching back, pushing their bikes. "Don't let a crowd gather. Before long, gapers'll show up, so keep 'em across the street."

Officer Hannigan, a rangy blonde in her early twenties with purple eye makeup and coral lipstick, opened the door before Hoke and Sanchez reached the front porch. She had licked or gnawed most of the lipstick from her long lower lip.

"Don't you have a hat either?" Hoke said.

"It's in the car." She flushed. "Besides, Sergeant Roberts said it was optional whether we wore hats or not."

"No," Hoke said, "it's not an option. Any time you're wearing a sidearm, you'll keep your head covered. If you want me to, I'll explain the reasons why to Sergeant Roberts."

"I'd rather you didn't."

"Where's the decedent?"

"Down the hall, in the small bedroom across from the master bedroom. We didn't go into the room, but I looked

5

at it—the boy, I mean—from the door. He's an OD all right, and was DOA as reported.''

"That's very helpful, Hannigan. Let's go into the dining area, and we'll see what else you can tell us.''

The living room, except for two squashy, lemon-colored beanbag seats, was furnished with antique-white rattan furniture, with yellow Haitian cotton cushions on the couch, the armchair, and the ottoman. There were vases of freshly cut daisies on three low, white Formica-topped tables. The beige burlap draperies were closed, and three circular throw rugs, the same color as the draperies, were spaced precisely on the waxed terrazzo floor. The dining area, which held a round Eames pedestal table and four matching chairs, was curtainless. The open vertical Levolors filled the room with bright morning sunlight. A blue bowl in the center of the table held a half-dozen Key limes.

"All right,'' Hoke said, as he sat at the table, "report.''

'Report?''

"Report.'' Hoke took a limp package of his specially cut-short Kools out of his jacket pocket, looked at it for a moment and then put it back. Sanchez, unsmiling, stared at the young woman but did not sit down. Hannigan clutched her handbag with both hands and cleared her throat.

"Well, we received the call on the DOA at oh-seven-thirty. I was driving, and we started right over. There was a mix-up, I guess, and at Flagler we got another call to abort. But just a few minutes later, before I could find a turnaround, we were told to continue.''

"Do you know why?''

"No. They didn't say.''

"There was a boundary dispute, that's why. A block away, on Ficus Avenue, the Hialeah boundary begins. So at first they thought the DOA should go to Hialeah instead of Miami. But after they rechecked the map, Miami won the body. We would have preferred, naturally, to give it to Hialeah.''

Hoke took out his notebook and ballpoint. ''Who discovered the decedent?''

''The boy's mother, Mrs. Hickey. That's Loretta B. Hickey. She's divorced, and lives here alone with her son.''

''What's the dead child's name?''

''He isn't a child. He's a young man, nineteen or twenty, I'd say, offhand.''

''You said 'boy' before. How old are you, Hannigan?''

''Twenty-four.''

''How long you been a police officer?''

''Since I graduated from Miami-Dade.''

''Don't be evasive.''

''Two years. Almost two years.''

''Where's the mother?''

''Now?''

''If you keep twisting the strap on your handbag, you'll break it.''

''Sorry.''

''Don't be sorry; it's your purse. The boy's mother.''

''Oh. She's next door with a neighbor. Mrs. Koontz. The young man's name is . . . was Jerry Hickey. Gerald, with a *G*.''

Hoke wrote the information in his notebook. ''Has the father been notified?''

''I don't know. Joey, Officer Garcia, didn't notify anyone, and neither did I. Mrs. Koontz might've called him. But we were just told to—''

''Okay. Unlatch that death grip on your purse and dump the contents on the table.''

''I don't have to do that!'' She looked at Sanchez for support, but Sanchez's disinterested expression didn't change. ''You have no right to—''

"That's an order, Hannigan."

Hannigan hesitated for a moment, chewing some more on her lower lip. With a shrug, she emptied the handbag on the table. Hoke poked through the contents with his ballpoint, separating items that ranged from a half-empty package of Velamints to three wadded balls of used tissues. He picked up the ostrich-skin wallet. Tucked between a MasterCard plate and Hannigan's voter's registration card, in a plasticene card case, were two tightly folded one-hundred-dollar bills.

"That's my money," she said. "I won it at Jai alai last night."

"Did Garcia win, too?"

"Yes! Yes, he did. We went together."

"Sit down." Hoke indicated the chair across the table as he got to his feet. "Put your stuff back in your purse."

Hoke opened the front door and beckoned to Garcia. As Garcia ambled toward him, Hoke fanned the two bills in his left hand, and extended his right. "Let me see your share, Garcia."

Garcia hesitated, his brown face mantling with anger.

"He wants to see our Jai alai winnings!" Hannigan called shrilly from the dining area.

Garcia handed over his wallet. Hoke found eight one-hundred-dollar bills, folded and refolded into a tight square, behind the driver's license.

"That what you call an even split, Garcia? Eight for you, and only two for Hannigan?"

"Well—I found it, not Hannigan."

"Where?"

"In plain sight, on top of the dresser. I—I didn't touch nothing else."

"You and Hannigan are assholes. Stealing a ten-dollar bill is one thing, but don't you think Mrs. Hickey would miss a thousand bucks and scream to the department?"

8

Garcia looked away. "We—we figured the two of us could just deny it."

"Sure. The way you did with me. Ever been interrogated by an Internal Affairs investigator?"

"No."

"You're lucky then you didn't try to lie to me. Now hustle your ass next door and get Mrs. Hickey. Bring her back over here."

"What—what about the money?"

"The money's evidence."

"What I mean, what about me and—?"

"Forget about it. Try and learn a lesson. That's all."

Hoke returned to the dining area. "Hannigan, we're going to examine the body. While we're in the bedroom we can't watch the silverware and you, too, so go back to your car and listen to the radio."

The concrete-block-and-stucco house had three bedrooms and one bathroom. Two of the bedrooms were half the size of the master bedroom. The bathroom could be entered from the hallway, and also from the master bedroom. At the back of the house there was also a Florida room that could serve as a second living room, with glass jalousies on three sides. The back lawn sloped gently to the square milky lake. A sliding glass door led from the master bedroom to the Florida room, and across the hall from the larger bedroom was the spartan room occupied by the dead Gerald Hickey.

Mrs. Hickey's bedroom held a round, unmade king-sized bed, with a half-dozen pillows and an array of long-legged nineteenth-century dolls. There was a pink silk chaise longue, a maple highboy with a matching dresser and vanity table, and a backless settee. The vanity table, with three mirrors, was littered with unguents, cold creams, and other cosmetics. The round bed was a tangle of crumpled Laura Ashley sheets in a floral pattern not observed in nature,

9

with a wadded lavender nightgown-and-peignoir combination at the foot of the bed.

Sanchez picked up one of the long-legged dolls. Hoke sniffed the anima of the owner—Patou's Joy, perspiration, cold cream, bath powder, soap, and stale cigarette smoke.

"You ever notice," he said, "how a woman's room always smells like the inside of her purse?"

"Nope." Sanchez dropped the doll on the bed. "But I've noticed that a man's bedroom smells like a YMCA locker room."

"When were you"—Hoke started to say "inside a man's bedroom" but caught himself—"inside the Y locker room."

"When I was on patrol, a long time ago. Some kid claimed he'd been raped in the shower." She shrugged. "But nothing ever came of the investigation. No doubt someone cornholed him, but we figured he claimed rape because the other kid wouldn't pay him. It became a juvenile matter, and I was never called to court."

"How long were you on the street?"

"Just a little over three months. Then I spent a year guarding manholes all day so Southern Bell could hook up wires under the street. Then, because I was bilingual, they made me a dispatcher. Seven years listening to problems and doing nothing about them."

"Okay . . . let's take a look at the body. You can tell me what to do about *it*." Hoke closed the door to the master bedroom and they crossed the hallway.

Jerry Hickey, with his teeth bared in a frozen grin, was supine on a narrow cot. Except for his urine-stained blue-and-white shorts, he was naked. His arms hugged his sides, with the fingers extended, like the hands of a skinny soldier lying at attention. His feet were dirty, and his toenails hadn't been clipped in months. His eyes were closed. Hoke rolled back the left eyelid with a thumb. The iris was blue.

On a round Samsonite bridge table next to the bed there were three sealed plasticene bags of white powder and shooting paraphernalia—a Bic lighter, a silver spoon, and an empty hypodermic needle with the plunger closed. There was the butt of a hand-rolled cigarette in an ashtray, and three tightly rolled balls of blue tinfoil. Hoke put the butt, the tinfoil balls, and the square packets of powder into a Baggie, which he stuffed into the left-hand pocket of his poplin leisure-suit jacket. The right-hand pocket was lined with glove leather and already held several loose rounds of .38 tracer ammunition, his pack of short Kools, three packages of book matches, and two hard-boiled eggs in Reynolds wrap.

Hoke stepped back a pace and nodded to Ellita Sanchez. There was a knotted bandana tied around the dead man's upper left arm. She examined the arm without loosening the crude tourniquet and looked at the scabs on his arm. "Here's a large hole," she said, "but the other track marks look older."

"Sometimes they shoot up in the balls."

"You mean the scrotum, not in the balls." Sanchez, with some difficulty, pulled down the stained boxer shorts and lifted the man's testicles. There were a half-dozen scabs on the scrotum.

"This malnourished male," she said, "about eighteen or nineteen, is definitely a habitual user." She pointed to a row of splotchy red marks on the dead man's neck. "I don't know what these are. They could be thumb marks or love bites."

"When I was in school," Hoke said, smiling, "we called 'em hickeys. That's what we used to do in junior high in Riviera Beach. Two of us guys would grab a girl in the hall between classes, usually some stuck-up girl. While one guy held her, the other guy would suck a couple of

11

splotches onto her neck. Then"—Hoke laughed—"when the girl went home, it was her problem to explain to her parents how she got 'em."

"I don't get it." Sanchez appeared to be genuinely puzzled. "Why would you do something like that?"

"For fun." Hoke shrugged. "We were young, and it seemed like a fun thing to do to some stuck-up girl."

"Nothing like that ever happened at Shenandoah Junior High here in Miami. Not that I know of, anyway. I saw girls with hickeys at Southwest High, but I don't think any of them were put there by force."

"You Latin girls lead a sheltered life. But the point I'm trying to make is, these marks look like hickeys to me."

"Maybe so. From the smile on his face, he died happy."

"That's not a smile, that's a rictus. A lot of people who aren't happy to die grin like that."

"I know, Sergeant, I know. Sorry, I guess I shouldn't joke about it."

"Don't apologize, for Christ's sake. I don't know how to talk to you sometimes."

"Why not try talking to me like I'm your partner," Ellita said, compressing her lips. "And I didn't like that crack about my sheltered life, either. Growing up in Miami and eight years in the department, I don't even know what sheltered means. I realize I'm still inexperienced in homicide work but I've been a cop for a long time."

"Okay, partner." Hoke grinned. "What's this look like to you?"

"This is just an overdose, isn't it?"

"It looks that way." Hoke closed his fingers and made tight fists, reaching for something that wasn't there. He crossed to the closet. A pair of faded jeans and a white, not very clean, short-sleeved *guayabera* were draped over the closet door. Hoke went through the pockets of the shirt and pants and found three pennies, a wallet, and a folder of Holiday Inn matches. He added these items to the Baggie and then looked at the top of the dresser against the wall. There was no suicide note in the room, either on the card table or on the dresser, but there were two twenties and a ten on the dresser top.

Hoke pointed at the money without touching it. "See this? Amateurs. Our two fellow police officers left fifty bucks. A professional thief would've taken all of it. But an amateur, for some reason, hardly ever takes it all. It's like the last cookie in the jar. If there'd been twenty-two bucks on the dresser, they'd have left two."

Hoke added the bills to the stack of hundreds and handed the money to Sanchez. "Later on, when you write the report, lock all this dough in my desk. I'll get it back to Mrs. Hickey later."

The top dresser drawer contained some clean shorts and T-shirts, and a half-dozen pairs of socks. The other drawers were empty except for dust. The narrow closet held a dark blue polyester suit, still in its plastic bag from the cleaners, two blue work shirts, and one white button-down shirt on hangers. There were no neckties. There were no letters or other personal possessions. The only clue to the dead man's activities was the book of matches from the Holiday Inn—but there were two dozen Holiday Inns in the Greater Miami area, with two more under construction.

Hoke was puzzled. If there had been a suicide note, Mrs. Hickey could have found it and flushed it down the john. That happened frequently. A family almost always thought there was a stigma of some kind to a suicide, as if they, in some way, would be blamed. But this didn't look like a suicide. This kid, with a thousand bucks and more heroin to shoot up with when he awoke, should have been a very happy junkie. It was, in all probability, an accidental overdose, perhaps from stronger heroin than Jerry was used to taking. One less junkie, that was all.

But Hoke still wasn't satisfied.

"Take a look in the bathroom," Hoke said to Sanchez. "I'll call the forensic crew."

Hoke called Homicide from a white wall phone in the kitchen. The OIC of the forensic crew would inform the medical examiner, who would either come out or wait at the morgue. In either case, there would be an autopsy.

Hoke lit a Kool, being careful not to inhale, and went outside. The two girls with the bicycles had disappeared. Hannigan, wearing her cap, sat in the front seat of the police car with the door open. Hoke wondered what was holding up Garcia and Mrs. Hickey. He cut across the lawn. As he stepped through a break in the Barbados cherry hedge between the two yards, the front door opened and Garcia came out, hanging on to a struggling, giggling woman. The woman's face was reddened and blotchy and streaked with tears. She had a fine slim figure and was taller than Garcia. Her wide-set cornflower-blue eyes were rolling wildly. She was, Hoke estimated, in her late thirties. She wore a pair of green cotton hip-huggers, a yellow terrycloth halter—exposing a white midriff and a deepset belly button—and a pair of tennis shoes without socks. Her long, honey-colored hair was tangled. She stopped giggling suddenly, raised her arms above her head, and slid through Garcia's encircling arms to the grass. With her legs spread, she sat there stubbornly, sobbing with determination.

"Where's your hat, Garcia?" Hoke said.

"I left it in the house. It fell off."

"Get it and put it on. When you wear a sidearm with a uniform, you're supposed to be covered at all times."

A short, matronly-looking woman with steel-gray hair edged shyly out of the doorway, making room for Garcia to reenter the house. She was wringing her hands, smiling, and her face was slightly flushed. She wore red shorts and a T-shirt. She was at least forty-five pounds overweight.

"It's all my fault, Lieutenant," she said. "But I didn't mean it."

"Sergeant, not lieutenant. Sergeant Moseley. Homicide. What's all your fault? Mrs. Koontz, isn't it?"

She nodded. "Mrs. Robert Koontz. Ellen."

"What's all your fault, Mrs. Koontz?"

"Lorrie—Mrs. Hickey—was very upset when she found Jerry dead. She came over here, so I thought it would be a good idea to give her a drink. To calm her down a little, you know. So before I called nine-eleven, I poured her a glass of Wild Turkey."

"How big a glass?"

"A water glass, I'm afraid."

"Did you put any water in it?"

"No. I didn't think she'd drink all of it, and she didn't. But she drank most of it, and then it hit her pretty hard. I don't think I've ever seen anyone ever get so smashed so quick." Mrs. Koontz giggled, and then put her fingers to her mouth. "I'm sorry, Sergeant, I really am."

"You should've put some water in with it."

Sanchez knelt on the grass beside Mrs. Hickey, and handed her a wadded tissue to wipe her face.

"Perhaps you and Officer Sanchez can get Mrs. Hickey back into your house?" Hoke said. "I can't talk to her that way. Put her to bed, and tell her I'll be back this evening. It'll be best to have her out of the way when the lab group gets here anyway."

"I'm really sorry about her condition—"

"Don't be. The world would look better if everybody drank a glassful of Wild Turkey in the morning."

Hoke signaled to Garcia, who had retrieved his hat from the house. They walked to the police car, and Mrs. Koontz and Sanchez helped the sobbing Loretta Hickey into Mrs. Koontz's house.

There were a dozen area residents standing across the street on the sidewalk. The neighbors, muttering to one another, stared at the two houses.

"Keep those people over there, Garcia," Hoke said. "I'll lock the back door, and you, Hannigan, can stay in the back yard to keep people from coming around to peep in the windows. You stay out front, Garcia, and don't answer any questions."

Hoke returned to the Hickey house and opened the refrigerator. There was no beer, but he settled for a glass of Gatorade, which he topped off with a generous shot of vodka from an opened bottle he found in the cabinet above the sink. He sat at the Eames table in the dining area, put his feet on another chair, and drank the Gatorade-and-vodka like medicine.

Sanchez returned to the house, sat across from Hoke, and made some notations in her notebook. "Except for some Dexedrine, and it was in a prescription bottle for Mrs. Hickey, there's nothing of interest in the bathroom. Hickey obviously hasn't taken a bath in some time, and Mrs. Hickey hasn't had time, I suppose, to take a shower this morning."

"We'll see how the P.M. goes, but it's probably a routine OD. I'll talk to Mrs. Hickey tonight, and we can work on the report tomorrow."

"You didn't have the right to make Hannigan dump her purse, Sergeant."

"That's right. I didn't."

"How'd you know she and Garcia took the money from the dresser?"

"I didn't. How could I know?"

"The way you acted. You seemed so positive."

"I just had a hunch, that's all."

16

"If she reports you, you'll be in trouble. I'm your partner, but I'm also a witness. It puts me—"

"Do you think she will?"

"No. It's just that . . ."

"Just that what?"

"If you hadn't found the money, you could've been in a jam. Or if they'd stuck to their phony story that they'd won the money at Jai alai, you—"

"In that case, I'd've turned it over to Internal Affairs. Then, when Mrs. Hickey reported the money missing, Garcia and Hannigan would've been suspended for an investigation. Sometimes a hunch pays off, and sometimes it doesn't. Pour yourself a Gatorade-and-vodka and relax."

"I don't drink," Sanchez said. "On duty."

"Neither do I. I'm taking the rest of the day off to look for a place to live. I'll take my car, and you can wait for forensic. Garcia can give you a ride back to the station in their car."

"We've got a meeting with Major Brownley at four-thirty."

Hoke finished his drink and grinned. "I know." He washed his glass at the kitchen sink and put the wet glass on the wooden dryer rack. "I'll see you then. But until then, I'm on comp time."

2

Although Miami is the largest of the twenty-seven municipalities that make up the Greater Miami area, it does not have the desirable, middle-class residential areas or the affordable neighborhoods that the smaller municipalities have. There are several expensive, up-scale neighborhoods, but very few policemen, even those with working wives, can afford these affluent enclaves. There are slum areas and black neighborhoods with affordable housing, but WASP policemen with families avoid them, as they avoid the housing in Little Havana.

When a neighborhood becomes black or Latin, Anglo policemen move out with their families. Latin cops prefer Little Havana and have no problem in finding decent housing for their extended families, but the middle-income housing where married WASP cops prefer to live is in short supply, now that Miami's population is more than 55 percent Latin. As a consequence, the Anglo family men in the department had moved out of the city to the burgeoning Kendall area, to suburban South Miami, to the giant condo complexes in North Miami, and to the new and affordable subdivisions in West Miami.

The city's policemen were required to carry their badges and weapons at all times, to be ready to make an off-hours arrest or assist an officer in trouble. But with so many men living out of town, few were actually available. It seemed logical to the new chief of police that if all thousand Miami police officers were living within the city limits, there would be a marked drop in the crime rate. There had in fact always been an official rule to this effect, that a cop had to reside within the city, but until the new chief had taken over it had never been enforced. Now, uncompromising deadlines had been established for all of the Miami police officers living in the other municipalities to move back to the city. To most cops, the rule was unreasonable and unfair, because many of them had purchased homes in the other communities. Many resigned rather than move back, and had little difficulty in finding new police jobs in their adopted municipalities, although most took a pay cut. Others, with too much time in the department to resign, left their families in the other cities and rented small, cramped apartments or moved in with their Miami relatives. Still others, after desperate searches, of course, found suitable housing.

The strict enforcement rule had resulted in the loss of more than a hundred officers, many of them highly competent veterans. Because of city budget problems, the department was already short more than 150 people, so the force was reduced to approximately 850 full-time policemen. With this personnel shortage, plus the difficulty in recruiting new minority policemen, who had a priority under the Affirmative Action plan, it now seemed imperative for the new chief to maintain the rule. The damage had been done, but at least most of the remaining cops now lived within the city limits and were available during their off-duty hours.

Hoke Moseley, however, had a special problem. As a sergeant, his annual salary was $34,000. For a single, divorced man, this should have been enough to live on fairly well in Miami. But because of the terms of his divorce settlement, Hoke had to send half of his salary— every other paycheck—to his ex-wife, who lived in Vero Beach, Florida. Ten years earlier, when Hoke had signed the agreement—which also gave his ex-wife, Patsy, the full-time custody of their two daughters—he had been willing to sign almost anything to get out of his untenable marriage. At the time of their separation, he had been living rent-free with a young advertising woman named Bambi in her two-bedroom condo in Coconut Grove, a desirable neighborhood within the city limits. But later on, after the divorce, and after he had broken up with Bambi, he realized how foolish he had been to agree to the pre-divorce settlement. He still had to pay the income tax on $34,000 out of the $17,000 he had left, plus paying out money for the pension plan, PBA dues, Social Security, and everything else. The everything else included medical expenses for his two daughters, and these bills had been costly over the years, especially dentists' and orthodontists' bills. Patsy also sent him the bills for the girls' new Easter and Christmas outfits, school clothes, and for the summer camp the girls liked to go to in Sebring, Florida, which included horseback riding— an extra fee. If Hoke had only had his own lawyer, instead of sharing Patsy's, and had opted for alimony instead of a pre-divorce settlement, he could have at least taken alimony payments off his income tax. But Patsy

20

had hired a sharp woman lawyer who had persuaded Hoke to sign the financial agreement.

After Bambi, he had been forced to live in cheap efficiency apartments, and he had even tried living in private homes with kitchen privileges. But he had gone deeper into debt as the years passed. He ran up large dental bills himself as his dentist tried vainly to save his teeth, but at last they were all extracted, and he was fitted with a complete set of grayish-blue dentures. These fragile-looking teeth were so patently false that they were the first thing people noticed about Hoke when they met him.

Two years earlier, before the department had been taken over by the new chief, Hoke had found a solution that had solved some of his financial problems. Howard Bennett, the owner-manager of the Eldorado Hotel, a seedy Art Deco establishment in South Miami Beach, had taken Hoke on as security officer. Hoke was given a rent-free two-room suite, and all he had to do was to spend his nights in the hotel, and most weekends. He had a view of Biscayne Bay and the Miami skyline from his window, and he could take the MacArthur Causeway into Miami and reach the downtown police station in fifteen minutes. Or less, depending upon the traffic. On the other hand, Miami Beach was not Miami, and Major Willie Brownley, the Homicide Division chief, had told Hoke to move back inside the city.

"It's imperative that you get out of the Eldorado as soon as possible," Major Brownley had told him. "Next to Coral Gables, South Beach probably has the highest crime rate in Dade County. And sooner or later, in that crummy neighborhood, you're going to get mixed up in a shooting or something and have to make an arrest. Then, when it comes out that you're a Miami cop, and not a Miami Beach cop, I'll be blamed because you aren't supposed to be living there in the first place."

"It's a quiet place, the Eldorado," Hoke had said. "Mostly retired Jewish ladies on Social Security."

"And Mariel refugees."

"Only five left now, Willie. I got rid of the troublemakers. But I'll get out. I just want to know how much time I've got, that's all."

"Two weeks. You've got comp days coming. Take a few days off, find a place to live, and get the hell out of there. You're the only man left in my division who hasn't got a Miami address."

"I've got a Miami address. Officially, my mail goes to Bill Henderson's house."

"But I know you're still living in the Eldorado."

"I'll be out in two weeks, Willie. Don't worry about it."

"I'm not worried. Two weeks, or you'll be suspended without pay till you're back in the city."

A week had gone by already, and Hoke still hadn't found a rent-free place to live. He had contacted several downtown hotels about the sort of arrangement he had with the Eldorado, but he had been turned down flat. The fleabag transient hotels downtown weren't suitable for Hoke. The better hotels wanted full-time security officers only and weren't willing to provide a free room to a part-time security officer with irregular hours—not when they could rent out the same room for seventy-eight dollars a night or more.

Maybe, Hoke thought, the Safe 'n' Sure Home-Sitting Service in Coconut Grove would be the solution. It was worth a try, and if it didn't work, he would have to find a room in a private house again, with kitchen privileges—some place with a private entrance. The way rents had increased in the last few years, he could no longer afford a cheap efficiency apartment: There were no *cheap* efficiencies. Once again, Hoke marveled at the brilliance of Patsy's lawyer. No specific sum of money had been mentioned in the divorce agreement. It stated merely that Hoke

22

would send every other paycheck, properly endorsed to Ms. Patsy Mayhew (his wife had resumed her maiden name), including any and all cost-of-living increments and raises. Ten years ago Hoke had been a patrolman earning $8,500 a year. He had lived much better, with Bambi, on half of that sum than he was living on now at $17,000. But ten years ago he had never dreamed, nor had any other police officer, that he—or even sergeants—would ever be paid $34,000 a year.

Who could have predicted it? On the other hand, his oldest daughter would be sixteen now, and his youngest fourteen. In two more years, his new lawyer told him, when his oldest daughter became eighteen, he would petition the court and see if he could change the arrangement. Patsy's salary (she had an executive job of some kind with a time-sharing hotel chain in Vero Beach) would also be taken into consideration by the judge—when the time came. But right now, his lawyer advised him, nothing could be done. Hoke would just have to live with the agreement he had so unwisely signed.

"Too bad," the lawyer had said, shaking his head. "I wish I'd been your attorney at the time. When a couple getting a divorce decides to share the same lawyer, he has two fools for his clients, but one of them is more foolish than the other. I would never have allowed you to sign such a dumb and binding agreement."

Hoke had more than an hour to kill before his appointment in Coconut Grove with the house-sitting service. It was too early for lunch, but he was starving. He stopped at a 7/Eleven, bought a grape Slurpee, and then ate his two hard-boiled eggs and slurped the Slurpee in his car in front of the store. This was his usual diet lunch, and it was as unsatisfactory as his diet breakfast, which called for two poached eggs and half of a grapefruit. He could get by on this diet fare all day, but could rarely stick to

23

it by nightfall. By the end of the day he was always too hungry to settle for the three ounces of roast beef and can of boiled spinach his diet called for, so he usually ate something that tasted good instead—like the Colonel's extra-crispy, with a couple of biscuits and gravy. But even so, Hoke had lost weight and was down to 182 pounds. He had given up a daily six-pack habit, and that had helped, but he felt deprived and resentful. He was also trying to quit smoking, in an effort to lower his blood pressure and save some money, but that was harder to do than it was to diet. Although, now that cigarettes cost $1.30 a pack, it made a man think twice before lighting up a cigarette worth six and a half cents. Hoke stubbed out his short Kool, put the butt in his shirt pocket for later, and drove to Coconut Grove.

Hoke parked on Virginia Street, not far from the Mayfair shopping complex, and put his police placard on top of the dashboard in lieu of dropping a quarter in the meter. The Safe 'n' Sure Home-Sitting Service, the outfit Hoke was looking for, was only a short distance away from the Mayfair's parking garage. Hoke had selected this agency from one of six display ads in the Yellow Pages. Not only was Coconut Grove a desirable place to live, but out here he might be lucky enough to get a residence with a swimming pool.

Ms. Beverly Westphal, the woman Hoke had talked with on the telephone, was on the phone again when Hoke came into her office. He was fifteen minutes early. A tinkly tocsin above the door announced his entrance. The small room—the front room of what was undoubtedly Ms. Westphal's private residence—looked more like a living room than an office. The first impression was reinforced by the round oak table that served as her desk. The desk held a metal tray and the remains of a pizza, as well as her telephone, nameplate, and a potted philodendron.

Ms. Westphal was about thirty, and she wore Gloria

Vanderbilt jeans, a black U-necked T-shirt with the word MACHO across the middle in white block letters, and green-and-red jogging shoes. A small pocket watch dangled from the T-shirt. She didn't wear a brassiere beneath the T-shirt, and her breasts had prolapsed. Her brown eyes were popped slightly, Hoke noticed as she hung up the phone. She was the kind of woman with whom Hoke would avoid eye contact if he happened to see one like her in a shopping center.

Ms. Westphal told Hoke to pull a chair up to the table.

"At least you're a WASP, Sergeant Moseley."

"Yes, and I'm not bilingual."

"That isn't important. I've got more Latin house sitters now than I can use, but there's a shortage of WASP sitters at present. There's a thousand-dollar security bond, and if you don't have a thousand dollars—"

"I don't have a thousand dollars."

"—I can get you a bond for a hundred in cash."

"I can raise that much."

Ms. Westphal summarized the situation for Hoke. Three years before, when white flight had begun in earnest, it was easy to move away from Miami. A house could still be sold for a handsome profit then, and the happy seller moved to Fort Lauderdale or Orlando or far enough north to avoid hearing any Spanish. But white flight had increased as the crime rate increased, especially after the influx of Castro's 125,000 Marielitos, and the newer and higher interest rates kept young couples from buying used homes. Nevertheless, the inflated prices were holding steady. A used home sold eventually, but instead of a quick turnover, sellers often had to wait for a year or more to find a buyer. But people who wanted to move away still moved, and if they couldn't sell their house or rent it, they needed someone to watch the empty residence to discourage burglary and vandalism.

Ms. Westphal had separate lists of homeowners. One

was a group that had moved and didn't want their houses to remain unoccupied while their agents were trying to sell them; the other was a shorter list of homeowners who wanted to take vacations of from two weeks to two months in North Carolina, and didn't want their houses left unoccupied. Homeowners on both lists paid her fifteen dollars a day for the service. Out of this amount, the sitter received five dollars a day. At the end of each two-week period, she gave the sitter seventy dollars in cash.

"If there's anything I hate," she said, "it's fooling around with all of that withholding tax and minimum-wage bullshit paperwork."

"I understand," Hoke said. "Using cash eases your paperwork burden, and the government's."

"Exactly. What d'you know about house plants?"

"I've never owned one."

"That's an important duty. You have to take care of the house plants. But the owners usually leave detailed instructions, so all you have to do is follow them."

"I can do that."

"What about dogs and cats?"

"Cats are okay. I lived with one once, but I've never owned a dog."

"Well, this place I'm sending you to has a dog that goes with it. You'll have to feed and water the dog as well as the house plants. The last five people I've sent out there have turned the place down. I don't understand what the problem is. None of them would say why they backed out. It may be the dog. But you, being a cop and all, should be able to handle a dog."

"As I told you on the phone, Ms. Westphal, I'll be coming and going at odd hours, so it's probably a good idea to have a dog on the place. I don't mind the dog."

"That's about it, then." Ms. Westphal handed Hoke her business card, with the address of the house scribbled on the back. "But if you tell me no, too, you'll have to give me a reason. Otherwise, I'm going to ask Mr. Ferguson to try another agency.''

"What is it? A house or an apartment?''

"It's a small house, but it's quite lovely. Two bedrooms, one bath, with a kidney-shaped pool in back. There are some orange trees, too, but you won't have to worry about the yard. Mr. Ferguson's got a gardener for that. You'll have to spend your nights there, but the fact that you come and go at different times is a plus. The house has a TV and air conditioning, but there are no nearby stores. You've got a car, haven't you?''

"A 1973 Le Mans, but it's got a new engine.''

"Good. I'm going out now myself, but I'll be back by two or two-thirty. Talk to Mr. Ferguson. Then come back here and we'll work out the bond arrangement and the contract.''

The mailbox on Main Highway had the number and Mr. Ferguson's name stenciled on it. There was a gravel driveway in a sigmoid loop, and the house was hidden completely from the road by palmettos and a thick stand of loblolly pines. As Hoke parked in front of the house, Mr. Ferguson, together with his dog, a bushy black-and-burnt-orange Airedale, came out of the house. The moment Hoke got out of the car, the dog, slavering, gripped Hoke's right leg tightly with his forelegs, dug his wet jowls into Hoke's crotch, and began to dry-hump Hoke's leg in a practiced, determined rhythm. Mr. Ferguson, a red-faced, red-haired man in his early forties, wearing a gray, heavy cardigan sweater despite the eighty-five-degree temperature, lit his pipe with a kitchen match.

Hoke tried to shake the dog loose. "Ms. Westphal sent me out about the house-sitting job.''

"I know,'' Mr. Ferguson said after he got his pipe going, "she called me. Come on inside.'' Mr. Ferguson started toward the door, and Hoke managed to kick the amorous

27

Airedale viciously enough to dislodge him when Mr. Ferguson turned his back. But the dog darted ahead through the door before Hoke could close it. The moment Hoke closed the door, the dog was on him again, his forelegs clamped like a vise around Hoke's right thigh. Hoke took out his pistol.

"If you don't get this animal off me, I'm going to kill him."

"No need to do that," Mr. Ferguson said. "Rex! On the table, boy!"

The dog released Hoke's leg at once and jumped to a chair, then onto the kitchen table, which still held the dirty dishes from Mr. Ferguson's lunch. Mr. Ferguson reached between the dog's legs, above the red, pencil-sized penis. "Old Rex gets horny living here without a mate, but if you jack him off once or twice a day, he stays mighty quiet." The dog climaxed, and Ferguson wiped the table with a paper napkin. Rex jumped to the chair, then to the floor, and crossed to a corduroy cushion under the stove.

"What I want to do," Mr. Ferguson said, "is go up to stay with my mama in Fitzgerald, Georgia. She's dyin' of cancer, you see, and the doctors only give her six or seven months to live. I don't think it'll be that long, but however long it takes, I'm gonna stay with her. She's all alone up there, with no friends, so I have to go up whether I want to or not. A man only has one mama, you know."

"Why not bring her down here? Wouldn't that be better than leaving your job and your house?" Hoke shivered. The air conditioning was set for sixty or lower; no wonder Mr. Ferguson was wearing a sweater.

"No, I can't do that. She's too old, and she don't want to leave her friends up there."

"You just told me she didn't have any friends."

"She has friends, all right, but they're all dead and in

the cemetery. Mama's eighty-six years old. But she's got her own little house, and sick as she is, she wouldn't want to come down here to Miami. And I can't take Rex up there with me. Mama don't like dogs, and she never did. And I know she wouldn't 'low Rex in the house. I hate to leave Rex down here, but I don't see no other way out of the situation. Do you?''

"You could hire somebody to stay with her.''

"No, I couldn't do that. Jesus Christ Himself couldn't get along with that old woman. Nobody'd stay with her for more'n a day or two. No, I have to go. A man's only got one mama. Want to see the rest of the house? I got a pool out back. Rex likes to dive for rocks. You can throw a rock in the deepest part, and he'll dive right in and bring it to you. Labrador retrievers do that, but not many Airedales.''

"I've got another appointment, Mr. Ferguson. Ms. Westphal will call you later.''

"You gonna sit my house for me?''

"I don't think so. I've still got a couple of other options.''

"That's too bad. Rex liked you a lot. I could tell.''

Hoke drove back into the Grove, parked behind the Hammock Bar, and drank two draft beers before returning to the Safe 'n' Sure office. After his experience with the frigging dog, Hoke felt entitled to the drinks. Except for Rex, the house would have been ideal.

Ms. Westphal unlocked the front door, and they went into the office together. "Sorry you had to wait," she said. "What I need is a secretary. I was going to buy an answering machine, but most people won't talk to them anyway.''

"I don't want to sit Mr. Ferguson's house.''

"You, too? What's the problem out there, anyway?''

"Well, part of the deal is that you have to jerk the dog off every day. I don't know why he didn't tell you about that in the first place. But Mr. Ferguson owns a concupiscent Airedale.''

"What kind of Airedale?''

"Sex-crazed. He humps your leg, and he won't let go till you jack him off.''

"How long does it take?''

"Less than a minute. Closer to thirty seconds than a minute.''

"What's the big deal then, Sergeant? I used to jerk guys off in junior high. Oh, don't look so surprised. If you didn't, you never got a second date. It seems to me that getting a lovely home to live in free, and five dollars a day besides, should be worth a minute of your time every day.''

"Not to me it isn't. If it ever got out in the division that I—look, I'm just not interested.''

"Let's talk a minute. I'll tell you what. It'll only take me ten minutes to get over there. Why don't you take the house, and then when the dog jumps your leg you can call me. I'll drive over and handle it for you.''

"Why don't you sit the house yourself? Then you could get a secretary and let her live here. You'd have someone here to answer your phone when you were out, and you'd have a nice house with a pool for a few months.''

"That isn't a bad idea, you know.''

"I know. What else do you have?

"I've got a duplex in Hialeah.''

"No, it's got to be in Miami. Not necessarily in the Grove, but within the city limits.

"All I've got in the Grove right now is a week at Grove Isle. A two-hundred-and-fifty-thousand-dollar condo, complete with sauna.''

"A week isn't enough. I need a place for at least a month or two.''

"I'll call you. But you should've told me you didn't like dogs. It would've saved a trip out to Mr. Ferguson's house.''

"Until I met Rex, I didn't know I didn't like dogs. But please call me soon, because I need a place before the end of the week."

"I'll see what I can do."

But from the cool tone of her voice, Hoke had a hunch, as he headed downtown on Dixie Highway, that it would be a damned cold day in Miami before she called him again.

3

H oke shared a small office at the Homicide Division
with Ellita Sanchez. The upper half of the wall that faced
the squad room was glass, and there were several wanted
posters affixed to the glass with Scotch tape. Most of the
space in the little office was taken up by a large double
desk, the kind favored by small real-estate firms. There
was a D-ring bolted to the desk so that suspects could be
handcuffed to it. A glass top covered the desk, and lists of
telephone numbers and various business cards were scattered beneath the glass for easy reference. As a consequence, even when the desk was cleared, it looked messy.
The desk was rarely cleared, however. There was a two-
drawer filing cabinet, two metal swivel chairs, and one
customer's straight chair that was usually piled high with

copies of the two daily Miami newspapers. The IBM Selectric typewriter was, of course, on Ellita's side of the desk.

On the wall facing Hoke's side was an unframed poster of a masked man pointing a pistol. Beneath the picture, in large boldface, was the current Greater Miami Chamber of Commerce slogan: MIAMI'S FOR ME! Technically, this small office, the only enclosed office in the division other than Major Willie Brownley's much larger glass-walled office, belonged to Lieutenant Fred Slater, the executive officer and number-two man for Major Brownley. But Lieutenant Slater, who preferred a desk in one corner of the bull pen, where it was easier to keep an eye on everybody, had given the small office to Hoke Moseley and Bill Henderson to use. A few weeks earlier, when Major Brownley had broken up their partnership, Hoke had been assigned Ellita Sanchez as his new partner, and Sergeant Bill Henderson had been moved to the bull pen. Sergeant Henderson's new partner, Teodoro "Teddy" Gonzalez, was the newest investigator in the division, and Henderson was supposed to break him in to homicide work, as Hoke was supposed to break in Ellita Sanchez. Bill and Hoke had worked together as partners, even after Henderson had been promoted to sergeant, for more than three years. They had worked well together, but because neither of them spoke Spanish, and both refused to learn the language, Major Brownley had broken them up and assigned them bilingual partners. Hoke, being senior to Henderson, had kept the little office, and Henderson and Gonzalez now occupied two beat-up metal desks next to the men's room. There was no women's room; Ellita had to take the elevator down to the second floor.

With more than half of Miami's population a mixture of various Latins, but mostly Cubans, and with more Salvadoran and Nicaraguan refugees coming in daily, the change in partners had been inevitable. Bill and Hoke hadn't been

33

happy about the switch, but they had accepted it without complaint because there was nothing they could do about it. Altogether, there were forty-seven detectives in Homicide, and, thanks to Affirmative Action, the balance was about even between Anglo and Latin officers. Not counting Major Brownley, who was black, there were three black detectives, and one of these was a Haitian. The Haitian detective, a Sorbonne graduate, spoke French fluently, as well as Creole and English, but he had less work to do than any of the others. The Miami Haitian population, about 25,000, was the most peaceful ethnic group in town. The occasional homicides in Little Haiti usually involved somebody from outside their district shooting one of them for fun from a passing car.

When Hoke came into the office, Ellita Sanchez, with the help of a small hand mirror, was applying a coat of American Dream to her lips. Except for this vividly red and wet-looking lipstick, Ellita used no other makeup. Because the corners of her mouth turned down slightly, unless she was smiling the two tiny red lines that tugged at the corners of her lips sometimes made it seem, at first glance, as though her mouth were dribbling blood. Hoke wondered if anyone had ever told her about this effect.

"How'd it go?" Hoke said.

"We'll know more later. The assistant M.E. said he thought it was an OD, not a suicide, but not for the record. I sent for Hickey's file. According to the computer, he's got a record, so I asked for a printout."

Hoke handed her the Baggie with the items he had picked up in Hickey's room. "Send the tinfoil balls and the bags of powder to the lab to be checked out. Send the roach, too, if you want—or take it home and smoke it."

"I don't smoke pot, Sergeant." Ellita put the roach into her purse.

Hoke went through Hickey's wallet, a well-worn cowhide fold-over type, and removed a driver's license, expired; a slip of paper with a telephone number, written in pencil; a cracked black-and-white snapshot of a mongrel with a ball in its mouth; a folded gift coupon for a McDonald's quarter-pounder, expired; a Visa credit card in Gerald Hickey's name, expired; and a tightly folded twenty-dollar bill that had been hidden behind the lining of the wallet.

"Not much here." Hoke passed the twenty across the desk. "Put this bill with the others."

"I've already sealed the money in an envelope."

"In that case, you'll have to unseal it, won't you?"

Ellita cut the flap of the brown envelope with the small blade of her Swiss army knife, took out the money, flattened the twenty, and added it to the other bills. She placed the money in a new brown envelope, threw the mutilated envelope into the wastepaper basket, and then sealed the money inside. She wrote "Gerald Hickey" and "$1,070" on the outside of the envelope before passing it to Hoke across the desk. Hoke put the envelope in the side pocket of his leisure jacket, and shook his head.

"I didn't mean to snap at you. But I had a weird experience this afternoon, and I still haven't found a new place to live. Why do you think, Sanchez, that Hickey would carry a picture of a mongrel dog in his wallet?"

Ellita stood up, leaned over the desk, and frowned at the items on the desk. "Everything else is expired, so I'd say the dog is probably dead, too. Maybe it was once his dog, and it died, so he wanted to keep the picture as a *memento mori.*"

"A *memento mori* is a human skull, not a picture of a dog. But you may be right. There was no indication of a dog living at the Hickey house. Pass me the phone."

Hoke dialed the number on the slip of paper.

"Hello."

"I'd like to speak to Jerry Hickey," Hoke said.

"Who?"

"Jerry Hickey."

"He don't live here no mo'." It was a black woman's voice.

"Who is this, please?"

"Who is you?"

"I want to buy Jerry's dog. When he left, did he leave his dog with you?"

"He didn't have no dog. I don't 'low no dogs here. Who is this?"

"When did Jerry move?"

The woman hung up the phone.

"You're probably right about the dog, Sanchez." Hoke handed her the slip of paper. "Get the address of this number from the phone company. It doesn't mean anything to us, but I can pass it on to Narcotics. It might be a lead for them. Jerry had to get the heroin somewhere. He hadn't been living at home long. I'll find out how long this evening when I talk to his mother."

Ellita nodded. "You want some coffee, Sergeant?"

"Do you?"

"We've got a half hour before we meet with Major Brownley."

"I know that. I asked if you wanted some coffee."

Ellita nodded.

"In that case," Hoke said, "I'll go. You've gone the last three times, and it isn't supposed to work that way. Bill and I always took turns. I've been taking advantage of you. How many sugars?" Hoke got to his feet.

"None. I keep Sweet 'n' Low here in my desk."

Hoke took the elevator downstairs to the basement cafeteria. For some reason, he thought, Ellita seemed to be afraid of him. Several times lately he had noticed her staring at him, and she looked frightened. He couldn't understand it, because he had been leaning over backward to be friendly with her. Maybe it was the meeting coming up with Major Brownley. Most of the detectives in the division were afraid of the major. As a rule, Brownley kept his distance, either by communicating with his detectives through Lieutenant Slater or by sending out memos. It was unusual for Brownley to call a special meeting this way. As he filled two Styrofoam cups with coffee, Hoke wondered vaguely what the old fart wanted.

4

Major Willie Brownley, the first black ever to be appointed to that rank in the department, leaned back in his padded leather chair and got his cigar drawing well before he said anything. His face, the color of an eggplant, but not as shiny, was lined with tiny wrinkles. His cropped hair was gray at the temples, but his well-trimmed mustache was still black. The whites of his eyes were the color of a legal pad. He looked of indeterminate age, but Hoke knew that Willie Brownley was fifty-five, because Hoke had worked for the major when he had been a captain in charge of Traffic. The major wore his navy-blue gabardine uniform even on the hottest days, with the jacket always buttoned, and his trim military appearance made him look younger than his age.

The three detectives sat facing Brownley's desk, with Henderson on the right. Henderson was a large, paunchy man who almost always wore a striped seersucker jacket with poplin wash pants. Although he was officially six feet, two inches tall, he appeared six-four because he wore Adler's elevator shoes. Henderson thought the extra two inches made him look slimmer. They didn't, really, but the extra height did make him look more formidable. Henderson was an affable man, but his front teeth, both uppers and lowers, were laced with a tangle of silver wire and gold caps. When he smiled, these brutal metal-studded teeth were more than a little frightening, particularly when he questioned a suspect. But his smile rarely changed, whether he was interrogating someone or eating a bowl of chili.

Hoke and Ellita sat closer together on the left of the desk, facing the major. Ellita had a yellow legal pad and a ballpoint pen. Before they went to Brownley's office, Hoke told her it might be a good idea to take a few notes.

Brownley dropped the burnt match into an ashtray made from a motorcycle piston, looked at Hoke, shook his head, and smiled. "Hoke, you must be the last man in Miami wearing a leisure suit. Where'd you find it, anyway?"

"There was a close-out in the fashion district. I got this blue poplin and a yellow one just like it for only fifty bucks on a two-for-one sale. I like the extra pockets, and with a leisure suit you don't have to wear a tie."

"You don't wear a leisure suit to court, do you?"

"No. I've got an old blue serge suit I wear to court. Is that what this meeting's about, Willie? My taste in plain clothes?"

"In a way. What I'm doing is what they suggested in the Dale Carnegie course I took last year. I'm putting you all at ease by developing a relaxed atmosphere. You all relaxed now?''

Hoke shook his head, Henderson smiled, and Ellita said, ''Yes, sir.'' Hoke took the butt of the Kool from his shirt pocket, lit it, and dropped the match into Brownley's piston ashtray. He took two drags and then put out the butt.

''Until I tell you different,'' Brownley said, ''consider this meeting as confidential. It'll probably get out in a few days, about what you're doing, simply because of what you're doing, but I don't want the press to get wind of it. If anyone in the department asks you what you're doing, just say you're on a special assignment and let it go at that. Until we see where we're going, I think we can get away with that much, anyway.''

Brownley puffed on his cigar before he continued. ''You've all heard the rumors about the new colonelcies the chief's passing out, haven't you?''

Henderson shook his head. ''Colonelcies? There aren't any colonels in the department. Except for assistant chief—and we got three already—major's as high as we go.''

''I heard something about it the other day,'' Hoke said, ''but I didn't pay any attention to it.''

''It isn't official yet, but it's no longer a rumor. The chief's found a sneaky way around the no-raise budget this year. He's creating a new rank of colonel, and there'll be eight of them passed out. The new rank'll mean an extra eighteen hundred bucks a year for those promoted. It'll also mean eight major and captain vacancies. So although there's no money in the new budget for raises, a good many deserving officers will be getting more money when these promotions are okayed by the city manager.''

''What about the cop on the street?'' Henderson said. ''What'll he get?''

"He'll get zip. On the other hand, with more supervisors, it'll mean more vacancies for him, too, if he passes his exams high enough."

"It stinks," Henderson said. "I was in the infantry, and we only had one colonel, the regimental commander, for a fifteen-hundred-man regiment. We've got way less than a thousand cops, and we've already got a highly paid chief, three overpaid assistant chiefs, and now he wants eight new colonels. What we're gonna look like is a damned Mexican army, all generals and no privates."

"A police department's not a rifle regiment, Bill," Brownley said. "You can't equate a professional police officer with a grunt private. Most of our officers have got at least a junior college degree of some kind."

"I know, I know." Henderson scowled. "But what we need's more men on the street, not more brass sitting on their ass."

"You and Hoke both should take the exam for lieutenant. I've told you that before. Promotions are going to break wide open for qualified people. But that's your problem. What I want is one of the colonelcies. And I've come up with a way for you two"—he looked at Ellita, and smiled—"and you, too, Sanchez, to get it for me."

There were four stacks of rust-colored accordion files on the table against the wall. The major pointed at them. "I've been going through the old files. These are fifty old unsolved homicides. All of them go back a few years, some much longer than others. Some of these, I know, could've been solved at the time. But they weren't solved, or resolved in some way, because there wasn't enough time. There's never enough time. Most breaks, as you know, come in the first twenty-four hours. After three or four days, something else comes up, and after two weeks, unless you get a break accidentally, you're on a new case, or even three new cases. After six months, the homi-

41

cide's so far back in pending, it's colder than the victim.

"I'm not telling you something you don't know already. I didn't become the Homicide chief because I was a detective. I'm an administrator, and I was promoted for my administrative ability. It didn't hurt that I was black, either, but I wouldn't have kept my rank if I couldn't do the work. It seems to me, if we can solve some of these cold cases, it'll make our division and the entire department look even better than it is. And if that happens, they'll have to make at least one of those new colonels a black man. What I want is one of those silver eagles and another gold stripe on my sleeve."

"Time's always been the problem, Willie," Hoke said. "When we get a chance we work on old cases, but a new dead body is found damned near every day in a car trunk, a tomato field, an apartment—"

"I'm not finished, Hoke. Time is what I'm going to give you. You rank Bill, so you're in charge. But the three of you are going to get two full months to do nothing else but work on these fifty cold cases I picked out."

"What about the cases we're on now?" Henderson said. "We've got, me and Gonzalez, a triple murder in Liberty City, and no leads at all. Tomorrow we're supposed to—"

"Gonzalez will have to handle that one by himself. Hoke, you can give your current cases to Gonzalez, too. I know he lacks experience, but he'll report directly to Lieutenant Slater, and he'll get all the help from Slater he needs. I can't spare four men for this assignment, but the three of you, in two months' time, should get some positive results."

"Three months," Henderson said, "would be better."

"I know." Brownley smiled. "And six months would be better than three months, but you've got two. I've already gone through the old files and picked out these fifty. Take them with you, go through 'em again, and decide which cases to work first. You know more about the possibilities than I do. Any questions?''

"That office we've got," Hoke said. "It's too small for the three of us. Can we have one of the interrogation rooms to work in on a permanent basis?"

"Take Room Three. There's a table and some folding chairs in there already. It's yours for as long's you need it. I'll inform Lieutenant Slater. Anything else?"

"When Hoke and I turn all our cases over to Gonzalez, he'll shit his pants," Henderson said.

"He'll be all right with Slater. Just fill Slater in on what's been done so far. Slater knows what you all will be doing, but Gonzalez doesn't. Just tell him you're on a special assignment, Bill, and to do the best he can. You have any questions, Sanchez?''

"No, sir. I think it's a good idea, that's all."

"It would be a better idea if we had three months," Henderson said.

"Solve at least ten of these cases in two months, and I'll give you the extra month," Brownley said.

"Fair enough." Henderson picked up an armload of files and left the office.

After the cold cases were stacked in piles on Hoke's desk, he looked at them and shook his head. "It's five-thirty. We'll start going through them tomorrow morning in the interrogation room."

"If you want me to, I can take a couple home with me tonight to read," Ellita said. "I haven't got anything else planned."

"No. I want to think about how best to work things out. You guys go home."

Henderson broadened his smile slightly. "I think I'd better take Teddy out and buy him a drink before I give him the news. Did you notice Gonzalez through the window when we were in Willie's office? The poor bastard went to the can three times. He probably thought the meeting was all about him. But you can't blame him. If I'd been left out there, I'd've thought the same thing."

After Henderson and Ellita left, Hoke locked the office, got his Pontiac from the lot, and drove out to Green Lakes to pay another visit to Mrs. Hickey's house.

~~~~~~

5

The rush-hour traffic on Flagler Street was heavier than usual because of the rain. In July, during the rainy season, showers and thunderstorms begin at four or four-thirty every day and continue into the early evening hours. Hoke didn't mind the rain or the traffic, or the fact that he was working overtime without compensation. He appreciated doing anything that would delay his getting home to the Hotel Eldorado in Miami Beach—any delay, that is, that didn't cost money. The long nights at the Eldorado were dull, so he was always glad when he had an excuse to postpone going home.

The pile of old cases on his desk troubled him a little, but not very much. Brownley had had a good idea there, despite his selfish motivation, and Hoke looked forward to the two-month assignment. He didn't think they would be able to solve ten cases, but even if they could solve three or four, it would be better than none. He just wished that he had been the one to select the fifty cases to work on, instead of Willie Brownley. If he and Henderson had gone through all the cold cases, and there must be several hundred, they could have done a much better job of winnowing them than Brownley. On the other hand, the fact that Brownley had selected these particular files out of all the other unsolved cases gave Hoke at least a weak excuse for failure if they didn't resolve any of them at all.

The best way to work it, he decided, was to have each of them read all of the cases first. Each reader could then select the ten most likely cases to work on. If they all came up with the same three or four homicides on their lists, these would be the cases to work on first. If they all had the same half-dozen, it would be even better.

Hoke didn't know why Brownley had assigned Sanchez instead of Gonzalez to his team, but it was probably because he didn't think Slater could work well with a woman. Slater had a very short fuse, and Brownley undoubtedly felt that Slater would feel more comfortable chewing on Gonzalez's ass every day than he would Sanchez's. Regardless of the reason, Hoke was happy to have Sanchez instead of Gonzalez. She could spell, as well as type, so he would have her keep the daily notes and write the weekly progress reports that Major Brownley wanted. Sanchez didn't have much of a sense of humor, but he would be working with Henderson again, who did, and that was a big plus.

Loretta Hickey was no longer the distraught youthful mother Hoke had last seen sobbing on the lawn that morning. When she opened the door, she was rested, clean and sweet-smelling, and wearing a black-and-white silk djellabah. Sober, Mrs. Hickey was a handsome woman. Her long hair, freshly shampooed, still had damp ends, and she had brushed it straight back. Her high white forehead was shiny and without makeup, but there was a pink trace of lipstick on her full lips.

She asked Hoke for identification. He had to tell her his name and show her his shield before she would unlock the screen door. She stared at Hoke with bold blue eyes and without apparent recognition.

"Are you always this cautious?" Hoke said, stepping into the living room.

"No, not always." Her face relaxed a little. "But I thought it might be those two men coming back."

"What men?"

"They said they were friends of Jerry's, but I'd never seen them before. Neighbors have been coming by all afternoon, bringing food, but these two came at about three-thirty, when no one else was here. They got upset when I told them that Jerry was dead. Then they started looking in his room."

"That room is sealed."

"I told them that, but they broke the strip of paper and looked around in there anyway. They asked me if Jerry had left a package for them, and I told them no. Then one of them asked if the police had found twenty-five thousand dollars in the room! I told them that Jerry had a thousand, but no twenty-five thousand. But the thousand wasn't there either. That's when they started dumping the drawers out on the floor."

"What did they look like, these men? Did you ask them for ID?"

Mrs. Hickey shook her head. "No. I'd thought at first they might just be more neighbors. I didn't know half the people who brought food over this afternoon. And they didn't look like friends of Jerry's, either. They looked more like Yuppies, well-dressed with blow-dry

47

hair—like Brickell Avenue or Kendall types. One of them was wearing a silk suit, and the other had on a linen jacket. They were in their mid-twenties, I'd say. The one in the suit had black loafers, the other man wore brown-and-white shoes.''

Hoke grinned. ''The man with the black shoes did all the talking, right?''

Loretta Hickey nodded. ''How'd you know that?''

''I didn't. But guys who wear two-tone shoes have an ambivalent personality, and are indecisive.'' Hoke studied the drape of the silk djellabah and wondered if she was wearing a bra. ''What else did they say about the twenty-five thousand?''

''Jerry was supposed to deliver the money to them yesterday, but he didn't show up, and they'd been looking for him. I told them that Jerry had a thousand dollars, and I knew that, because he showed it to me when I came home from work yesterday evening. If he had more, he didn't tell me anything about it. The thousand was on the dresser when I found him this morning. I had assumed it was still there, because I didn't go back into the room again. But it was gone when we went into the room, so—''

''I have it in my pocket,'' Hoke said. ''Tell me, did you let Jerry in yesterday?''

''No, I wasn't here. I'd already gone to work, but he came to the house in the morning, he told me.''

''How'd he get in? There was no key with his effects.''

''He used the key I keep hidden in a fake rock. If you live all alone and happen to lock yourself out—and I've done it—you've got a problem. I'll show you.''

She opened the screen door and led Hoke outside. She picked up a gray stone about four inches long and handed it to Hoke. It weighed four or five ounces and had a flat bottom. Hoke opened the flat part by sliding it to one side and found the key concealed in the recess. He hefted the stone in his hand. "This is the phoniest fake stone I've ever seen. Where'd you get it?"

"I ordered it from a catalog. It's supposed to be granite. It looks real to me."

"Yeah, but we don't have any granite in south Florida. We've got gravel, and we've got oolite, but not any granite. A burglar who spotted this in your yard next to the house would know that it was a fake. What you should do is leave the key with a neighbor instead."

"I've done that. Mrs. Koontz, next door, has a key, and I've got a key to her house."

"In that case, I'd advise you to keep this phony stone inside the house. What else did these men say?" Hoke opened the screen door, and they went back into the living room.

"Nothing else. Mrs. Ames, from across the street, came over with a Key lime pie, and while I was around the back letting her in, they slipped out the front door and left."

"Did you see their car?"

"It was a convertible. The top was down. It was light green, an apple green."

"You didn't take down the license number?"

"No, I was talking to Mrs. Ames, telling her what had happened. It wouldn't have occurred to me anyway." She looked away. "Would you like a drink, Sergeant?"

"A beer would be okay."

"I've got vodka, and a six-pack of Cokes, but no beer."

"Make it a Coke, then. I usually drink beer or bourbon, but I can drink almost anything, except for Mr. Pibb."

Hoke followed Mrs. Hickey into the dining area and sat at the Eames table while she went into the kitchen. The table was loaded with food. There was a baked ham, studded with cloves; two cheesecakes; two Key lime pies;

and a large brown ceramic casserole dish filled with Boston baked beans, topped with parboiled strips of fatty bacon.

"You ever see so much food?" Mrs. Hickey said, coming back from the kitchen. She handed Hoke a tall glass of Coca-Cola over ice cubes. "On top of all this"—she made a sweeping gesture over the table—"there's a big tuna salad in the fridge and a half a watermelon." She blushed. "I've had two ham sandwiches already, and both with mayonnaise."

"That's natural. Death makes a person hungry. Those beans look good to me."

"Would you like some? I'll never be able to eat all this food by myself."

"I'm on a kind of diet. I'd rather have the beans, but I'll settle for some tuna salad."

"I'll fix you a plate."

Hoke didn't want the tuna salad either, but he thought it might help if he gave Mrs. Hickey something to do with her hands. She had to be embarrassed about her morning's performance, but she was covering it well. He needed to know more about Jerry Hickey. If Jerry had ripped off twenty-five thousand dollars, where was it? Of course, he might not have ripped off anything. The two guys could have been looking for him for something else, and told Mrs. Hickey that as a cover story. On the other hand, it was plausible. Drug people stiffed each other all the time, and a junkie like Hickey might not have considered the consequences of taking down a dealer. If these two dealers, or whoever they were, had been dumb enough to trust that kind of money to a junkie, they deserved to be ripped off. The kid, if he took the money, had hidden it somewhere, stashed it away, figuring that he would hide out here for a few days, then pick it up and take off. He had kept out a thousand, probably, as an emergency fund . . .

The tuna salad was attractively presented: a heaping portion on a lettuce bed, garnished with two deviled egg halves, green and black olives, and celery sticks. To keep Hoke company, Mrs. Hickey had a slice of Key lime pie. She took two bites, then got up and started the percolator in the kitchen.

"This is good tuna salad," Hoke said, "but I never put hard-boiled eggs in mine. I prefer the classic recipe. One pound of tuna, one pound of chopped onions, and one pound of mayonnaise."

Loretta Hickey laughed. "Oh! All that mayonnaise! I'm sorry. I guess I shouldn't laugh, but I couldn't help it."

"Don't ever apologize for laughing, Mrs. Hickey. Life goes on, you know, no matter what. That's what your neighbors were trying to tell you when they brought this food over."

"I know. And I don't want to seem callous. I should feel sorry about Jerry's death, but I always knew that something would happen to him sooner or later. So in a way, I'm just as glad it's over. I don't mean I'm happy about his death—don't get me wrong—but his father and I gave up on Jerry a long time ago."

"I understand, I think. What I'd like from you now is a little background information on your son—"

"Jerry isn't my son. That is, I wasn't responsible for him the way I would've been if he'd been my own son. Or even my legal stepson."

"That isn't quite clear. Gerald Hickey isn't your son?"

"No. I'm divorced. Jerry's my ex-husband's son. Only Jerry wasn't his natural son either. He was my ex-husband's adopted son. That is, Jerry was my ex-husband's ex-wife's son by her first husband. Harold, my ex-husband, adopted Jerry when he married Marcella, his first wife, because she had custody of Jerry from her first marriage. You see, when he married Marcella, she talked Har-

51

old into adopting Jerry. Then, after they were divorced, Marcella left town, and he had to keep Jerry because Jerry was now his legal responsibility. Harold didn't know where Marcella went, and he's never heard from her again. Jerry was fifteen when they were divorced, and then Harold married me about a year later, when Jerry turned sixteen. But I never adopted Jerry, so I wasn't his legal stepmother or anything like that. He just came with Harold and the house. This house.''

"You may not believe me," Hoke said, pushing his plate to one side, "but I can follow you. I run into a lot more complicated families than yours in Miami. Then you divorced Harold, right?''

"That's right. I never got along too well with Harold, but I always got along with Jerry because I didn't try to play the mother act with him. Jerry was too old for me to try that anyway, when Harold and I got married, and I'm not the maternal type. I got along with Jerry much better than Harold ever did, but then Harold was responsible for him legally.

"At any rate, when I got my divorce I also got the house—this one—as part of the settlement. Harold wanted a bachelor pad, so he asked me to keep Jerry, too. He gave me an extra two hundred a month in the agreement, so I let Jerry stay on. By that time Jerry and I were pretty good friends. He did pretty much as he wanted to do, and I didn't care. After he got his car, I didn't see him much. He got into a little trouble with the police, but his father always got him out of it. After he dropped out of school, he was sometimes away from the house for two or three weeks at a time. He ran around with a bunch in Coconut Grove, but he never brought any of them here. So to tell you the truth, Sergeant, I don't know all that much about what he was doing, or where he spent his time. But I wasn't legally responsible for him. I do know, or feel, that this place was a kind of a sanctuary for him. I never bugged him, and there was always food to eat here if he wanted to come home and eat it. Harold still sent me the two hundred every month, whether Jerry was here or not, even after Jerry turned eighteen.''

"Did you know that Jerry was on drugs?"

"I suspected it, but I wasn't positive. As I said, I wasn't legally responsible for—"

"Yes, you did mention that. Where did Jerry get his money to live on? Did he have a job?"

"Not lately. He used to get odd jobs now and then, at the Green Lakes Car Wash, and as a bag boy. He offered to help me once in the flower shop, but I turned him down. He wasn't a dependable boy, so I knew he wouldn't stay for more than a few days, and I didn't want to add another failure to his list. Harold mailed him a check once in a while, but that was after he quit school. While he was in school I gave him an allowance, but when he dropped out of school I stopped it. After his driver's license was suspended, he sold his car. He made about two thousand on the sale. But that was several months ago.'' She ate the last bite of her pie. "Anyway, it's all over with now, isn't it? Including my extra two hundred a month from Harold. That's what I wanted to ask you about.''

"What?"

"A favor. Somebody has to tell Harold about Jerry. And I just can't make myself do it. Would you call and tell him for me? I think he ought to be told soon, because it wouldn't be very pleasant for him to read about it in the papers or hear it on the radio.''

"Jerry's name won't be released to the papers until they've checked with us that his next-of-kin's been notified. The press is pretty decent about things like that. But I'll call him if you want me to.'' Hoke got to his feet. "Where does he live?"

"At the Mercury Club, in Hallandale. I'll get his number for you.''

Harold Hickey, Hoke thought, must have a bundle. The Mercury Club was right on the ocean, with tight security, and had its own small marina. The Mercury Club was still restricted, too: no Jews, blacks, or Latins. When all of the civil rights legislation was considered, it cost a great deal of money to keep a private club restricted nowadays.

Hoke dialed the number Mrs. Hickey gave him. After two rings, a voice came on the line. The voice was deep and husky; each word was enunciated self-consciously.

"This is a recording. I am Harold Hickey, attorney at law. I am temporarily unable to answer the phone in person. In a moment or so, when I finish speaking, you will hear a tone. At that time, if you are so inclined, you may leave your name, phone number, and message. I will return your call at my earliest convenience."

Hoke waited for the tone, and said: "This is Detective-Sergeant Hoke Moseley, Homicide, Miami Police Department. Your son Gerald died this morning under peculiar circumstances. For additional information, call me after ten P.M. at my residence, the Eldorado Hotel, Miami Beach. Don't give up too quickly." Hoke gave the number, then added, "If you don't call me at the hotel, you can reach me at Homicide, Miami police station, tomorrow after seven-thirty A.M."

Hoke racked the phone and turned away. Loretta had an expression of dismay. "What was that all about? Were you talking to a recording?"

"He wasn't there, so I gave the machine the information."

"Jesus! You told the recording Jerry was dead? I could've done that myself. Except that I'd never tell a recording anyone was dead. That'll be a shock to Harold when he plays it back. The reason I asked you to call him in the first place was I thought you could do it gently."

54

"There isn't any gentle way to tell someone that a member of his family's dead. The direct method's as good as any. Besides, if Mr. Hickey was sensitive, he wouldn't have a recording answer his telephone for him. By the time he calls me back, he'll have had time to digest the news."

"You don't know Harold." She looked away, toward the bedrooms. "But at least he didn't have to discover the body, the way I did."

"I think the coffee may be ready."

"Just a sec. I'll see."

When Loretta returned with the coffee and cups on a tray, Hoke handed her the envelope containing $1,070 and asked her to count it. He then asked her to sign a receipt.

"This money's yours, or your ex-husband's. Or you two can split it. But you'd better tell him about it."

Loretta Hickey nodded. "Suppose those two men come back? They might say it's theirs."

"If they come back, call me." Hoke put his card on the table. "Let me have your home and office number too.

She gave him the numbers, and Hoke wrote them down in his notebook.

"Is this money evidence, Sergeant?"

"No. I've got a list of the serial numbers, and that's all I'll need. If I were you, I'd put the money into your night deposit at the bank."

"I don't think I want to leave the house tonight. Can't you keep the money for now, and give it to me tomorrow at the shop?"

"I suppose." Hoke put the receipt into the envelope with the money, and returned the envelope to his jacket pocket. "Where do you work?"

"I have my own shop, The Bouquetique, a flower and gift shop in the Gables, on Miracle Mile. Do you know where it is?"

"I can find it, but I don't know exactly when I can get there. Did you make that name up all by yourself, or did you inherit it?"

"I made it up. It's a combination of bouquet and boutique."

"I suspected that. What do you sell besides flowers?"

"Smart things. Gifts. Vases, ceramics, turquoise jewelry from New Mexico. Little things like that."

"All right. I might have some more questions for you. Try and make a list of Jerry's friends—men and women— and I'll see you then. If I can't make it tomorrow, I'll call you. When was the last time you saw Jerry?"

"This morning—but you mean before that, don't you?" Hoke nodded.

"About a month ago. He came by one night and got two shirts, but he only stayed for a few minutes. He was living in the Grove, but he didn't tell me where, and I didn't ask. Somebody drove him over and waited for him outside. He was only here a few minutes. He just got the shirts and left."

"Who brought him—a man or a woman?"

"I don't know. I was working on some accounts here at the dining table, and didn't go outside with him when he left."

"It doesn't matter. If you're pressed for money, I can leave you some of this thousand."

"I'm not pressed for money, Sergeant. What makes you think that?"

"I didn't say I thought so." Hoke smiled. "I'm always pressed for money, so I guess I usually assume everybody else is, too. Meanwhile, if you think of anything else about your conversation with those two men, or if they pester you again, call me at the Eldorado Hotel in Miami Beach. I wrote the number on the back of my card."

"The Eldorado? That's in South Beach, isn't it?"

56

"Right. Just off Alton Road, next to the condemned Vizcaya Hotel, on the bay side."

"How can you possibly live in such a terrible place? If you don't mind my asking."

"When I got my divorce, my wife got the house, the car, the furniture, the children, the weed-eater, my tankful of guppies—the same old story."

"You're not married now, then?"

"No." And you've got a very nice house, Hoke thought.

"Perhaps you can come over for dinner one night? I've still got all this food."

"Why not?" Hoke finished his coffee and got to his feet. "There'll be a postmortem on Jerry, but we'll let you know when you can recover the body."

"That's all right. Harold'll take care of all that. So tell him, not me. I don't think he'll want a funeral, but he'll probably call me about that." She walked Hoke to the front door. "How come, Sergeant Moseley, you live in Miami Beach, anyway? I thought it said in the paper that all the Miami police had to live in the city."

"That's a long story, Mrs. Hickey. I'll save it for another time. I don't think those men will come back, but keep the bolt on the door anyway, and if they do come back, don't let them in. Just call me instead. All right?"

"I will. Good night, and I'll see you tomorrow."

"Tomorrow. And thanks for the tuna salad."

The rain had stopped, and the dark clouds had moved west over the Everglades. Hoke drove cautiously on the still-slick streets. At eight-thirty there was enough light left to drive by without his headlights, because of Daylight Saving Time. But when he reached the MacArthur Causeway, Hoke turned on his lights anyway. Some people drove like maniacs across this narrow link to Miami Beach.

Hoke hadn't been laid in four months, and Loretta

57

Hickey, all fresh and sweet-smelling from her shower, had made him horny. If he had stayed much longer, he might have made a move on her. But the timing wasn't right. Her emotions had been drained that morning. She had discussed Jerry as if he were a stranger. She had been coming on to him toward the end of their conversation, though. She knew how sexy she was in that thin floor-length robe. It was funny how some women were sexy and others were not. Ellita Sanchez, despite her ample bosom and good legs, didn't do it for him. But underneath, she probably smouldered. She was thirty-two, and still lived with her mother and father. He doubted if she had ever been laid. On the other hand, her bed was Cuba: The right man could fry an egg on her G-spot. Living at home that way, and saving her money, she would have one hell of a dowry for some macho Cuban to squander on a sexy mistress some day. At thirty-two, however, her chances of getting married in the Cuban community were negligible. Most of those Cuban girls were married by the time they were eighteen or nineteen. Ellita was no longer an old maid of twenty-five; officially, after thirty, she was a spinster.

Hoke parked in his marked slot in front of the hotel and glanced up at the electric sign. The neon spluttered, but it still spelled ELDORADO in misty rose letters. The shabby lobby was occupied by a half-circle of old ladies watching the flickering television, bolted and chained to the wall, and by four male Cuban residents playing dominoes at an old card table. By tacit consent, the live-in residents of the hotel kept to their own sides of the lobby. The only time the Cubans watched TV was when President Reagan, their hero, was on the tube. The noise at the card table stopped when Hoke crossed the lobby to the desk to check his mail. Eddie Cohen, the ancient desk clerk, was not behind the desk, and there was no mail in Hoke's box.

Hoke's thoughts kept returning to Loretta Hickey as he made his routine, if perfunctory, security check on each floor on his way up to his suite. After he made out his report for Mr. Bennett, which he would leave on the manager's desk in the morning, Hoke undressed and took a tepid shower in his tiny bathroom. Thinking of Loretta Hickey again, and about how she must look under her robe, Hoke masturbated gloomily in the shower. Christ, he thought unhappily, I'm getting too old to jerk off this way. I've got to get out of this hole and find a place where I won't be ashamed to bring a woman.

6

As usual, Hoke awoke without the aid of a ringing alarm at 6 A.M. It was a habit held over from his three years in the army. He invariably awakened at six, regardless of the hour he went to bed.

After his one year of junior college in Palm Beach, Hoke had enlisted for three years as a Regular rather than wait to be drafted. An R.A. man had an advantage over the draftees, and the Vietnam War had had little effect on Hoke, except that he probably wouldn't have enlisted in the army if it hadn't been for the war. He had spent three uneventful, but not unpleasant, years as an M.P. at Fort Hood, Texas. Most of that time had been spent at the front gate, saluting and waving cars on and off post. He had also pulled his share of guard duty, wandering around unlighted warehouses, but on the whole his had been a safe war. He had gone home twice to Riviera Beach, Florida, on leave, but spent his other furloughs in El Paso and Juarez, where he had some great times with his bunky, Burnley Johnson.

Hoke had never attended any of the army's special schools, which could have led to a promotion, nor had he applied for any. He made PFC when he completed basic training, and he was discharged as a PFC. He then went home to Riviera Beach, worked in his father's hardware and chandlery store for two years, and married Patsy, a girl he had dated at Palm Beach High School.

He finally quit at the hardware store when he realized that his father would never relinquish the management to him for as long as he lived. Hoke's salary was no larger than any of the other clerks', and Hoke's father, who had become wealthy from his real-estate investments on Singer Island (having bought up island property during the 1930s), refused to give Hoke a larger salary because he said it would smack of favoritism. The old man was tight, there was no question about that, but he had married an attractive well-to-do widow after Hoke's mother had died, and the two of them lived very well in a large house on the inland waterway.

Frank Moseley was seventy now, and he still went to the store every day. He had never given Hoke a share of the profits, nor did Hoke expect to get anything when he died. Hoke suspected that the bulk of the estate would go to the widow and to Hoke's two daughters, Sue Ellen and Aileen. The old man doted on his granddaughters, and Patsy was wise enough to drive down from Vero Beach often enough to maintain the old man's interest, yet not often enough to become a nuisance. Hoke had not seen his girls since Patsy divorced him and moved to Vero Beach. Patsy thought it would be better that way. The most recent photographs he had of the girls were from four years ago. He had never paid much attention to the children when they had lived together, Patsy said, and she didn't want their new lives upset by occasional, so-called duty visits.

Patsy was unfair in this regard, Hoke felt, but there was enough truth in what she said to discourage him from pursuing the matter legally.

Thanks to Hoke's M.P. background, limited though it was, he had no trouble getting into the Riviera Beach Police Department, and he and Patsy were happy enough during the three years he spent on the force as a patrolman. As a hometown boy—and a "Conch"—Hoke got along well with people, and Riviera Beach, before the 1970s boom and the unforeseen development of condominiums on Singer Island, was relatively crime-free. Patsy kept busy with the children all day, and Hoke drove a patrol car, alternating between day and night shifts. During his off-duty time, he either fished or went to the beach at Singer Island, the widest and nicest beach on Florida's east coast.

One night Hoke stopped a speeding Caddy. The driver dismounted with a gun in his hand when Hoke approached the car, and Hoke shot the man without even thinking about it. There were three kilos of cocaine in the trunk of the Caddy. The driver had been killed instantly; Hoke was cleared almost immediately and received a commendation from the chief. The rest of his police work at Riviera Beach was routine.

A few months later, after three years on the Riviera Beach force, Hoke applied for and was accepted by the Miami Police Department. It had been pleasant living in Riviera Beach, and Patsy had some family there, too, but with the girls growing up, Hoke needed the larger salary he could earn as a Miami policeman.

It was difficult at first. Hoke made more money, but it cost more to live in Miami. To earn extra money, Hoke volunteered for overtime, and he always worked the football games on Saturdays and Sundays in the Orange Bowl during his off-duty time. He neglected Patsy and the girls, but after she started to nag him and make his life unpleasant at home, he spent even fewer hours there. He met Bambi, began an intense affair, and studied for the sergeant's exam in the downtown public library. The girls were noisy at home, and he couldn't concentrate. Then Patsy joined a neighborhood "consciousness-raising" group, found out about Bambi, and their marriage was over.

Without any family obligations, except for endorsing and mailing every other check to Patsy, Hoke had prospered in the department. He had enjoyed his earlier work in Traffic and liked being a detective even better, especially after he was promoted to sergeant. But the life had taken a toll on his face.

Without his false teeth, Hoke looked much older than forty-two, and this morning, when he looked into the mirror, still thinking about Loretta Hickey, he wondered if she would ever be interested in him as a lover. She could hardly be interested, he thought, if she saw him without his teeth. His eyes were his best feature. They were chocolate brown, a brown so richly dark it was difficult to see his pupils. During his years in the Miami Police Department, this genetic gift had been useful to him on many occasions. Hoke could stare at people for a long time before they realized he was looking at them. By any aesthetic standard, Hoke's eyes were beautiful. But the rest of his face, if not ordinary, was unremarkable. He had lost most of his sandy hair in front, and his high balding dome gave his longish face a mournful expression. His tanned cheeks were sunken and striated, and there were dark, deep lines from the wings of his prominent nose to the corners of his mouth.

Hoke took his dentures out of the plastic glass where they had been soaking overnight in Polident, rinsed them under the faucet, and set them in place with a few dabs of Stik-Gum. He looked a little better, he thought, with the blue-gray teeth, and he always put his dentures in before shaving. One thing he knew for certain, he looked much trimmer and felt much better at 182 pounds than he had at 205.

The window air conditioner labored away while he dressed (today he wore the yellow leisure suit), and then he made a final check of the room to see if he had forgotten anything. Today was Friday, and his sheets wouldn't be changed until Saturday morning. The sitting room was a mess, and there was a pile of dirty laundry in the corner of the bedroom. The Peruvian maid would pick up his laundry when she changed the sheets and bring it back on Saturday evening. There was a sour, locker-room smell in both rooms.

Hoke checked his .38 Chief's Special, slipped it into his holster, and clipped the holster into his belt at the back. He would be reading most of the day, so he left his handcuffs and leather sap on the dresser before going down to the lobby.

As Hoke took his daily report into Mr. Bennett's office, Eddie Cohen, the desk clerk, called to him from the desk.

"Sergeant Moseley," the old man said, "you had a call about three A.M., but I told the lady I couldn't wake you up unless it was an emergency. She said it wasn't an emergency, and she didn't give her name. But I wouldn't wake nobody at three o'clock in the morning for nothing."

"Thanks, Eddie. What did she sound like? The caller, I mean?"

"Like a woman. It was a woman's voice, that's all."

"Okay. If she happens to call back today, try and get her name and number. The plug on my air conditioner was pulled out again when I got to my room last night. I've told you before not to pull it out. The room was like a damned oven with the burners on high when I came home."

"Mr. Bennett sends me around to pull out the plugs when nobody's home. If no one's in the room, it just wastes energy, he said."

"I understand your position, Eddie, but that rule doesn't apply to me. It takes about two hours for that beat-up air conditioner to cool off the suite. Also, tell Emilio to set some rat traps around the dumpster again. I spotted two Norways in the back corridor last night."

"It ain't the dumpster they're after." Eddie shook his head. "These old ladies put their garbage in the hallways instead of taking it down to the dumpster."

"Never mind. Have Emilio set the traps. I put it in my report to Mr. Bennett. He can pay off the inspectors, but if one of these old ladies ever gets bitten by a Norway, they'll come down on us again."

Hoke got into his car, wondering why he should be concerned. Within a week, he'd have to get out of the hotel anyway. He didn't know where he would be, but he would be somewhere else. With all of the money he owed, a suspension without pay would be a disaster. And any time his check to Patsy was more than a day late, he got a threatening call from her bitchy lawyer.

When Hoke got to the station at seven-thirty, he learned that Ellita was already there and had moved all of the cold case files down to the interrogation room. He sent her down to the cafeteria to get coffee and a jelly doughnut. He hadn't felt like poaching eggs, and boiling two more, on his hot plate this morning; now his stomach rumbled with hunger. He divided the huge pile into three more or less even stacks without counting them. He also got some legal pads and Bic ballpoints from his office. Sanchez returned with three coffees and Hoke's doughnut.

"Sergeant Henderson's still out there in the bullpen talking to Lieutenant Slater and Teddy Gonzalez," she said, "but I brought coffee for him, too. Are you going to brief Teddy on what we've been doing?"

"Gonzalez'll be busy enough as it is. For now, we'll hang onto our own cases. There's only the one child-abuse case and a suicide. We can complete them and handle the cold cases, too."

"But Major Brownley said—"

"I know what he said. But there's no hurry on our pending cases. After we get the P.M., we can close out the Hickey overdose case, too. I talked to Mrs. Hickey last night and found out that the kid was in over his head. Two guys came around yesterday afternoon and told her that Hickey had ripped them off for twenty-five thousand bucks."

"There was only a thousand in his room."

"I know. I'm giving it to her today. What I figure, Hickey stashed the money somewhere, and then was so excited by the idea that he gave himself a stronger fix than he thought he was getting."

Ellita nodded. "It could've happened that way. But Mrs. Hickey could've also taken the extra twenty-four thousand and left the thousand on top of the dresser."

"No." Hoke shook his head. "She wouldn't do that."

"You told me yesterday that an amateur never takes it all, and that only pros take everything."

"That's true as a general rule, but it doesn't apply to Mrs. Hickey. I talked to her for a long time, and she isn't the kind of woman who'd steal from her stepson."

"Jerry isn't her son?"

"No, she inherited him from her ex-husband, along with the house, when they got divorced."

"It's a possibility, just the same."

"No way. She's a successful businesswoman, with her own flower shop in the Gables. Forget about it. We've got a lot of work to do."

Sanchez watched him and sipped her coffee.

Hoke took off his jacket and draped it over the back of the folding chair. He had been wearing the same short-sleeved flowered sports shirt for three days, and there were three concentric white rings of dried sweat under the armpits. He wouldn't have a clean shirt until Saturday evening. The windowless room was cool enough, with plenty of cold air coming through the ducts, but he realized that if he could smell the dried perspiration on his shirt, Ellita could, too. So what? He could smell her overdose of Shalimar perfume, with an extra overlay of added musk. Like most Cuban women, she used too much perfume.

"Just take a stack," Hoke said, "and read them all. When I get through my stack we'll exchange. After we've read all the cases, we'll each vote on the three most likely cases to work on. Then we'll see what we've got. Take your time, Ellita. My idea's to discover the ten most likely cases. If we all come up with the same ten, we'll have a consensus. But we won't look at each other's choices till we've each gone through all fifty of them. I don't want to prejudice you or Bill by telling you my choices as we go along."

"You won't. But we won't get through all these cases today."

Hoke shrugged. "We've got two months. But the ones we do agree on, even if it takes us a week, will save us a lot of useless running around later."

They went to work, not speaking, and taking occasional notes. Bill Henderson joined them at nine-thirty. Hoke briefed him on the plan, and Henderson moved his stack down to the far end of the table.

"That extra cup of coffee's yours, Bill," Hoke said.

"Thanks, Ellita," Henderson said, removing the plastic lid. He sipped the coffee and made a face. "Christ, it's stone cold. I'll go down for some more. Anybody else ready for more coffee?"

"I'll get it," Ellita said, getting up. "I didn't think you'd be out there so long with Slater and Gonzalez."

When she was gone, Henderson got up and sat on the table next to Hoke. "I was already late this morning in the first place, and then I had to argue with Slater. He wanted

67

me to go over tomorrow afternoon to Miami Beach and guard wedding gifts at a reception. There's fifty bucks in it, less Slater's ten percent for giving you the job, but you have to wear your uniform. That isn't bad, Hoke, fifty bucks for drinking champagne for three hours while you just stand around. But I couldn't take it because I promised Marie I'd take her and the kids to the Metrozoo. Now if you can use fifty bucks, Hoke, you could get the job if you asked Slater.''

''My uniform's too loose on me now, Bill. But I wouldn't take it anyway. When I made sergeant, I promised myself I wouldn't do any more moonlighting. I'm not uptight about it, and I could use the dough, but I resent Slater's ten percent rake-off. I've told him so, and that's why he never asks me to take any moonlighting jobs. So if I asked him for this one, he'd think I'd changed my mind.''

''I know what you mean. I was just passing along the suggestion. The other reason I'm late, I had to talk to my son this morning. I had a note from his P.E. coach that Jimmy won't take a shower after P.E.''

''How old is Jimmy now?''

''Fourteen. I asked him about it, and he said he doesn't want the other boys looking at his thing.''

''Is it too big or too small?''

''I don't know. He won't show it to me either. But he was stubborn about it, so I gave him a note to take to the coach, telling him that Jimmy has scabies. I said he couldn't take showers until he got through using sulfur ointment to get rid of it.''

''He'll have to take a shower sooner or later.''

''I know. But Jimmy's sensitive, Hoke. Daphne's a year younger, and she's tougher than he is. If they'd let her, she'd take a shower with the boys in Jimmy's place.''

''That's because your wife's in NOW. Does Marie let Daphne read her *Ms.* magazines?''

"Daphne doesn't read anything. And she hasn't learned a fucking thing in school. Last week, she asked me when we were going to have the next Bicentennial celebration. She still reads at the third-grade level. But she isn't dumb. She can watch a mystery on the tube, and tell you who the guilty person is before the first commercial. I thought she might have dyslexia, but I had her tested and her eyes are okay. She just doesn't like to read. But Jimmy's read my entire Doc Savage collection already, and most of my Edgar Rice Burroughs Mars books."

"I don't know whether my daughters can read or not."

"Do you ever miss 'em, Hoke? The girls?"

"No. I mean, I do once in a while . . . but I don't. They were real little when they left, and I didn't know them that well. I'm just not a family man."

The three of them worked until eleven-thirty, and then Hoke checked his in-box in the office. There were two phone messages to call Harold Hickey, in addition to the regular distribution. The second telephone message from Hickey said he would be at home all day. There were no lab reports, and nothing pressing to answer in the mail.

Hoke told Henderson and Ellita that he was going out for a few hours, and suggested that the two of them break for lunch.

"I should be back before four o'clock, but I've got some house-hunting to do."

"Don't rush into anything, Hoke," Henderson said. "If push comes to shove, I can always put you up on a cot in my Florida room for a few days."

"Thanks, Bill, but I don't get along too well with Marie, as you know. She's always accusing me of making a sexist remark, and I never know what she's talking about."

"I didn't mean on a permanent basis. But it would be better to sleep in my Florida room for a few days than to get a suspension without pay."

"Thanks, Bill. If I have to take you up on it, I will.

Anyway, if I'm not back by four-thirty, lock the files up in my office and we'll start on 'em again Monday. Until we start work on an actual case or two, we'll just put in a normal eight-hour day.''

"I might come in tomorrow for a couple of hours," Ellita said.

"That's up to you. But you don't have to—anyway, I should be back before four.''

Hoke left the office and drove to Hallandale, but he took U.S. 1 instead of the I-95 Expressway. About once a month, when Hoke had to be in the north part of town, he stopped at Sam's Sandwich Shoppe for a tongue on rye. Hoke didn't abuse the privilege (once a month was just about right), but he liked to stop at Sam's because Sam always tore up his lunch check. Not only was the sandwich free, but except for Wolfie's in Miami Beach, Sam made the best tongue sandwiches in Dade County.

7

The guard at the sentry box outside the Hallandale Mercury Club wore a powder-blue uniform, a gold cap with a black bill, and a shiny black-patent-leather Sam Browne belt, complete with holster. There was no weapon in the holster. The man held a Lucite clipboard in his left hand and a one-ounce paper cup of Cuban coffee in his right. Droplets of coffee from the guard's thick mustache had dribbled onto the light-blue jacket.

Hoke stopped at the lowered black-and-yellow-striped semaphore arm. The guard looked at his clipboard, and at his coffee, then put the cup down, realizing that he would need his right hand to write on the pad in the clipboard.

"Ramon Novarro," Hoke said, "to see Mr. Harold Hickey."

The guard looked at his mimeographed sheet, found Hickey's name and apartment number, and wrote "R. Novarro" opposite Hickey's name. He checked Hoke's auto tag number, added that to the clipboard, and pushed a button that raised the arm.

"Apartment 406," the guard said.

Hoke drove through the gate, parked on the grassy verge, and walked back to the gatehouse. The compact complex of clubhouse and three separate low-rise apartment buildings was enclosed by a buff-colored ten-foot wall. The wall was topped with three strands of barbed wire. Two locked gates on the ocean side, opening to the marina and the beach, were marked "Members." Hoke assumed that members held keys to both gates.

"How do you know," Hoke asked the guard, "that my name's Ramon Novarro?"

"What?"

"I said, 'How do you know my name's Ramon Novarro?' You didn't ask me for any ID. You didn't look very hard to see if I was armed, either." Hoke took his .38 out of the belt holster, showed it to the guard, and returned it.

"In fact," Hoke continued, "you don't know who I am, or who I'm going to see. All you know is that Harold Hickey has an apartment here, and you knew that much before I drove up to the gate. Why didn't you call Mr. Hickey and tell him that a Mr. Ramon Novarro was here to see him? He might've told you that Novarro is dead, and has been dead, for several years."

Hoke showed the guard his shield and ID folder. "I'm a police officer. How much they pay you, three sixty-five an hour?"

"No, sir. Four dollars."

"For what you aren't doing, that's a good sum."

Hoke got back into his car, drove to the guest parking area in front of the clubhouse, and made a guess. If the three buildings were each three stories, and they were, Apartment 406 should be in Building Two on the first floor. He was right. He lifted and dropped the brass knocker on Hickey's front door three times. The door was opened by a Filipino houseboy, actually a wizened man of about sixty wearing pink linen trousers, a gray silk house jacket and a white shirt with a black bow tie. He led Hoke down the hallway, past the living room, and into Hickey's den-of-fice. The living room and the den were furnished with black leather and chrome armchairs and glass-topped tables. Hickey was seated in a black leather, deeply cushioned armchair. As Hoke came in, he got to his feet and switched off the television. Hickey wore a purple velour running suit and a pair of white rabbit-fur slippers. The air conditioning hissed quietly, and Hoke figured it was well below 65 degrees.

Hickey smiled, revealing expensively capped teeth, and the smile made him almost handsome. His black hair was worn long, in a modified Prince Valiant cut, but the youthful effect was spoiled by a baseball-size bald spot at the crown. Hickey was tall and lean. His nails had been buffed and polished, and there was a gold University of Miami ring on his left hand.

"I just got a strange call from the gate guard." Hickey smiled. "Words to the effect that a dead policeman was on the way to see me."

"Did he tell you his name?"

"Ramon Novarro. Wasn't he the actor who was killed by a hustler a few years ago?"

"He's dead, but I don't remember the circumstances. I remember seeing some of his films, from when I was a kid, but none of the titles. He was always running someone through with a sword."

"No matter. Sit down, Mr. Moseley. Would you like a drink?"

"A Tab."

"Two Tabs," Hickey said to the doorway. "You are Mr. Moseley, aren't you?"

Hoke nodded. "I was testing your gate guard. You people pay for security, but you don't get very much."

"I know. But a gate guard is a deterrent, if nothing else. We used to pay more for armed guards, and then one night a Nicaraguan guard at the gate shot a hole in the manager's car. The manager thought all the guards knew him, but he didn't take the turnover into account. So when he drove through the gate without stopping, a new guard took a shot at him. After that, we decided it would be best to have unarmed guards."

Hoke sat in a leather chair that faced the sliding glass doors to a bare travertine marble patio. There were two potted spider palms on the patio, but no chairs. Hoke pointed toward the patio with his chin.

Hickey smiled. "I never use my patio. If I feel the need of some sun, I go over to the pool by the clubhouse. That's why there's no furniture out there."

"No. I was just thinking you don't have much of a view from here, with the wall only twenty feet away."

"I didn't buy this place for the view. I bought it because I could finally afford to live in a place like this. I tried to call you last night, twice, but I didn't get an answer. You said on the phone that—"

"I'm sorry about that. There's only one desk man at the Eldorado, and when he's not at the desk there's no one on the switchboard. I'm sorry you couldn't get through. It's been inconvenient for me, too, at times. At any rate, when I called you from Mrs. Hickey's house, I didn't know at the time who you were. Later on, I remembered that you were one of the drug lawyers profiled in the paper a few months back."

"An inaccurate portrait. I handle drug cases once in a while, just like any other lawyer, but I specialize in taxes. Lately, I've been turning down drug cases. The dealers can

74

afford my fees, but they think they can get off simply because they've paid a large fee. I always tell them in advance that I can get a few delays, or get them out on bond, but if they're guilty, they're going to do a little time. Things have changed a lot down here, you know, with the Vice President's task force on drugs.''

The houseboy brought in two cans of Tab; each can was wrapped neatly in a brown paper towel, with the towel secured by a rubber band. The houseboy left, and Hoke removed the straw. He noticed a crude black-and-white drawing on the wall above Hickey's computer table.

"Is that an original Matisse?" Hoke asked, lifting his Tab.

"James Thurber. It's a woman. That thing in her hand is either a martini glass or a dog collar, I've never been able to decide which.''

"Looks more like a bracelet to me."

"Yes, it could very well be a bracelet."

Hoke sipped from the Tab. "I suppose you phoned Mrs. Hickey last night?''

"When I couldn't get you, yes."

"You know that Jerry died from an overdose of heroin?''

Hickey nodded. "That's what she said."

"What I'd like to know is the kind of relationship you had with your son, Mr. Hickey. How close you were to him, for example; whether you were the stern father, or what?''

"Why? What's that got to do with Jerry's death?"

"I don't know. It occurred to me last night that he might've met some of your clients, your drug dealers. If so, he could've made a connection through them, or one of them. He'd been on drugs for a long time.''

"Jerry never met any of my clients. He never came to my office because it was off limits to him. To be frank, we didn't have any relationship, not of the sort you mean. In

75

the first place, Jerry wasn't my real son. I suppose you know that already.''

''Your wife told me.''

''Ex-wife. Did Loretta also tell you how she happened to become my ex-wife?''

''No. But I didn't ask.''

''I found out she was fucking Jerry, that's how. He was seventeen at the time. I don't know how long it had been going on, but as soon as I found out about it I moved out. I didn't really care. In fact, it was a good excuse to get a divorce. She couldn't fight me about something like that in court, so we obtained a simple no-fault divorce. I made some concessions I didn't have to make, but a man always has to do that if he doesn't want to be distracted. I was just getting into making some big bucks, so I wasn't hurt financially. She got the house, of course, and one of the cars.

''Legally, you see, I got stuck with Jerry when my first wife divorced me. Jerry was her son, and I was asshole enough when we first got married to adopt him. So not only did I get rid of Loretta, I got rid of Jerry at the same time when my divorce came through. It was a good deal all the way around.''

''Except, perhaps, for Jerry.''

''Jerry had no complaints. He had a place to live, and no one ever hassled him. Loretta didn't want to keep him, but she couldn't very well get out of it. What happened between them wasn't any love affair, or anything close to it. She'd been drinking one day, and I suppose she got a little horny. Jerry, who was seventeen, happened to be available. It happened a few more times, I suppose. You know how it is, once you get it, you can always get it again. But it was all over by the time I found out about it, I'm pretty sure.''

''How'd you find out? It's none of my business, but I'm curious.''

76

"Mrs. Koontz, the next-door neighbor, told me. I didn't believe her at first, but then when I questioned Jerry he admitted it right away. 'I didn't think you'd mind, Mr. Hickey,' he said. And of course I didn't mind, because then I had an excuse to get out of a bad marriage."

"Your son called you 'Mr. Hickey'?"

"Most of the time, yes. I didn't want him to call me 'Dad' because he wasn't my real son. I don't see anything wrong with that. After all, I supported him, so I was entitled to a little respect."

"Yours wasn't exactly a loving relationship then?"

"He got some love from Loretta." Hickey smiled. "He admitted it, and so did Loretta after I confronted her with his confession. I made him put it in writing, in case she wanted to fight the divorce."

"How'd Jerry get on the spike without you finding out about it?"

"I did know about it. I recognized the signs right away. I advised Jerry to get off drugs at once. I also told him I'd pay for drug counseling. But he claimed he could handle it, and that was that. A lot of young people are into dope down here, you know."

"I know."

"I don't even smoke pot. But Jerry could get drugs anywhere in the city in five minutes, so long as he had the money."

"But you gave him the money."

"I gave him a small allowance after he quit school, but I advised him to finish high school. And I told him I'd put him through college. But when he dropped out of high school, I lowered his allowance. In this state, a father's no longer responsible for a child after he reaches eighteen. But I would've sent him to college. No one ever helped me." He leaned forward in his chair. "I put myself through the University of Miami by washing trays at night in the old Holsum Bakery in South Miami. And I did maintenance

77

work to get a free efficiency apartment. No one ever gave me a fucking penny. Miami offers a young man more opportunities than any other city in the United States. If you want to get ahead down here, you take advantage of them. Jerry fell by the wayside. It's not society's fault, and it's not Reagan's, and it's not mine.'' Hickey, sitting back, started to yawn; he put a hand to his mouth. ''Excuse me. But this is a sore point with me. Every day, if you look at the women's section of the paper, you'll see articles blaming the parents for the way their kids turn out. It's all bullshit.''

''It isn't easy to always know the right thing to do, I suppose. But then, I'm not a family man.''

''When can I get the body? I'd like to send somebody over to get Jerry cremated.''

''After the autopsy. I can recommend Minrow's Funeral Home, if you don't have anyone else in mind.''

''What do you get? A ten percent commission?''

Hoke didn't mind the question, not from a Miami lawyer. As it happened, Hoke didn't get any commission, but he usually recommended Minrow when someone asked, because he and Minrow had been neighbors when Hoke first moved to Miami. If he denied getting anything, Hoke knew that Hickey would merely consider him a fool.

''No,'' Hoke said. ''I just get a flat fifty bucks for each referral.''

''Okay. I'll call Minrow's and mention that you recommended him. It makes no difference to me.''

''At one time,'' Hoke said, getting to his feet, and placing the empty Tab can on the glass-topped desk, ''there was a number you could call in Miami, and a man would come by in a taxi cab. You paid him five bucks and he took the body away and you never heard of it again. But I don't think that number's in service any longer.''

''Is that the truth, Mr. Moseley, or are you trying to be funny?''

78

"Sergeant Moseley." Hoke pointed to a framed blue-and-green oleograph on the opposite wall. A blue man playing a violin floated upside down above a white house in a green sky. "Is that one of Jerry's crayon drawings, from when he was a kid?"

Hickey shook his head. "No, it's a Marc Chagall." He leaned forward and switched on the television. A commercial touting the new aviary at the Metrozoo appeared on the screen, and Hickey turned off the sound.

"I like the picture anyway," Hoke said, turning in the doorway. "Just one more question, Mr. Hickey, and I'll be on my way. Did Jerry ever carry any large sums of money for you?"

Hickey got to his feet. He shook his head. "No. I never wrote Jerry a check for more than a hundred dollars at a time. The most money he ever had was when he sold his car. I paid four thousand for his Escort, and he sold it for only two. He should've gotten a lot more than that."

"That almost always happens. You always pay more for a car than you sell it for."

"I know that. But I should've kept the title so he couldn't've sold it at all."

"We all make mistakes sooner or later, Mr. Hickey. Thanks for the Tab."

The Filipino appeared and escorted Hoke to the front door.

8

As Hoke drove back toward the city after cutting over to I-95, he wondered why he had wasted time talking to Harold Hickey. Hoke wasn't fond of lawyers, especially lawyers like Hickey who managed to get low bonds for their drug clients and then advised them to skip the country to avoid prison. On the other hand, someone had been furnishing Jerry with money. Jerry's father gave him an allowance, but he wouldn't have given the kid a thousand dollars. A thousand bucks for a drug dealer, on the other hand, was small change. And now that he was dead, the missing $24,000 was gone forever. It was possible that Jerry had been a small-time pusher in the Grove to help him support his own habit. But it still bothered Hoke that an experienced user, with a large sum of money and more drugs available, would take a deliberate overdose, or even OD accidentally. It just didn't fit the pattern.

Hoke returned to U.S. 1, and then stopped at an Eckerd's drugstore to buy a package of Kools. After he paid for the cigarettes, he showed the clerk his shield and asked if he could use the telephone. Since the pay phone rates had jumped from a dime to a quarter a few years back, Hoke, as a matter of principle, had never paid to use a phone again. He called Ms. Westphal at the house-sitting service. When she answered after the first ring, Hoke identified himself and asked if she had found any more prospects for him.

"I'm now willing," he said, "to take a short-time sitter's job, even if it's only a couple of weeks. How about that apartment on Grove Isle?"

"That's gone. I've got a garage apartment on Tangerine Lane in the black Grove. It'll be available next Friday for twenty-one days. It's owned by a Barbadian sculptor who's going up to New York for a one-man show. He uses the garage under his apartment as his studio, and he doesn't want his tools and things left unguarded."

"That's right in the middle of the black Grove, isn't it?"

"Not exactly in the middle. It's off Douglas a few blocks. But you're a policeman, and you've got a gun, so it shouldn't bother you to live in a black neighborhood."

"I told you I couldn't be there much in the daytime, except for weekends."

"Daytime doesn't bother Mr. Noseworthy. The man who lives in the house in front'll be home during the day."

"That's a pretty funky neighborhood, Ms. Westphal."

"Listen, Sergeant, I think you're a little too finicky for this kind of work. Perhaps you should look for another agency—"

"No, no, I'll take the garage apartment. Of course, I'd like to look at it first."

"There's nothing to see. It's got a bed, a sink, a hot plate and a refrigerator, and you use the bathroom in the house in front of the garage. There's no dog, if that's what's bothering you. If you don't want it, I can easily get a black house-sitter for a furnished apartment like this one."

"Okay, I'll take it. I'll drop by one day next week for the key."

Ms. Westphal gave Hoke the address and reminded him to bring a hundred dollars for the bond when he came by for the key.

"If you could give me my hundred-and-five-dollar salary in advance," Hoke suggested, "you could just hang onto the hundred for the bond and pay me five dollars."

"You're very droll, Sergeant." Ms. Westphal laughed and hung up the phone.

Hoke returned to his car. Major Brownley, he knew, would recognize the address in the black Grove and would wonder why in the hell he had moved there. He didn't want the major to know that he would be living rent-free as a house-sitter. He wondered if the Bajan sculptor had a phone. If not, he would have to make some kind of arrangement with the neighbors to take his phone calls. The problem was, in that neighborhood, not many people could afford a phone. He'd just have to wait and see. Moving, at least, was no problem. Except for a cardboard box full of his files and old papers, all he had to move were his clothes and his little Sony TV. And his hot plate; he'd better take his hot plate. Even if Noseworthy had one, Hoke would probably need his own for the next move, although he could hardly move down any lower than a garage apartment in the Coconut Grove ghetto. Yes, he could; the Overtown ghetto was worse.

When Hoke returned to the station, he stopped for a moment to say hello to Bill and Ellita and then he checked his mail. There was a printout on Gerald Hickey. Hoke sat in his office and read the rap sheet, which went back to Jerry's junior-high-school days.

In the eighth grade Jerry had gotten into a fight with a black student, claiming that his lunch money had been taken. A knife had been confiscated, but neither boy had been cut. No charges filed, but the officer who had been called by the principal had made a written report of the incident.

There were two separate arrests for "joyriding" in stolen cars. Jerry was merely a passenger each time, and stated he didn't know the car—in each incident—was stolen. No charges filed.

There was another arrest when a woman claimed Jerry had exposed himself to her while standing on her front lawn. The misdemeanor was reduced to committing a public nuisance when Jerry claimed he had merely stopped to urinate on the woman's lawn. Although the incident happened at 3 P.M., Jerry said he didn't see the woman sitting on her front porch ten feet away. Charge dismissed. Counsel for Jerry had been Harold Hickey.

Arrested for smoking marijuana, with two other juveniles, in Peacock Park, Coconut Grove. Charge reduced to loitering. No charges filed. Released in father's custody.

Two more pickups for "loitering" in Coconut Grove. No charges filed. Released at station.

Picked up in a Coral Gables parking lot. A glasscutter confiscated. Jerry claimed he found the glasscutter in the street, and that he didn't know what the tool was used for. No charges filed.

Picked up in the parking lot, Sears, Coral Gables store, for shoplifting. Subject's father paid for the item—a brass standing lamp, complete with parchment shade, with a blue eagle painted on it. Released to father's custody. No charges filed.

There was also a brief report from an interview with a psychiatric social worker:

Hickey, Gerald. Age: 16—4 mos. 68 inches tall. Wt. 147 lbs. Adopted. I.Q. (Stanford/B) 123. Intelligent, but rambles when asked direct questions. Sociopathic personality. Schizoid tendencies; unrealistic goals, i.e., wants to be "Russian interpreter at U.N." or a "marine biologist." Suppressed sexual anxieties. Admits to hustling gays for money, but not always "successful." Smokes pot daily. Mixes codeine with pot, but doesn't use PCP. Cooperative. Despite sociopathic attitude and quick temper, Jerry would probably thrive in a disciplined environment, e.g., live-in military school. Father can afford it. Therapy recommended.

s/t M. Sneider, MSW

Not much. Hoke wished now he had read the file before he talked to Harold Hickey. He could have asked him why he hadn't sent Jerry to a military school. Of course, at a military academy, a weak kid like Jerry would have been cornholed by the upper classmen, but they would have kept him off the spike. On the other hand, this was about the time of Hickey's marriage to Loretta, so Harold might have thought that she would be a stabilizing factor for Jerry. But that was speculation. Not a single overnight stay in Youth Hall or jail. In a legal sense, Jerry wasn't a juvenile delinquent officially. To become a bona fide juvenile delinquent, a kid had to be charged, found guilty, and the case adjudicated. If Jerry had been pushing dope, he had managed to avoid ever being apprehended for it.

Hoke phoned the lab and asked if they had completed the report on the contents of the Baggie that Sanchez had sent for analysis. He was promised a report for Monday, Tuesday at the latest.

"Make it Monday," Hoke said and hung up.

84

It was only three o'clock, and he should take the money to Loretta Hickey. But there were all those files to be read. Henderson and Sanchez would have made a dent in them by now, and he would have to catch up. Hoke looked up the number of the Bouquetique in Coral Gables, then wrote it in his notebook before dialing.

A childish, incredibly high voice answered. "Bouquetique. How may I help you?"

"Mrs. Hickey, please."

"She's designing in the back. May I help you?"

"Just take a message. Tell her that Sergeant Moseley will be in to see her tomorrow."

"Sergeant Moseley?" the tiny voice chirped.

"That's right. You are open on Saturday, aren't you?"

"Oh, yes! Saturday's our busiest day."

"Okay. I don't know what time, but it'll be some time tomorrow."

Hoke hung up the phone. The voice sounded like a little girl around six or seven years old, he thought. Why would Loretta Hickey employ a child to answer the telephone? Hoke went to join Bill and Ellita in the interrogation room.

Bill and Ellita were sitting close together at Bill's end of the table. Both were studying material from the same accordion file. Hoke lighted a Kool, but before he could sit down, Bill held up an eight-by-ten black-and-white glossy photograph.

"Remember this guy, Hoke?"

Hoke looked at the photo and grinned. It was a picture of an unsmiling middle-aged man—a head-and-shoulders shot—wearing an open-collared polo shirt.

"Captain Midnight."

"That's right," Bill said. "Captain Morrow. I was telling Ellita about him. He was the pilot we called Captain Midnight. We must've talked to him a half-dozen times three years ago."

"He was clean."

"He wasn't clean. He was eliminated as a suspect because we couldn't prove anything. Anyway, I'd been looking at his file just before Ellita and I went over to have lunch at the Omni. Otherwise, I don't think I'd have recognized him. The fucker was sitting on the bus bench at the southwest corner of Biscayne when we went in, and he was still sitting in the same place when we came back to get the car. But if I hadn't just been looking at his photo here, I wouldn't've recognized him. He's a bum now, Hoke. On a hunch, I sent Ellita over to talk to him because I figured he might recognize me. She asked him if he'd missed his bus, and he told her he was waiting for his wife."

"His wife's dead," Hoke said. "Her head was smashed in by a four-pound sledgehammer. He was our only suspect, Ellita, but we finally suspended the case."

"He did it, Hoke, I know he did," Bill said.

"We think he did it. We couldn't ever prove it, Bill. He passed the polygraph without a tremor. I know the machine can be beat, but in his case, if he did kill her, the indications were that he didn't know he'd killed her. After he passed the test, we had to drop it altogether."

"According to your notes," Ellita said, "he didn't have any reason to kill his wife. They'd only been married a year, and the neighbors claimed they were a happy couple. He didn't need money—not as a pilot earning fifty thousand a year."

Hoke sat down and flipped through the papers in the file. "We should be reading the other cases. We can vote on this one later if you want, if you want to put it on your list. But right now we should follow my plan."

"Tell him, Ellita," Henderson said.

"He was very confused, Sergeant Moseley," Ellita said. "I tried to talk to him, ask him a few more questions like 'Are you sure your wife's bus stops here?' and he just

86

repeated what he said the first time. Finally, he got angry. He said, 'You aren't my wife,' and walked away.''

"I signaled Ellita to go get the car," Bill said, "and I tailed him. He lives over on Second Avenue, down from the old Sears store, in Grogan's Halfway House, or what used to be the halfway house. It's just a rooming house now. Grogan lost his license and his city funds when the bag lady starved to death on the front porch. Do you remember that, Hoke?"

"Yeah. It was a legal problem. There was no law to cover it, although the paper wrote an editorial on the case. What happened, Ellita, was weird. There were about ten guys staying at the halfway house at the time. All of them were on parole, but some had jobs and others were on a methadone program and just lived there. Do you remember the bag lady case at all?"

"No. How long ago was it?"

"Seven or eight years. I don't remember exactly. Anyway, this old lady climbed onto the porch when it was raining. She was run down, physically, like most bag ladies, and she just laid there for four days. The guys in the halfway house, including Grogan, had to step over her for the first day or so, and then she managed to crawl over to the wall. The point is, no one helped her or gave her any food or water. She was too weak to move, so she just died there. Finally, after she died, someone told Grogan the woman was dead, and he called the rescue squad to pick up her body. When he was asked why he didn't call them the first day she showed up on the porch, he said he didn't mind her lying there. She didn't bother anybody, he said, but he would've called the police if she'd tried to come inside the house. When they were questioned, the parolees in the halfway house all claimed that they didn't see anything wrong with a woman lying out there, moaning, on the porch."

"And so Grogan lost his license for the halfway house?"

"Yeah, but not for that. If someone comes up on your front porch to get out of the rain, you can let him do it out of the goodness of your heart. That person isn't your personal responsibility. But a lot of people in town were pissed off because the old lady died. Four days is a long time. So housing inspectors were sent out, and they yanked Grogan's license for faulty wiring and drainage problems."

"But Grogan's house is still there, Hoke," Henderson said. "Only now his place is a rooming house, and that's where Captain Morrow lives. Ellita picked me up in the car, and we came back here. I went over his file and I think we should talk to Captain Midnight again. The man owned a hundred-thousand-dollar home, he had money in the bank, and he was an airline pilot. Where did all of that go in only three years? He looks like he's been on the street for months. And he looks at least twenty years older than he did the last time we talked to him. If he's sitting around on a bus bench waiting for his dead wife, he's confused and disoriented. Maybe he'll admit now that he killed her if we lean on him a little. The time to kick a man, Hoke, is when he's down. You know that."

"Maybe he was waiting for a new wife. He could have gotten married again, you know."

"Tell him, Ellita," Henderson said. "Did he look like a married man to you?"

"No one would marry a bum like that. He's a sick man, not a drunk, not talking to himself or anything like that, more like a man lost somewhere in his own thoughts."

"Let's go talk to him, Hoke," Henderson said. "You know he's guilty and so do I. If we can crack a case on our first day, Willie Brownley'll shit his pants."

"Okay. But let me look at the file for a minute."

Everything in the file led to Captain Robert Morrow as a prime suspect. After dinner he had left his house, he said, to get a package of cigarettes. While he was at the 7/Eleven, he drank a cup of coffee, a large one, and talked to the Cuban manager. His house was only two blocks away, and he was gone for only twenty minutes—twenty-two minutes at most. When he returned home, he found his wife in the kitchen. Someone had taken his four-pound sledgehammer from the garage and hit his wife over the head with it while she was washing pots and pans at the sink. Death was instantaneous, with a hole in her skull big enough to hold an orange. From the way it looked, she hadn't known what hit her. The sledgehammer, without prints, was on the floor beside her body. When he discovered her body, Captain Morrow had telephoned 911 and waited outside on the front lawn until the police arrived, smoking two of the cigarettes from the package of Pall Malls he had bought at the 7/Eleven.

He had shown little or no emotion about his wife's death, but he had explained that to Hoke and Henderson. "After two years in 'Nam, I don't find the sight of a dead body particularly upsetting," he had said.

He had understood his Miranda rights, but he talked freely anyway, without a lawyer present. "I didn't do it," he claimed. "If you charge me, I'll get a lawyer, but I can't see paying a lawyer who'll just tell me to remain silent. I haven't done anything to remain silent about."

Hoke and Bill had talked to the neighbors, to the Morrows' friends—they didn't have many acquaintances—and Mrs. Morrow did not, apparently, have any enemies. Nothing had been stolen from the house, not even the three-thousand-dollar diamond ring that Mrs. Morrow had taken off her finger before washing the pots and pans. The ring was still on the counter right next to the sink.

What had bothered Hoke and Bill most, however, was why Captain Morrow had gone to the 7/Eleven to buy cigarettes. He had a carton of Pall Malls, with only two packs missing, in his dresser drawer. Also, there was a pot of coffee in the Mr. Coffee machine in the kitchen. The pot was half full, and the red light on the base of the coffee maker showed that it was still warm enough to drink. He had, for some reason, lingered in the convenience store, establishing an alibi with the manager before returning home. Two witnesses had seen him on his walk to the store and back, but that merely confirmed that he had been in the store.

The case had been frustrating. Hoke and Bill had talked to Morrow several times. At one point, Hoke had advised him to confess and to plead "post-Vietnam stress syndrome," which would mean, in all probability, a lighter sentence or a commitment of a year or two to a psychiatric hospital.

"I didn't do it," Captain Morrow said. "And I don't have any stress problems. If I did, they wouldn't have me flying a 707 back and forth to Rio."

After the pilot passed the lie detector test, they had put the case away, pulling it out occasionally only to take another look at it. But there were no more leads, and it looked as though Captain Morrow had managed to get away with murder.

"Why not?" Hoke said. "It won't hurt to talk to him again. Bill and I will do the talking, Ellita. But you check out a micro-cassette recorder from Supply and keep it in your purse. Just record everything that's said, and don't get too close to him. You got handcuffs, Bill?"

Bill nodded.

"I didn't bring mine today. I didn't think I'd need 'em."

9

From the looks of Grogan's rooming house, an ocher concrete-block-and-stucco two-story structure on Second Avenue, very few repairs, if any, had been made since Grogan had lost his city contract to run a halfway house. The unpainted concrete porch, almost flush with the cracked sidewalk, held two rusty metal chairs. They were occupied by two aging winos. There was no rail, and as soon as Hoke, Henderson, and Ellita stepped onto the porch, the winos stepped off the other end of the porch and started briskly down the street. Hoke wore high-topped, lace-up, double-soled black shoes, which gave him away as a cop if his face did not. Henderson usually reminded people of a high-school football coach. Ellita, of course, although she wore sensible low-heeled black pumps, was not so obviously a police officer. Today she wore a red-and-white vertical-striped ballerina-length skirt with her cream-colored silk blouse.

A black-and-white TV crackled in the living room, but although the set was on, no one was in the room to watch it. There were some battered chairs of wicker, and a low coffee table piled high with old *Sports Illustrated* and *Gourmet* magazines. There was a sign on the wall saying "Thank you for not smoking," and there were no ashtrays in the room; nevertheless, there were more than a dozen cigarette butts ground into the scuffed linoleum floor.

The landlord was in the kitchen. He was sitting at a table by the window, overlooking a backyard that contained a wheelless 1967 Buick on concrete blocks, a discarded and cracked toilet, and a pile of tin cans. The backyard was enclosed by a wooden fence, but only the top third of the fence was visible because of the jungly growth of tall grass and clumps of wild bamboo. The proprietor, a gray-haired man in his mid-sixties, was eating a bacon-and-fried-egg sandwich.

Hoke showed the man his badge. "Are you Mr. Grogan?"

"You're looking at him. Reginald B. Grogan. What can I do for you, Officer?"

"We'd like to talk to Captain Morrow."

"No Captain Morrow here. People come and go, but I haven't had a boat captain here since I lost the methadone people."

"He's an airplane captain. A pilot."

"No pilots either. Never had one of them. People here now are mostly day laborers, although a couple are on Social Security. But no Morrow."

Henderson showed Grogan the photograph of Captain Morrow but pulled it back when Grogan reached for it. "Your fingers are greasy. Just look at it."

"You can't eat a bacon-and-egg sandwich without getting a little grease on your fingers." Grogan peered at the photo, squinting. "That looks something like Mr. Smith, but Mr. Smith's a lot older than that."

"Smith?" Hoke said.

"John Smith. Lives upstairs, last door on your right down the hall. Right across from the john." Grogan bit into the sandwich, and a trickle of undercooked yolk ran onto his chin.

"Mind if we talk to him?" Hoke said. "We don't have a warrant. We just want to talk to him."

"Sure. Go ahead. I'm eating my second breakfast now, or I'd show you up. Besides, my fingers are greasy. But you can't miss his room. It's right across from the john. He's paid up through Sunday, but I don't know if he's in or not."

Upstairs, the house had been modified by plywood partitions to make ten small bedrooms out of four larger ones, but the bathroom at the end of the corridor had not been altered. Two dangling unshaded light bulbs, one of them lighted, illuminated the narrow corridor. The door to the room across from the bathroom was closed. Hoke tapped on the door. No answer. He tried the knob, then opened the unlocked door.

John Smith, né Robert Morrow, was sitting on the edge of a narrow cot. He was using a metal TV table as a desk, and was writing with a ballpoint in a Blue Horse notebook. He looked up when the three detectives entered the room, but there was no curiosity in his face or eyes. His disheveled gray hair needed cutting, and he hadn't shaved in several days, but he wasn't dirty. His khaki work pants and his blue work shirt were both patched, but they were clean. He tapped his right foot, and as he did so the upper part of the shoe moved but the sole did not, because it was detached from the upper. The room was about eight feet by four, and a four-drawer metal dresser, painted to look like wood, completed the furnishings. Because the room was at the end of the building it had a window, and the jalousies were open. The tiny room was filled with light from the afternoon sun. With four people in the room, it was very crowded. Bill stood in the open doorway. Ellita moved to the dresser and leaned against it. Hoke smiled as he bent over and put out his right hand to shake Morrow's. Morrow shook hands reluctantly.

"It's good to see you again, Captain," Hoke said. "Do you remember my partner, Sergeant Henderson? That's Ms. Sanchez over there. She was talking to you earlier—"

"She was harassing me, and I had to leave my bench. But I've got no complaints against her. A man can't just sit in his room all the time. But it's quiet here in the daytime, so I usually work here anyway. If you don't mind, I'd rather you'd all go away."

"What kind of work are you doing?" Hoke said.

"You can remain silent if you want to," Bill added.

"What you say could even be held against you."

"That's right," Hoke said. "You don't have to tell me anything."

"That's a fact," Bill said, loud enough for Ellita to get it on tape.

Hoke rubbed his chin. "If you've got enough money, you could have a lawyer present."

"He doesn't need any money, Hoke," Bill said. "If he can't pay, we can get him a lawyer free."

"This is a benevolent state." Hoke smiled. "The government will pay for a lawyer if you're broke. Do you understand?"

"Why do I need a lawyer?" Morrow frowned. "I haven't done anything illegal."

"It's just that we don't know what you're working on," Hoke said. "Maybe it's legal and maybe it isn't."

"My system," Morrow said, compressing his lips, "isn't for sale!" He closed his notebook and slid it under

94

the slipless pillow. He crossed his arms in front of his chest.

"It looks to me," Hoke said, glancing around the room, "like your system, whatever it is, isn't working. You seem to be living under—what's the term?—reduced circumstances, Captain. The last time we talked to you, about three years ago, you were living in a nice neighborhood with a swimming pool in your backyard."

"That's because they changed the wheels on me. My system is foolproof, but they got onto me and rigged the wheels."

"When did you invent your system?" Bill asked from the doorway. "Before or after you killed your wife?"

"Before. Frances just didn't understand, that's all. I told her we could become millionaires within a year or so, but she wanted me to keep flying. She didn't have faith in me. She wouldn't let me resign from the airline, or even take an extended leave of absence. And she refused to sign the papers so I could sell the house."

"We always wondered why you killed her, but could never come up with a motive," Hoke said. "Let me take a look at your notebook for a moment. I promise not to use your system."

"You can believe Sergeant Moseley, Captain Morrow," Henderson said. "He's got his own system."

"He couldn't understand mine anyway." Morrow shrugged. "Even if I explained it, you still wouldn't understand it. Look at the notebook all you like." He handed Hoke the Blue Horse notebook.

Hoke paged through it. There were long columns of figures on each page, with the arabic numbers written as small as possible with a ballpoint pen. The numbers 36, 8, 4, and 0 were circled on each page.

"You're right, Captain," Hoke said, passing the notebook to Henderson. "It's too complicated for me." Henderson riffled through the pages, shook his head, and returned the notebook to Morrow.

"If we promise not to use it, will you explain some of it to us?" Hoke said.

"Do you promise?" Morrow narrowed his eyes.

Henderson raised his right hand, and so did Hoke.

"I promise," Hoke said.

"Me, too," Bill said.

Morrow pointed to Ellita. "What about her?"

"I won't tell anyone either," Ellita said, raising her right hand. "I promise."

Morrow wet his lips. "It's too complicated for a woman to understand anyway. Frances couldn't understand it, and I tried my best to explain it to her."

"Is that why you killed Frances?" Bill asked. "Because she was too dumb?"

"Frances wasn't dumb!" Captain Morrow raised his voice. "She was a receptionist for a lawyer when I met her, and she had a high-school diploma. But mathematics are beyond a woman's comprehension. They're too emotional to understand arithmetic, let alone logarithms. Here, let me show you." Morrow opened his notebook and pointed to the vertical columns of figures. "It's not that hard to understand, not if you have the patience. Even you two men should be able to grasp the basics. You bet the eight and the four three times, then you bet thirty-six five times. Meanwhile, you watch the Oh, the house number. The Oh and the double-Oh are both house numbers, but the single Oh is the one you watch. If the Oh doesn't come up during your first eight bets on the three numbers, then you start to play the Oh only, and double up until it hits. Four, eight, and thirty-six come up more often than any of the other numbers, and I can prove it by my notebook. So you'll break even, or pull ahead a little while you wait for the Oh to miss eight times. After eight times, the Oh's odds change, and it only takes a few turns of the wheel, doubling up, before it hits. Then, what you've done, you've made a nice profit for the day. If you play my system every day, betting with fifty-cent chips, you'll earn about five hundred dollars a day. No one understands roulette any better than I do.''

''Where'd you play roulette?'' Hoke said. ''Nassau?''

''Aruba. After I sold my house I moved to Aruba and rented a little beach house. I just rented it. I could've bought it, but I didn't. Sometimes, when the wheel wasn't right—it's dry in Aruba, but there's more humidity some days than others, and humidity affects the wheel, you see—I'd fly over to Curaçao. I'd play the casinos there. But I liked Aruba best. I had a housekeeper, and learned enough *Papiamento* to tell her what I wanted for lunch and what to get at the store. I got up late, swam some, ate lunch, took a nap, and then had another swim. Then I would eat dinner at one of the hotels, and play in the casino till midnight. I put in a six-hour working day, and my system worked fine. When I won five hundred, I quit for the day. Otherwise, on slow days, when I only won two or three hundred, I still quit after putting in six hours of play. After six hours, it's hard to maintain your concentration, you see.''

''You must've made a lot of money,'' Bill said.

''I did. But then something happened. What I think is they got onto me and changed the wheels or something. I started to lose, but it wasn't my system's fault. My system's foolproof. All you need is concentration and patience. One mistake, one bet on the wrong number out of sequence, and it won't work. And that's what I don't understand. I never varied from it. Before I took my leave of absence from the airline, I'd already tested the system in Nassau, in San Juan, and in Aruba, you see. I'd fly deadhead down there and spend a weekend in the casinos. It never failed me, and that's what I tried to explain to Frances. I *hated* flying. Flying a plane's the most boring

97

job in the world, and roulette was our ticket out. But Frances just couldn't understand.''

"But your wife was two months pregnant," Hoke said. "Maybe she wanted the security your job offered her?"

Morrow snorted. " 'There is no security,' General Douglas MacArthur once said, 'there's only opportunity.' Besides, I told her there'd be no problem in Aruba with the baby. It would be just as easy to get an abortion in Aruba as it was in Miami. Or, if she wanted to, I told her, she could have her abortion in Miami, and then join me later in Aruba.''

Ellita started to cry. She didn't make a sound, but tears rolled down her cheeks. Hoke and Bill looked at her, and then at each other.

"Excuse me," Ellita said, breaking in sharply. "But I've got to go to the bathroom across the hall. Would you guys mind waiting till I get back before you go on? I don't want to miss any of this conversation, and I . . . I think your system's brilliant, Captain Morrow.''

Captain Morrow smiled, and got to his feet. "Not at all." He sat down again as Ellita left the room and closed the door behind her.

"Did you lose it all, Captain?" Hoke asked.

Morrow nodded. "I think we'd better wait for the little lady. She said she didn't want to miss anything.''

"Sure." Hoke nodded. Henderson broadened his metal-studded smile, and then offered Morrow a cigarette.

"No thanks. I don't smoke.''

Ellita opened the door, and took her place against the dresser. "Thanks for waiting," she said.

Morrow nodded and pursed his lips. He looked blankly at Hoke.

"Did you lose all the money?" Hoke said.

Morrow nodded. "Except for a thousand dollars I left here in Miami. I've been living on that. They wouldn't extend my leave of absence, so next week I've got to find another flying job somewhere and get requalified. Then, when I get another stake together, I'm going to Europe. But this time I won't stay so long in one place. I'll go to Monte Carlo for a few days, and then to Biarritz. The system works on any roulette table, so long as they don't change the wheel.''

"You won't have to go back to flying again, Captain," Henderson said, unhooking his handcuffs from his belt. "We're going over to the station now, and then, after we get your confession typed and you sign it, about eight years from now—it takes about eight years for all the appeals, right, Hoke?"

"About eight years." Hoke nodded.

"About eight years from now," Bill went on, "they'll burn your gambler's ass in the electric chair."

Bill handcuffed Morrow's hands and pushed him toward the doorway. Ellita snapped her purse closed.

"Can I have my notebook?" Morrow asked.

"Sure." Hoke picked up the notebook, unbuttoned the top button of the pilot's shirt, and dropped the notebook in.

Then, while Henderson and Sanchez escorted Morrow to the car, Hoke got six dollars back from an unhappy Grogan (for the two nights' rent Morrow had paid in advance), gave the landlord a receipt, and added the six dollars to the thirty-seven dollars left in Morrow's wallet.

10

B ill Henderson had Captain Morrow handcuffed to the desk in Hoke's office. While Ellita typed a condensed confession for Morrow to sign, Hoke telephoned Major Brownley at home.

"It isn't necessary for you to come down, Willie," Hoke explained. "I'll get an assistant state attorney over here and get Morrow booked for first degree."

"Is he dangerous? I mean, dangerous to himself? If he is, you'd better have him locked up in the psycho cell at Jackson."

"He's disoriented, but not suicidal. Altogether he lost more than two hundred thousand bucks, including the insurance money he collected on his wife. Losing the money's just about all he can think about. Everything else seems irrelevant to him now, and the confession's just a minor annoyance. If we put him in a psycho cell, it might weaken the case. I think the best thing to do is just book him and then let the judge decide whether he wants a psychiatric evaluation or not. Morrow didn't ask for a lawyer, but I called the public defender's office anyway, and they're going to send someone over. But the confession'll be signed before anyone gets here. Sanchez has just about got it typed now. Besides, we still have his confession on tape.

"You read him his rights?"

"It's on the tape."

"You did a good job, Hoke."

"Henderson spotted him, not me. It was just a fluke, Willie, a lucky accident. We didn't even know Morrow was back in the city. So I don't think it's a good idea to put out any PR about our special assignment yet. Hell, we haven't finished reading through the cases you picked out."

"The papers'll pick up on it soon, Hoke. Morrow's wife was pregnant when he killed her, and reporters love stuff like that."

"But we can still release this first one as just another routine case for the division. Later on, if we get lucky again, we can fill them in on the cold-case business. So why not just say we've been working on this case for a long time, which we have, and let it go at that?"

"Okay. If the public defender gives you any flak, have him call me. I'll be home all evening."

Hoke went down to the cafeteria and got four cups of coffee. By the time Hoke got back to the office, Morrow's confession was signed, all five copies, and had been notarized by the division secretary. Ellita and Henderson had signed it as witnesses.

The assistant state attorney was a happy man, but the public defender, a young woman who had passed the bar recently, was not. If they had called her in time, she complained, she would have advised Captain Morrow not to sign the confession.

"Why not?" Hoke said. "We had it on tape anyway, and this makes it easier to follow."

"Are you going to ask Captain Morrow any more questions?"

"No. All we need to know's in your copy of the confession. But if we do, we'll call you first, now that you've advised him to remain silent."

"You guys think you've got away with something, don't you?"

"The important thing is that Morrow didn't. He killed a young woman of twenty-five who was carrying his child. She never did any harm to anyone, and she didn't deserve having her head crushed by a sledgehammer just so this sonofabitch could gamble away their savings."

"He's unbalanced now, and he had to be insane at the time of—"

"Maybe so, but if you plead him not guilty by reason of insanity, he'll fry for sure. I'd advise you to plead guilty to second degree and let him take a mandatory twenty-five years. But I don't care what you do. Right now, unless you want to talk to him some more, we're taking him over to the jail."

Hoke told Ellita to lock up the cold cases in the office and go home. He and Henderson would take Morrow to the lockup.

Henderson took Morrow's arm and guided him out of the office. Ellita got to her feet, blocking Hoke from the door. "Did you people say anything while I was out of the room at Grogan's?"

"No, but I didn't think it was very professional for you to take a side trip to the can in the middle of an interrogation."

"It was all I could think of to do," Ellita said. "The

battery in the recorder went dead, so I had to get out of the room to change it, that's all."

"Did you have an extra battery?"

"Of course."

"Okay, then. That's professional. Did you get it all on tape?"

"Everything, if you didn't talk while I was out of the room."

Hoke patted her awkwardly on the shoulder. "You did the right thing, Ellita. Go on home."

* * *

On the way to the Dade County Jail in the car, Morrow cleared his throat. "I signed the confession, the way you wanted and all, so I'd like to ask you guys a favor."

"Sure, Captain," Henderson said. "What can we do for you?"

"Well." Morrow licked his lips. "I'd appreciate it if you guys didn't tell the airline about this matter. If they found out I was a gambler, they'd put the word out on me, and I'd never get another crack at flying again. Airlines are like that. They consider gambling as obsessive behavior, you know, and if it ever gets on your record, they won't rehire you as a pilot."

"I won't tell the airline," Bill said. "How about you, Hoke?"

"I won't tell 'em either."

"Thanks," Morrow said, "thanks a lot." Relieved, he sat back and studied his notebook until they got to the jail.

It was after 11 P.M. when Hoke got back to his suite at the Eldorado. He was exhausted from the long day, and he was hungry. He heated a can of chunky turkey-noodle soup on his hot plate and sat at his small Victorian desk to eat it out of the pot.

Above the desk there was a painting of three charging white horses pulling a fire wagon. There was a brass chimney on the back of the wagon, spewing white smoke. The nostrils of the horses flared wildly, and the crazed eyes of the horses showed whites all around. Hoke liked the picture and never tired of looking at it when he sat at the small desk. The little sitting room was busy. The previous tenant, an old lady who had lived in the suite for twelve years before her death, had furnished the room with small items she had picked up over the years at garage sales. There was a mid-Victorian armchair stuffed with horsehair, and a Mexican tile-topped table holding Hoke's black-and-white Sony TV. There were several small tables on long spindly legs (tables that are called either wine or cigarette tables), and each table held a potted cluster of African violets. There was a patterned, rose-colored oriental rug on the floor (a Bokhara, and quite a good one), but it had faded over the years and was spotted here and there with coffee and soup stains. On flat surfaces, including the built-in bookcases, there were abalone ashtrays, stuffed and clothed baby alligators, seashells, and a black, lacquered shadow box on the wall contained several intricately intaglioed mezzusahs, including one that had been made from a cartridge used in Israel's Six-Day War with Egypt. There was more than enough room on the bookshelves for Hoke's books: Except for a copy of *Heidi* (overlooked by Patsy when she left him), Harold Robbins's *A Stone for Danny Fisher*, and a *Webster's New Collegiate Dictionary*, Hoke didn't keep any more books in his collection. When he bought and read an occasional paperback novel, he dropped it off in the lobby so that one of the guests could read it.

There were purple velvet draperies for the single window, but they were pulled back and secured by a golden cord so they wouldn't interfere with the efforts of the laboring window air conditioner. The walls were crowded with pictures, watercolors of palms and seaside scenes for the most part, but Hoke's second-favorite picture was a copy of *Blue Boy*, with the boy's costume fashioned of real

104

parrot feathers. Each fluffy blue feather had been painstakingly glued in place by someone, and when a breeze from the air conditioner reached the picture and ruffled the feathers, the figure shivered. The face, however, was not the boy in the original picture, but a photograph of Modest Moussorgsky's head, scissored from an encyclopedia, complete with the composer's magnificent mustache. The walls were papered with pink wallpaper, and dotted with tiny white *fleurs de lis*.

The bathroom was also small, but the sitz-bath tub had a shower as well. There was also the little windowless bedroom. Most of the bedroom was taken up by a three-quarter-sized brass bed, but there was still room enough for an eight-drawer walnut dresser. The closet was roomy enough for Hoke's old uniforms and blue serge suit, and he kept a cardboard box of his papers in the closet as well.

This small suite was Hoke's sanctuary, and he was reluctant to leave it. Not only was it rent-free, it was home. He wondered if Mr. Bennett would let him take the *Blue Boy* and the fire horses when he left, and decided that he would not. If the pictures were removed, they would leave lighter-colored square spaces on the wallpaper, and would have to be replaced with others.

After washing the small boiler pan and the spoon in the bathroom basin, and putting the utensils back in the highboy drawer, Hoke bundled up his laundry, wrapping it all in his yellow leisure suit jacket. The Peruvian girl, a maid with no English, would pick up his laundry in the morning, including his gray sheets, and have it all back to him by Saturday night. She would wash and iron his two poplin leisure suits, put them on hangers, and by Monday morning he would be all set for another week's work.

Hoke took a long shower, put on his last clean pair of boxer shorts, and decided to watch *The Cowboys*, an old John Wayne movie he had seen before and enjoyed. He poured the last two ounces of his Early Times into a glass, added water from the basin tap, and put the empty liter bottle into the wicker wastebasket under the desk. He drank half the drink and turned on his Sony before sitting in the Victorian armchair. The telephone on the desk buzzed.

It was Eddie Cohen. "I hope I didn't wake you . . ."

"I wasn't asleep. Who's calling?"

"No one's calling. It's these two girls. There're two girls down here, and they say you're their father."

"What?"

"I thought they was kidding me at first, and I told them you wasn't married. Then one showed me your picture, and it's you all right, wearing a police uniform."

"Two girls?"

"Teenage girls. They don't look nothin' like you, Ser-geant. But they say they're your daughters. You want me to bring 'em up, or do you want to come down?"

"I'll be right down."

Hoke put on a pair of khaki Bermudas, a gray gym T-shirt, and slipped into his shoes without putting on any socks. There were no clean black socks left in the drawer. He put his wallet and ID case and badge into his pockets, and slipped the holstered .38 into the belt at his back. His keys were on the desk, and he dropped them into his right front pocket. He went into the bathroom, put his dentures in, and quickly combed back his thinning hair.

In the elevator down, he recalled the 3 A.M. phone call from the woman Eddie had told him about. That must have been Patsy, he thought, but she had claimed it wasn't an emergency. If sending his daughters down to Miami in the middle of the night wasn't an emergency, what would Pat-sy consider an emergency? But then, maybe the caller hadn't been Patsy. Something was up.

The desk was well-lighted by overhead fluorescent tubes, but most of the lamps in the lobby had been switched off. The TV set was dark, and there were no Cubans playing dominoes. On Friday nights, the resident Cubans went out

106

to nearby bars to spend their weekly paychecks. Some-times, when they got drunk and brought women back, Ed-die Cohen had to call Hoke to quiet them down, since the resident pensioners were usually in bed by nine or nine-thirty.

The two girls, both wearing shorts, T-shirts, and tennis shoes, were standing by the desk. Hoke wouldn't have rec-ognized either of the girls on the street, but he figured that the taller girl was Sue Ellen, and the smaller was Aileen. Despite Cohen's observations, the girls bore a greater re-semblance to Hoke than they did to their mother, now that Hoke had a look at them. They both had Hoke's sandy hair—an abundance of it—and Sue Ellen had an overbite. With her mouth closed, her two upper teeth rested on her lower lip, where the teeth had left permanent tiny dents. Both girls were slim, but Sue Ellen was well-rounded at the hips, and she needed the brassiere she was wearing under her "Ft. 'Luderdale" T-shirt. Aileen was more gangly, with a boyish figure, and there were no adolescent chest bumps yet beneath the thin cotton of her T-shirt. They weren't pretty girls, Hoke thought, but they weren't plain either.

Aileen's generous mouth was filled with gold wire and tiny golden nuts and bolts. Her teeth were hardly visible, because the places that weren't covered by gold wires were concealed by stretched rubber bands. She wore a black elastic retainer, with the cords stretched across her cheeks, and headphones, with a cord leading down to a Sony Walk-man on her red webbed belt. Both girls appeared a little anxious. Sue Ellen looked down at the photo in her hand, and then looked back at Hoke again before she favored him with a tentative smile.

"Daddy?"

"You're Sue Ellen, right?" Hoke said, shaking her hand. "And this is Sister." Hoke smiled at the younger girl.

"We don't call her that anymore," Sue Ellen said.

"Aileen," the younger girl said. She shook hands with Hoke, and then backed away from him. But Hoke didn't let her get away. He hugged Aileen, and then hugged Sue Ellen.

Hoke turned to Eddie Cohen, who was grinning behind the desk. "These are my daughters, Eddie, Sue Ellen and Aileen. Girls, this is Mr. Cohen, the day man and the night man on the desk, and the assistant manager."

"How do you do," Sue Ellen said. Aileen nodded and smiled, but didn't say anything. She took off the earphones and switched off the radio.

"Where's your mother?" Hoke said.

"She should be in L.A. by now," Sue Ellen said. "She tried to call you, she said, but couldn't get ahold of you. But I've got this letter . . ." Sue Ellen took a sealed envelope from her banana-shaped leather purse and handed it to her father.

Hoke unsealed the envelope, but before he could remove the letter, a Latin man of about thirty-five or -six pushed through the lobby doors, shouting as he approached the desk. "What about my fare? I can't wait around here all night! I gotta get back to the terminal."

"Did you girls fly down from Vero Beach?" Hoke said.

Sue Ellen shook her head. Her curls, down to her shoulders, swirled as she looked toward the cab driver. "We came down on the Greyhound. We got into Miami about seven, and we tried to call here a couple of times"—she looked at Eddie Cohen—"but no one answered the phone. We had a pizza, and then we went to a movie. Then, after the movie, we decided to take a cab over here."

"You girls shouldn't be wandering around downtown Miami at night. Don't ever do that again."

"We were all right. We checked our suitcases in a locker at the bus station before we went to the movie."

The suitcases were next to the desk: two large Samsonites and two khaki-colored overnighters.

"What about my fare?" the cab driver said. He was wearing a white dress shirt, with the sleeves rolled up to his elbows, and tattered blue jeans. There were blue homemade tattoos on the backs of his dark hairy hands. He put his hands on his hips and pushed his chin out.

"How much is it?" Hoke said.

"I'll have to take another look, now. The meter's still runnin'."

"I'll go with you. Eddie, wake up Emilio and have him take a folding cot up to my room—and the girls' suitcases."

"I've got some empty rooms on your floor," Eddie said.

"I'm aware of that." Hoke shook his head. "But Mr. Bennett would charge me for them. The girls'll stay in my suite."

Hoke followed the driver outside, reached through the window, and punched the button to stop the meter. The charge on the meter was $26.50.

"How long you been waiting?" Hoke asked.

The driver shrugged.

Hoke looked into his wallet. He had a ten and six ones. Hoke showed the driver his shield and ID. "I'm Sergeant Moseley, Miami Police Department. I'm going to inspect your cab."

Hoke opened the back door and looked inside. The back seat had a small rip on the left side, and there were three cigarette butts on the floor. All of the cab's windows were rolled down.

"Did you turn on the air conditioning when the girls got into the cab?"

"No, but they didn't ask."

"That's a Dade County violation. You're supposed to turn it on when passengers get in, whether they ask for it or not. The floor's dirty in back, and the seat's ripped. Let me see your license."

After exploring his wallet, the driver reluctantly handed Hoke his chauffeur's license. It was expired.

Hoke, holding the license, jerked his head toward the lobby. "Let's go inside. Your license has expired."

At the desk, Hoke got a piece of hotel stationery, a ball point, and took down the man's name, José Rizal, and license number, and the number of his cab. "If you came across the MacArthur Causeway, José," Hoke said, "a trip from the bus terminal wouldn't have been more than ten or eleven dollars. So you must have come over to Miami Beach by way of the Seventy-ninth Street Causeway to run up a tab of twenty-six bucks."

"There was too much traffic on Biscayne, and I couldn't get on the MacArthur."

"Bullshit." Hoke returned the driver's license and handed him six one-dollar bills. "I don't have my ticket book with me right now, but if you'll come by the Miami police station on Monday morning, I'll pay you the rest of your fare and write out your ticket for the county violations and your expired license."

For a long moment the driver stared at the bills in his hand, and then he wadded them into a ball and put them in his pocket. He turned abruptly and walked to the double doors. At the doorway the cabbie turned and shouted:

"Lechon!"

He ran out the door, got into his cab, and spun the wheels in the gravel as he raced out of the driveway. Hoke knew that he would never see the driver again.

"Did he cheat us, Daddy?" Sue Ellen asked.

"Not if you enjoyed your unguided tour of Miami Beach."

Hoke then opened and read the letter from Patsy:

Dear Hoke,

I've had the girls for ten wonderful years, and now it's your turn. I'm going out to California to join Curly

110

Peterson. We're going to get married at the end of the season. The girls were given a choice, and they said they'd rather live with you instead of with me and Curly. Perhaps they'll feel differently later, and can spend the Xmas season with us in California. Anyway, you can take them for the next few months, and if they don't come out to Glendale at Xmas-time, I'll see them when spring training begins again in Vero Beach. It's about time you took some responsibility for your girls, anyway, and even though I'll miss them and love them, they want me to have my share of happiness and I know you do, too.

I'm pretty rushed right now, getting ready to leave, but I'll send down their shot records and school records and the rest of their things before I catch my plane. Whatever else you were, you were always responsible, and I know that our girls will be happy and safe with you.

Sincerely yours,
Patsy

Sue Ellen took a package of Lucky Strikes out of her purse, then searched in the clutter for her Bic disposable lighter.

"Let me have one of your Luckies," Hoke said. "I left my pack upstairs."

Sue Ellen handed him the pack, lit her cigarette, and then Hoke's. He returned her package.

"Who's Curly Peterson?" Hoke said.

"That's the man mom's been living with—you know, the pinch hitter for the Dodgers. Sometimes he plays center field. She met him two years ago when the Dodgers came to Vero for spring training. He just renegotiated his contract, and he'll get three hundred and twenty-five thousand dollars a year for the next five years."

"How much?"

"Three hundred and twenty-five thousand a year."

111

"That's what I thought you said. I remember the name vaguely, but I can't picture anyone named Curly Peterson. I don't follow baseball much anymore. There're too many teams anyway."

Aileen looked at the floor and made a circle on the carpet with her right foot. "He's a black man."

"He isn't *real* black though," Sue Ellen said. "He's lighter than a basketball."

"Just the same," Aileen said, "he's a black man."

"He isn't as dark as Reggie Jackson. They both gave me autographed pictures, so I can prove it."

"He's mean, too," Aileen said, still looking at the floor.

"Curly isn't really mean, he's just inconsiderate," Sue Ellen argued, "as Mom said. He's had a lot on his mind, renegotiating his contract and all."

Hoke's mind was frozen. For a moment, he had difficulty in getting his thoughts together.

"What's his batting average?" Hoke said, clearing his throat.

"Two-ninety, and he's got a lot of RBI's."

"That's pretty good for a pinch hitter. He took you to all the games, did he?"

"We had passes to all the spring-training games in Vero."

"Do you like baseball?"

"Not particularly. And we didn't like Curly either. But Mom's gonna marry him, not me."

"Why don't you like him?"

"Well, one time he was having his lawyer and his agent over to dinner, and he told Mom he wanted everything just so. Me and Aileen helped, cleaning the house and all, and Curly came over early to check everything over. We vacuumed, dusted, and even washed the fingermarks off the doors. Then Curly took out his Zippo lighter, got up on a chair, and flicked his lighter in the corner of the ceiling. When he did that, the spider webs in the corner turned black and you could see them. You couldn't see 'em before, but the smoke from the lighter turned 'em black, you see. He didn't say nothing about how nice the rest of the house looked. He just showed us the cobwebs, and said, 'You call that clean?' Then he went off with Mom in the kitchen.''

"It was a mean thing to do," Aileen said.

"That wasn't the only awful thing he did, Daddy," Sue Ellen said. "That's just a sample. But I didn't mind too much because, if you didn't take it personally, it was kinda funny. I guess I didn't like Curly because he didn't like us—me and Aileen, I mean. We were in his way. He was there to see Mom, not us, but there we were, always hanging around. We were just a big nuisance to Curly."

"Do you girls know what's in this letter?"

Sue Ellen shook her head. "No, but I don't want to read it. On the bus coming down, me and Aileen agreed that we weren't going to be played off between you two."

Hoke put the letter back into the envelope. "What did she say to you when you left?"

"Not much. Just that we were to come down here, and not to talk to anyone. That she'd send the rest of our things down later. She was so excited that Curly actually sent for her, she didn't say much of anything. Mom wouldn't admit it, but I don't think she thought Curly'd ever ask her to marry him. But when he did, she couldn't get out of Vero fast enough."

Eddie came down the hall from the dining room, which had been closed for years and served now as a catchall storage room. He was carrying a folding canvas cot by its webbed handle.

"Emilio's not in his room," Eddie said. "I'll get you some sheets and towels."

"That's okay," Hoke said. "I'll get the sheets, and put the cot together when I get upstairs. You'd better stay down here with the switchboard."

Hoke got the sheets and a thin cotton blanket from the linen room, as well as bath and face towels. Hoke and the girls took the suitcases, the cot, and the linen upstairs in the elevator.

"This is an awful big hotel to only have one old man like Mr. Cohen working," Aileen said.

"It's only half full now, but even so, the Eldorado's got the smallest staff on the beach," Hoke said. "But the dining's room closed, and so's the kitchen. Only permanent residents live here, and if they want any maid service, they have to pay extra. Not many of them can afford to pay extra, so we only have two maids during the daytime. Emilio does all the maintenance, like cleaning the corridors and taking care of the yard. He's a Cuban, a Marielito, so Mr. Bennett gives him a free room for the work he does, but no salary."

"How can he eat with no salary?" Sue Ellen asked.

"Tips. And he also has some kind of a government refugee allowance, too."

Hoke made up the brass bed with clean sheets and gave the bed and the cotton blanket to the girls. He had to move the Victorian chair and two spindly tables in the sitting room to make room for the cot. The girls, who were used to having their own beds, didn't like the idea of sleeping together. They argued about who would sleep on the outside; neither girl wanted to sleep next to the wall. Hoke realized that they were tired and irritable, as well as excited, but he finally told them to shut up and go to sleep.

But Hoke couldn't sleep. There was no mattress, and the canvas cot was stiff and uncomfortable. He was also too worried to sleep. When he moved to that small garage apartment in the Grove ghetto, could he take the girls there, too? He wanted a drink, and considered walking over to Irish Mike's, where he could drink on his tab, but he decided against it because the girls might wake up, wonder where he was, and get frightened.

114

It was a rotten trick for Patsy to send the girls down to him without any warning. If Curly Peterson—Hoke's mind froze again momentarily—was making $325,000 a year and didn't want the girls around, why couldn't the ballplayer cough up enough money to put them into a private school somewhere?

Unable to sleep, Hoke slipped on his khaki shorts again and took the elevator to the roof. There was a duckboard patio on the roof, and at one time there had been a bar as well, but very few residents came up to the roof now. Hoke looked across the bay at the Miami night skyline, which was beautiful at this distance. A warm wet breeze came from the ocean, and it felt good on his bare back. To his right, Hoke saw the lights on the four small islands that made up the connecting links for the Venetian Causeway. Straight ahead was the dotted yellow line of light bulbs of the MacArthur Causeway. On his left, farther south, Hoke could see the lights of Virginia Key and Key Biscayne. He lit a Kool, and remembered the old joke that had circulated after Nixon sold his house on Key Biscayne.

"What's the difference between syphilis, gonorrhea, and a condominium on Key Biscayne?"

"You can get rid of syphilis and gonorrhea."

But more to the point, how could he get rid of these two darling but unwanted girls—at least until he got straightened out? In the morning, he would call his father. Frank had four bedrooms in his big house on the inland waterway in Riviera Beach. Maybe the old man would take them for the summer, or even for a month or two until he could work something out. Even two weeks would help a lot. By that time, maybe he would have a decent place to live in Miami. But now, with the two girls, he would need at least a two-bedroom apartment, or maybe a small house in a safe, quiet neighborhood. Next Friday was payday, and his next paycheck was supposed to go to Patsy—then he felt a

115

little better, a swift surge of relief. Now that Patsy had sent him the girls, the agreement was canceled. Finished.

Feeling a little better, but not much, Hoke butted his cigarette for later, went back to his canvas cot, and fell asleep.

11

H oke took the girls to Gold's Deli for breakfast. It was only two blocks away, so they walked. On their way over to Washington Avenue, Hoke pointed out the dilapidated condition of the old apartment houses and small hotels, and explained that there had been a moratorium on new construction for several years because there was supposed to be a master plan for complete redevelopment. But no redevelopment funds came through, so the owners of the buildings made only enough repairs to satisfy the fire marshal. He also told them to notice the population mix; young Latins and old Jews predominated.

"South Beach is now a slum, and it's a high-crime area, so I don't want you girls to leave the hotel by yourselves. If you had a doll, and you left it out overnight on the front porch of the hotel, it would probably be raped when you found it in the morning."

Both girls giggled.

"Maybe that's stretching it a little, but between First and Fourteenth Street, South Beach is not the real Miami Beach you see in the movies. If you were looking out the window of the cab last night, and paying attention, you'd've noticed the difference. North of Sixteenth there are tourists out on the streets, lights, open stores and restaurants, and so on. But as soon as you reach Fifteenth, heading down this way, there are no people anywhere at night. On the corners, you'll see two or three Latin males, maybe, but none of the old people leave their rooms after the sun goes down. And I don't want you girls to go out alone at night either."

"Why do you live here, then?" Sue Ellen said.

"We're moving next Friday. The owner of the hotel had a security problem with Marielitos, so I was just helping him out temporarily, that's all."

In Gold's, the girls ordered Cokes and toasted bagels with cream cheese. Hoke ordered two soft-boiled eggs and a slice of rye toast.

"Did your mother give you any money?" Hoke said, while they were waiting to be served.

"Fifty dollars apiece," Sue Ellen said, "after she bought our bus tickets."

Hoke held out his hand. "Let me have it."

Sue Ellen had forty-two dollars, and Aileen had thirty-nine and some change. They handed over the money reluctantly.

Hoke counted it. "Where's the rest of it?"

"We spent some coming down," Sue Ellen said. "Then we had a pizza and went to a movie."

"I played Donkey Kong in the bus station," Aileen said.

Hoke gave each girl a dollar bill. "Until you get jobs, and I'll help you find work when we get back to Miami,

118

I'll give you both a dollar a week as an allowance. But for a while, money'll be rather tight."

"You can't do much of anything with a dollar," Aileen said.

"I don't want you doing much of anything. I've got to go over to the station after breakfast. You can either go with me, or stay in the hotel, where Mr. Cohen or Emilio can keep an eye on you."

"Can we swim in the pool?" Sue Ellen asked. "I noticed the sign in the corridor pointing to the pool."

"There's a pool out back, on the bay side, but Mr. Bennett had it filled with sand. If you have a pool, you see, you have to have maintenance and insurance. The bay's too polluted for swimming, and I don't want you girls going over to the ocean by yourselves."

"At home, we had our own pool," Aileen said.

"Did you girls really choose to live with me, or did your mother send you down here against your will?"

"We said we'd rather live with you, Daddy," Sue Ellen said.

"All right, then. Just remember that I don't make three hundred and twenty-five thousand a year. But my job's got other compensations."

"Like what?" Sue Ellen said.

"Well, for one thing"—Hoke smiled—"I've got my two daughters back."

Apparently it was the right thing to say. Sue Ellen smiled. Aileen covered her golden mouth with her hand, so Hoke knew that she was smiling, too.

The girls decided to go with Hoke instead of hanging around the hotel. But Hoke made them change from their shorts into dresses before driving across the MacArthur Causeway.

"Tomorrow afternoon we'll go up on the roof, and you can watch the cruise ships come in through Government

119

Cut. We've got more cruises out of Miami than any other place in the world.''

"I've never been on a cruise,'' Sue Ellen said.

"Me neither,'' Aileen said.

"I went once, for a weekend in Nassau. It isn't worth the money. A weekend in Nassau's like a weekend in Liberty City.''

"Where's Liberty City?'' Aileen asked.

"It's just a black ghetto in Miami—one of the biggest.''

When they got to the station, Hoke took the girls into the interrogation room, and then got them some typing paper and pens from his office.

"I'll be working in my office, doing some paperwork, but you girls can draw pictures to pass the time. I know you like to draw.''

Sue Ellen laughed. "I'm sixteen years old, Daddy.''

"You used to like to draw.''

"That was a long time ago. I remember. I also remember the time you handcuffed me to the table in the patio.''

"I never did that.''

"Yes you did, too. I remember. And I cried.''

"You were only six when you left Miami. My handcuffs wouldn't close around your little wrists. They were only about this big around.'' Hoke made a circle with his thumb and forefinger.

"That's why you put the cuff around my ankle instead. I remember lots of things. You'd be surprised.''

"All right, then, if you don't want to draw, write letters to your mother. I'll get some envelopes later.''

Hoke returned to his office and telephoned his father in Riviera Beach. On Saturdays, the hardware store was only open until noon, but Frank Moseley rarely went in until ten, so Hoke knew he could still catch the old man at home.

"It's Hoke, Dad,'' he said, when Frank answered.

"How are you, son? Did the girls get there all right?''

120

"Sure. They're with me now, I'm at the police station. Did Patsy tell you she was sending them down to me?"

"Yes, she called me, and she said she'd call you."

"She didn't. The girls arrived last night, and I didn't have a clue."

"That's funny. She told me she'd call you and explain."

"Well, she didn't. Things are a little awkward for me right now, Dad, and I was wondering if you and Helen could take the girls for a couple of weeks."

"We aren't going to be here, son. If you hadn't called me, I would've called you on Monday. But in ten days, Helen and me are taking a round-the-world cruise on the *Q.E. II*. Twelve thousand dollars apiece for an inside stateroom, but the boat goes everywhere. I've never had a real vacation, except for the week of our honeymoon, when Helen and I went to St. Thomas. And Helen wanted to go on the *Q.E. II*, so that's that."

"I think that's great, Dad. In ten days, you say."

"That's right. The boat leaves from New York, but it stops in Fort Lauderdale. You can bring the girls up to Port Everglades to see us off, and we'll have a little going-away party in the stateroom. They say it's quite a ship, and I know the girls would like to see it. My tickets are in the mail, and when I get them I'll leave boarding passes for you, with the stateroom number and so on. You can meet us on the ship."

"If I can make it, I'd like to see it. How's Helen, by the way?"

"Excited. She's got a wardrobe trunk and two suitcases packed already, more than enough stuff for three months. She made me buy a tuxedo. On the ship, you wear a tux every night."

"Not on the first night, Dad. The first night out, as I understand it, is informal."

"I know that much from watching *Love Boat*. But Helen says it won't be the first night out for us because the first night out will be from New York, so I'll have to wear mine. But I don't mind. I look pretty good in it for an old man. Something like that DeLorean fellow, only I'm a lot better-looking." The old man laughed.

"I'd like to see you in it."

"I'll show it to you on the boat. I don't like the suspenders though. They hurt my shoulders."

"Don't wear 'em then. With the jacket on, nobody'll know."

"Helen will. She said if you don't wear suspenders, the pants don't hang right. But I'll be okay. You give the girls love from Grandpa, and I'll see you all on the boat."

"If I can't make it, I'll let you know."

"Try and make it. I think you'd like to see the boat, but I also know how busy you are. If you send me your size, Hoke, I'll get a suit made for you in Hong Kong."

"I don't need a suit, Dad."

"Send me your measurements. I'll get you one anyway. A man can always use a new suit, and in Hong Kong they're dirt cheap. Helen'll get presents for the girls."

"It was nice talking to you, Dad. Give Helen my best regards."

"I'll tell Helen you called . . . I'm awful sorry—" Frank started to cough, and then he gasped for a moment before catching his breath. "Excuse me. I'm—I'm really sorry about Patsy and that colored ballplayer."

"I don't want to talk about it, Dad."

"Right. Me neither. Well, you give the girls my love, hear?"

"I will, Dad. And have a bon voyage."

"Thanks. I've got to get down to the store. There's a lot to do before I leave."

"Sure. And if you send postcards, mail 'em here to the station. I'm moving, but I don't have my new address yet."

"I can call you from the boat. There'll be a phone in

the stateroom, so I can call the store every day. So we'll be in touch, son.''

"Sure, Dad. I've got to get to work myself.''

Hoke hung up the phone, wondering how Helen had managed to talk the old man into a round-the-world cruise. It was probably the phone in the stateroom that did it, he concluded. The fact that Frank could call every day and pass on some unneeded advice to his manager had been the clincher. Nevertheless, even though Frank wouldn't be able to take the girls, Hoke was happy for the old man. Christ, Frank had all the money in the world from his real-estate deals. It was about time he spent some of it.

Hoke rechecked the paperwork on the Captain Morrow case, wrote a short covering memo to Major Brownley, and then took the file case into Brownley's empty office and left it on the chief's desk.

Hoke took the next case from his unread stack of files and opened it. There had been an argument in a bowling alley, and a man named Rodney DeMaris, an ex-Green Beret captain, had gone out to his car, returned to the bowling alley with a .357 magnum, and shot a bowler named Mark Demarest five times in the chest. The five holes in Demarest's chest, fired at close range, could be covered by a playing card. Hoke looked at the Polaroid shot of Demarest's chest, taken at the P.M. by the pathologist, and marveled at the tight pattern. DeMaris had then driven away and disappeared. Hoke wondered why Brownley had selected this old case, dating back five years, and then he found a Xeroxed page from a detective's notebook stating that a man who looked something like DeMaris had been seen in town two weeks ago, driving a green 1982 Plymouth. The officer had tried to stop the driver, but the suspect had evaded him on I-95. That wasn't much of a lead; the detective didn't even get the license number of the Plymouth. The detective wasn't positive that the man had been DeMaris, but the fact that the suspect refused to stop

123

had reinforced the possible identification. Hoke decided not to waste any time on that one. What was he supposed to do—drive around town looking for a green Plymouth? Hoke put the file to one side, and reached for the next one.

The phone rang. It was Ellita Sanchez, and she was crying.

"I'm so glad you answered, Sergeant Moseley," she sobbed. "I've been trying to call your hotel . . ." Ellita was crying so hard Hoke had difficulty understanding her. She was also talking over band music—some kind of frantic salsa. He could hear horns honking and street noises in the background.

"Where're you calling from? I can hardly hear you."

"Just a second—don't hang up!"

"I'm not going to hang up. Try and calm down a little."

As Hoke listened, trying to pick Ellita's voice out of the background noises, Lieutenant Slater came into his office. His white, pockmarked face loomed above the desk like a dead planet. He wore a blue shirt with a white collar and white barrel cuffs, and the vest and black raw-silk trousers of his five hundred-dollar suit.

"What're those girls doing down in Number Three?"

"Just a minute, Slater, I'm talking to my partner."

"I'm at the little cafeteria outside the La Compañía Supermarket at Ninth Avenue and Eighth Street," Ellita was saying. "Can you come right away?" She had stopped crying and her voice was calm.

"I guess so. What's the matter?"

"I'll tell you when you get here. It's an emergency, of my own, and I don't know what to do. Do you have any money?"

"A little. How much do you need?"

"A dollar. I've had three coffees, and I want to give the cafeteria lady a quarter for using her phone."

"I've got that much. I'll be there as soon as I can."

"Please hurry."

124

"I'll be right there. Everything will be all right."

Hoke put the phone down. Slater was still glaring down at him.

"Those girls are my daughters, Lieutenant. Why? What's the matter?"

"You should've checked them in with me, that's what's the matter."

"You weren't at your desk when we came in."

"I was at my desk when you sneaked that file into Major Brownley's office."

"I didn't sneak it in, I took it in."

"Everything's supposed to go through me. Otherwise, I won't know what's going on around here."

"Take a look at it if you like. It's the Morrow file."

"I'm not allowed in Brownley's office when he's not there, and neither are you."

"For Christ's sake, Slater. I'm on a special assignment with Henderson and Sanchez. You know that, because Brownley filled you in when he assigned Gonzalez to work with you. What do you want from me?"

"I want you to follow the chain of command, Sergeant. You're no better than anyone else around here."

Hoke nodded, realizing suddenly why Slater was so angry. He had not been asked by Brownley to attend the meeting about the cold cases, nor had Brownley, in all probability, consulted him about their selection.

"Okay, Lieutenant," Hoke said. "I'm supposed to send Brownley a weekly progress report. I'll see that you get a Xerox of it next week. Okay?"

"See that you do. And don't go into the major's office again when he's not there."

Hoke got up and smiled. "Come on, Slater. I'll introduce you to my girls."

Hoke took him to the interrogation room, introduced the girls, and then handed his daughters two dollars apiece. "Lieutenant Slater'll show you where the cafeteria is downstairs, and vouch for you so you can eat there. I've got to leave the station for a while, so you girls can have lunch down there. Try the special. On Saturday it's usually macaroni and cheese. Isn't that right, Lieutenant?''

"I don't know. I don't eat in the cafeteria. I've got an ulcer."

"Anyway, girls, go with the lieutenant. I appreciate you taking the girls down, Slater."

"That's okay. I'll just go and get my jacket first."

"When'll you be back, Daddy?" Sue Ellen asked.

"As soon as I can. It's a little emergency. Nothing for you to worry about."

Eighth Street was only one-way at Ninth Avenue, so Hoke drove west on Seventh Street, turned south on Ninth Avenue, and took the first empty parking space he could find. He put his police placard on the dashboard and walked to the corner. Ellita was on the sidewalk, outside the pass-through counter of the tiny supermarket cafeteria. Music blared from a radio on a shelf behind the counter. Ellita was wearing tight Jordache jeans with a U-necked white muscle shirt. Her bare golden arms were devoid of the bracelets and gold watch she habitually wore. Her gold circle earrings dangled from her ears, however. It was a common Miami joke that doctors could always tell Cuban baby girls when they were delivered at the hospital: They were born with their ears already pierced. Hoke had never seen Ellita in tight jeans before, but she looked good in them, he thought. The full skirts she wore on duty had disguised her voluptuous figure. Ellita smiled when she saw Hoke, and he noticed that she wasn't wearing lipstick.

"We can't talk here," she said. "Where's your car?"

"Around the corner—"

Ellita took his arm and started toward the corner. She stopped abruptly. "Just a second. Let me borrow that dollar."

Hoke gave her a dollar bill. Ellita passed it through the window to the old lady behind the counter, said something in rapid Spanish, and rejoined Hoke by the supermarket entrance. They walked to the car.

"Where's your purse?" Hoke said. "Did you leave it back there on the counter?"

Ellita shook her head, bit her lower lip, and began to cry.

Hoke unlocked the door and Ellita got into the front seat. Hoke got behind the wheel and took the placard off the dashboard.

"There should be some Kleenex in the glove compartment," he said. He slid the placard under the front seat.

"I'll be all right." Ellita wiped her eyes with the backs of her fingers. "I called you, Sergeant, because . . . because I didn't know what else to do."

"You can call me Hoke, Ellita. After all, we're partners, and this isn't an on-duty situation—or is it?"

"You know how much I respect you, Sergeant—"

"Even so, I'm only ten years older than you. I'm not your father, for God's sake."

Ellita started to cry again. Hoke opened the glove compartment and found a purse-sized package of Kleenex.

"Here."

Ellita wiped her eyes with a tissue. Her familiar perfume and moschate odor was overwhelming within the confines of the car, especially with the windows rolled up. Hoke started the engine and switched on the air conditioning. As Ellita raised her arms to blow her nose, Hoke noticed the damp tufts of jet-black hair beneath her arms. Ellita didn't shave her armpits; that was something else he hadn't known about his partner. It had been a long time since Hoke had spent any time in the front seat of a car with a weeping woman. He found Ellita's underarm hair a little exciting, and remembered again that he hadn't been laid in more than four months. After Ellita's problem was straightened

127

out, there might still be time to drive over to Coral Gables and give Loretta Hickey her money, and maybe set up something . . .

"All right," Ellita said calmly. She sat back and looked straight ahead, staring at a red Camaro parked in front of them. The bumper had a strip on the right side reading, DIE YOU BASTARD. On the other side of the bumper was the logo for the Cuban Camaro Club. "My father threw me out of the house, Hoke."

Hoke grinned. "How could he do that? You pay the rent on the whole house, you told me."

"You don't understand. In a Cuban family, he's the father, and it's always his house, his rules."

"What did you do? Did you have an argument, or what?"

"This is embarrassing. But if I can't tell you, I guess I can't tell anyone. The trouble is, I told my mother, and I should've known better. She told my father and he threw me out of the house. I don't have my purse, my pistol, my checkbook, my car keys—nothing! All of a sudden, there I was, outside of the house on the porch. He locked the door, and I couldn't get back in. I waited awhile, then I knocked on the door because I could hear my mother crying inside. I said, 'I'm your daughter, and I've got to get my things.' He said, 'I have no daughter.' Then he wouldn't say another word. He gets like that sometimes. He's very stubborn and unreasonable. Last year, when he flew up to Newark to visit my aunt—his sister—he got into trouble with the airline because he wouldn't fasten his seat belt."

"Why not?"

"He thought if he fastened the belt, people would think he was afraid. He finally fastened it when the stewardess told him the captain used his, too. But for a while there, they were radioing for clearance to taxi back to the terminal."

Hoke smiled, shook his head, and took out his cigarettes.

"But he's my father, Hoke. He's made up his mind, you see, and now he won't change it. Maybe, eventually, when he gets used to the idea, he might change it, but right now he's angry and bitter. He thinks I've betrayed and disgraced him, which I guess I have, but right now I need my checkbook, weapon, badge, and car."

"He knows, doesn't he, that a cop's supposed to have his—her weapon with her at all times?"

"Of course he knows that, but at the moment he isn't thinking rationally. Later on, after my mother works on him, he'll calm down a little, but it'll never be the same between us again." She shook her head. "Don't worry. I'm not going to cry again."

"What did you do to him? You don't have to tell me, of course."

"I'm pregnant, Hoke. Seven weeks. I've known for a week now, and this morning I told my mother. I *told* her not to say anything to him, but I should've known better. She tells him everything."

Hoke nodded and lit a Kool. "That explains why you started crying when I was talking to Captain Morrow in his room. You didn't know his wife was pregnant when he killed her—"

"Of course I knew!" Ellita widened her eyes. "I read the file. I'm not that unprofessional, Hoke. I was crying out of frustration because of the damned battery on the tape recorder . . ."

Hoke saw that he had touched a nerve. He decided to try to make Ellita feel better about having told her mother.

"You couldn't hide a pregnancy from your father, Ellita. He'd've found out sooner or later, unless you got an abortion. But you've still got plenty of time for that."

"I can't get an abortion, Hoke. A baby's got a living soul."

"Soul or no soul, a lot of women do. What's the father got to say about it?"

"The father doesn't know about the baby. He doesn't even know my last name. I don't know his last name either, but I can find out easily enough. His first name's Bruce. That's all I know right now."

Hoke smoked his Kool and sat back. He didn't have to ask any more questions. She was going to tell him about it now anyway, whether he wanted to hear it or not.

"I didn't date Bruce, Hoke. It was just one of those things that happens. All I ever do, it seems, is work, go home, sleep, and then pull my shift again. I should've moved out and got my own apartment years ago. But Cuban girls don't do things like that, because we can't give our parents a valid reason. How come, your parents want to know, you want to rent an apartment and be lonely, and go to all that expense, when you can live comfortably at home? It makes no sense to them for an unmarried girl to leave home. With a son it's a little different, but even then they don't like it. But it didn't make any sense to me either, economically. I'm very comfortable at home. I pay the rent on the house, but my parents pay for everything else— utilities and food. I've got my own bedroom, my own TV set and stereo. My mother works part-time in Hialeah, at the Golden Thread garment factory. My father's with Triple-A Security. He's not just a security guard, either. He's in personnel and hires all the Latin guards because he's more or less bilingual."

"He has a little English, you mean."

"Enough. Much more than my mother. We speak Spanish at home. What I'm trying to say, I guess, is that I somehow got into a rut, a comfortable rut. But for the last two years, ever since my thirtieth birthday, I felt that life was passing me by. It was ridiculous to be a thirty-year-old virgin, and yet I never met anyone I liked, or who liked me well enough to—well, to pressure me. And it didn't

130

help that I had to be home by ten-thirty when I did go out."

"You're kidding. Ten-thirty?"

"You don't know Cuban fathers. It's his house and his rules, I'm telling you."

"But you pay the rent—"

"That doesn't matter. What else would I do with my money—living at home? With three incomes, even though my mother just does piecework, there's plenty of money for whatever we need. My mother cooks and cleans the house, and I don't do much of anything. I studied hard at Miami-Dade. Except for the one F I got in philosophy, I had straight As."

"I know. I checked your records. And so, one night, you went out, and—"

"That's right. On a Friday night, which is the big night in Coconut Grove, not Saturday—"

"I know, Ellita. If you don't get something lined up on Friday night, you don't have anyone for the weekend."

"I went to the Taurus, and it was jammed. I met Bruce in the bar. He bought me a drink, and then I bought him one. He was nice-looking. Blue eyes. He wore a suit and tie. A detail man for a pharmaceutical firm, he said. We went to his apartment instead of getting a third drink. This wasn't any Silhouette romance, Hoke. We went straight at it, Bruce because that's what he does on Friday nights, and me because I wanted to have the experience. It was a little exciting, I guess, but not what I expected."

"And because you were drunk you didn't take any precautions."

"I wasn't drunk, Hoke. I wasn't even high. Bruce had a vasectomy, he told me. I didn't believe him at first, and then he showed me the two little scars on his balls."

"On his scrotum, you mean."

"On his scrotum, right." She managed a little laugh. "We did it twice. Then I took a shower in his apartment,

131

got dressed, and I was still home before ten-thirty. Bruce was very nice, a lot younger than me, about twenty-five, I'd say.''

"But a liar."

"I guess so. Now. But he did have those two little scars. Maybe he had the operation and it didn't take.''

"More likely, he didn't want to wear a raincoat. I can find out for you. Remember where he lives?''

She nodded. "I know where he lives, but I don't want to see him again. I don't want him to know I'm pregnant. I'll just go ahead and have my baby and take care of it. But right now I'm scared. I've never been away from home overnight before by myself, can you believe that? And I don't have my gun, my badge, my checkbook, or my car. I'll need my clothes, too.''

Hoke sat for a moment, thinking. Then he put the car in gear.

"All right, let's go, Ellita. I'll get your stuff for you.''

12

Ellita didn't want her parents or neighbors to see her, so Hoke parked a block away from the Sanchez residence and walked the rest of the way to the house. It was much bigger than Hoke had expected, a three-bedroom concrete-block-and-stucco house with a flat, white gravel roof and an attached garage. The front lawn was freshly mown, and there were beds of blue delphiniums on both sides of the front porch. Ellita's brown Honda Civic was parked in the driveway. Old man Sanchez probably kept his own car in the garage. His house; his rules.

Hoke opened the gate in the white picket fence and glanced curiously at the shrine to Santa Barbara in the yard. The shrine was fashioned of oolite boulders and mortar; in the recess there was a blue vase of daisies and ferns at the

133

feet of the not quite life-sized plaster statue of Santa Barbara.

The front door opened before Hoke could ring the bell. Mrs. Sanchez waited in the doorway. If she had been crying, as Ellita claimed, she didn't look like it. She was a handsome woman, about two inches shorter than Ellita, and her black hair was streaked with gray. Her features were delicate, and she had brown luminous eyes.

"I'm Sergeant Moseley, Mrs. Sanchez. I've come to pick up some of Ellita's things."

"Come in, Sergeant." Mrs. Sanchez stepped back. "Ellita's told us a lot about you."

Hoke entered the living room. There was a bright yellow velvet couch against the wall; a matching easy chair was in one corner, and there was an abundance of black wooden furniture, carved with pear and leaf patterns, in both the living room and dining room. The wall-to-wall carpeting was pale blue. Dominating the living room, however, was a life-size plaster statue of St. Lazarus in front of the fireplace. A fireplace in Miami was rarely if ever used, so the Sanchezes had probably decided that St. Lazarus was a better decorating solution than a pot of tropical plants. On the carpeting surrounding the statue, and beneath the saint's outstretched, imploring hand, there were dozens of coins, most of them quarters. It took eight quarters to park and four more quarters to ride the Metrorail, so St. Lazarus would be a good candidate as the patron saint of Metrorail, Hoke thought.

"Is Mr. Sanchez at home? I'd like to talk with him."

Mrs. Sanchez pursed her lips and shook her head. "He's in his room. This is not a good time, Sergeant. This is a very *bad* time."

"I understand. But tell him I'd like to talk to him later. Ellita's my partner, you know, and we think a lot of her in the department. And in the division. You should be very proud of your daughter, Mrs. Sanchez. I've got two daugh-

134

ters of my own, and I'd be happy if they turned out as well as Ellita.''

"Thank you." She touched his arm. "I'll show you Ellita's room."

Ellita's room was the master bedroom at the back of the house, and on the right of the corridor. She had her own bathroom, too. Her parents, being so old, probably wanted their own separate, if smaller, bedrooms, and wouldn't mind sharing a bathroom. There were three sets of curtains on the bedroom windows. In addition to the layered curtains, there were heavy crimson draperies. The unmade double bed was layered with pink sheets, a blanket, a comforter, and a rose bedspread spaced with embroidered dark red roses. There were four pillows on the bed, and a reading lamp was clamped to an ornately carved black walnut headboard. The color TV was on a wheeled cart, so Ellita could watch it from the bed, or from the red velvet upholstered La-Z-Boy. There was an oil painting of the Virgin in a gilt frame above the vanity table, with a lighted votive candle on a shelf below the painting. There was a framed color poster of Julio Iglesias on the opposite wall. The stereo, in a blond wooden cabinet, was directly beneath Julio's poster.

Mrs. Sanchez slid back the louvered doors to the walk-in closet. "Her clothes are here."

"I'll need her purse, too. It's important that she has her ID, badge, and weapon. And her checkbook."

Mrs. Sanchez brought Ellita's purse from the dresser. The .38 and ID with the badge were in the purse, and so were Ellita's keys, checkbook, and wallet. There was a corner desk, and Hoke looked through the drawers. Ellita had a NOW checking account, as well as a regular checking account, so he added this checkbook to the purse. He also found two white passbooks; they were two $10,000 Certificates of Deposit. She would need them, too. He picked up Ellita's gold wristwatch from the bedside table, and dropped it into his jacket pocket.

"Does she have a suitcase?" Hoke asked. "Maybe you can help me pick out some clothes?"

"There's a box in the garage." Mrs. Sanchez hurried out of the room.

Hoke took two cream-colored silk blouses from the closet, the kind with long sleeves, and tossed them on the bed. He removed a black skirt and a red skirt from the closet, and added them to the blouses. That's all Ellita would need for a couple of days. In midsummer, she wouldn't need any jackets or sweaters. He went through her dresser, however, and picked out a purple silk night-gown, two pairs of black silk panties, and two brassieres. He took a peek at the size, 38-C. He added a jar of Eucerin, a toothbrush, and a tube of Colgate to the pile, but he did not include the atomizer of Shalimar or Ellita's bottle of musk. She was wearing enough perfume already, he thought, to last her for a week. Stockings, she would need stockings. There was a pair of pantyhose drying in the bathroom. He tossed the pantyhose on the pile, and then couldn't think of anything else.

Mrs. Sanchez returned with a cardboard box that had once held a dozen boxes of Tide.

"Ellita has a train case," she said. While Hoke packed the clothing into the cardboard box, Mrs. Sanchez got the train case, a red-and-blue plaid one, down from the closet shelf and packed it with cosmetics and vials from the vanity table, including the Shalimar and the musk and a plastic tree that held a dozen pairs of earrings.

"I guess this'll do for a few days," Hoke said, "but if you would pack the rest of Ellita's stuff, she can come by for it one day when Mr. Sanchez isn't home."

Mrs. Sanchez started to cry. She ran into Ellita's bathroom and closed the door.

Hoke decided not to wait for her to come out. He put

the box under his left arm and carried the train case in his right hand as he walked down the corridor to the living room.

Mr. Sanchez, a short, stocky man with black hair and a gray mustache, wearing green poplin wash pants and a white long-sleeved *guayabera*, was standing in front of St. Lazarus. His short arms were folded across his chest, and he stared at Hoke without expression.

"Mr. Sanchez? I'm Sergeant Moseley, your daughter's partner."

"I have no daughter." Keeping his arms crossed, Mr. Sanchez turned his back on Hoke and faced the statue.

"In that case, we have nothing to talk about."

Hoke left the house, put the box and the train case down beside the Honda Civic, dug the keys out of the purse, and unlocked the car. He put the box, purse, and case on the back seat, then shoved the front seat back as far as it would go before maneuvering himself into the driver's seat.

He drove down the block and parked behind his Pontiac. Ellita was standing on the curb. Hoke handed her the keys and her wristwatch after he got out of the car.

"What do you want to do now?"

"I don't know," she said. "I guess I should find a motel or something, and then look around for an apartment."

"Don't you have a girl friend or a cousin or someone who can put you up for a few days?"

"I've got some girl friends, but they live at home too. Because of the situation, their parents wouldn't want them to get involved. The same for relatives—even more—because of my father, you see."

"Your father's a fucking asshole."

"Please, don't say that, Sergeant Moseley. You just don't understand him, that's all."

"I don't want to understand him. He wouldn't even talk to me, for Christ's sake. What's more natural than a woman getting pregnant? That's what women *do*!"

"My mother'll have the priest talk to him. That might help some. But I doubt it."

"Jesus!" Hoke said, laughing. "I forgot all about the girls. They're still down at the station, and I was going to suggest that we have lunch and discuss what you should do!"

Hoke told Ellita about his daughters, about how they had arrived in the middle of the night.

"Why not stay at the Eldorado with us over the weekend?" he said finally. "By Monday you can phone your mother and see how your father feels about things. Maybe by Monday he'll want you back, once he realizes that he'll be stuck for the house rent."

"No, he won't. He knows I'll continue to pay the rent."

"Even after he threw you out?"

Ellita nodded. "My mother lives there, too, you know."

"How much do you pay?"

"Five-fifty a month."

"You can rent a damned nice one-bedroom apartment for that much—already furnished."

She shook her head. "Does the Eldorado have any empty rooms?"

"Plenty. You know where it is. Drive on over, and I'll meet you in the lobby after I pick up the girls. But don't sign in—I'll negotiate a deal for you."

Hoke got into his car and let Ellita drive away first before he switched on the engine and the air conditioner.

He didn't understand women at all, he decided. He had considered Ellita Sanchez a mature, responsible woman, and he had discovered in her a young, frightened child, in some things no more grown-up emotionally than his own teenage daughters. But she was his partner, so he would have to look after her until she decided what she wanted to do.

And Hoke had other things on his mind. He wanted to see Loretta Hickey sometime this afternoon. There were only a couple of loose ends to tie up on Jerry Hickey's OD, and then he was almost certain he could get something on with Loretta. He could tell when a woman was coming on to him, and it wouldn't take much effort on his part to get Loretta bedded.

Hoke drove back downtown to the station. He drove cautiously, as a man had to do to survive in Miami traffic, but when the way was obviously clear, he drove through red lights and only paused at stop signs to shift.

13

Slater and the two girls were at the lieutenant's desk. The executive officer was showing them slides of homicide victims on a viewer he had set up. Some of the slides were in color and others were in black and white, but the photos were graphically clear on the lighted, eight-by-ten-inch glass screen.

"I've been showing the girls some pictures, Hoke," Slater said. "Explaining some cases. You worked on the Merkle shotgun case, didn't you? The one we called the 'Laura' case because her face was unrecognizable?"

"That was Quevedo's case," Hoke said, "but I did some legwork for him. I think we all did. They caught the perp when he tried to sell the gold chain. It was a driveway killing, girls. This guy followed Mrs. Merkle home from the supermarket because she was wearing a heavy gold chain around her neck. He shot her for the chain and about forty bucks worth of groceries. Any woman who wears a gold chain is asking for it in Miami. And if she wears it every day, she can count on somebody snatching it eventually. But this guy was a crazy. He didn't have to kill her. You girls don't wear neck chains, do you?''

Sue Ellen and Aileen, still staring wide-eyed at the gory face on the screen, shook their heads.

"Don't do it, girls," Slater said. "They usually work in pairs, driving around town till they spot someone. Then one guy jumps out, snatches the purse and chain, gets back in the car, and they drive off. They're hard to catch because the woman usually gets hysterical and can't remember, half the time, whether the perps were black or white. Our problem with Mrs. Merkle was that even though we knew who she was, we couldn't prove it for a while. There were no fingerprints of hers on file either, so we couldn't get an ID. She was unrecognizable, as you can plainly see, and we were trying to identify her from an oil painting—a portrait—instead of a photo. But the people who knew her said the painting didn't look like her, and they wouldn't give us a positive ID. That's why we called it the 'Laura' case, from the old movie with Clifton Webb. It was a pretty good movie, too. If it comes back on late TV some night, you girls oughta see it.''

Hoke laughed. "We kidded Quevedo about falling in love with the oil painting. Eventually he got so pissed we had to stop. What made it so funny was that Quevedo had never heard of the movie, so he didn't even know what we were kidding him about. Besides, no one could've loved that face in the painting.''

Slater laughed. "I remember now. I'd forgotten about that part of it.''

"I appreciate you looking after the girls, Lieutenant. But I'll take 'em off your hands now.''

"Your partner okay, Hoke? No trouble?"

"No, no, she's fine. She just wanted me to take a look at a guy she thought she recognized at the supermarket. But he was gone before I got there. Thank the lieutenant, girls."

"Thank you, Lieutenant Slater," Sue Ellen said. "Especially for the dessert."

"Thank you," Aileen said.

They went back to Hoke's office as Slater began to put his slides away.

"We got the special," Sue Ellen said. "Macaroni and cheese, but didn't have enough money left over for dessert. So Lieutenant Slater bought us apple pie."

"That was nice of him, but don't ever let him get you anything else. Slater's not into altruism, so—"

"What?"

"Never mind." Hoke sat down behind his desk and looked at Sue Ellen. "I'll just say that Slater likes to have everybody under some kind of obligation to him . . . but don't worry about it. Did you finish the letters to your mother?"

"I couldn't think of anything to write," Sue Ellen said.

"Me neither," said Aileen.

"Bring the paper and pens with you. You might be able to think of something later. We've got to get back to the Eldorado now, and then you can meet my partner. She's going to be staying at the hotel with us for a few days."

"You've got a lady detective partner?" Aileen said.

"That's right, and she's a good one, too."

"Think I could be a detective? When I grow up?"

"No. The best career for a girl is marriage. Even my partner, who's a very good detective, probably wishes she was married now. But don't mention that to her."

Hoke unlocked his desk drawer, retrieved the envelope of money for Mrs. Hickey, and then drove the girls back to the Eldorado Hotel.

Ellita Sanchez was waiting for them in the lobby, and Hoke introduced her to Eddie Cohen as his partner. There was an empty room two doors down from Hoke's suite, and Hoke told Eddie to give Ellita the professional rate—or 10 percent off the ten-dollar daily room charge.

"I don't think Mr. Bennett'll go for that," Eddie said.

"If he doesn't," Hoke said, "tell him to talk to me."

After Ellita registered, they went upstairs. Hoke carried Ellita's cardboard box, and Sue Ellen carried the train case. The small room was hot and musty, but the window air conditioner worked after Hoke switched it on and kicked it a couple of times. Hoke registered the expression on Ellita's usually impassive face; he detected depression beneath her attempt to smile. The scarred linoleum floor had sections missing, and the furnishings, a metal cot with a thin mattress and patched sheets, a straight ladder-backed chair, and a dented three-drawer metal dresser—all painted dead-white—completed the inventory. The cracked gray walls had been painted with a cheap water-based paint, and the walls were powdery to the touch. The faucets in the bathtub and sink dripped. The washbasin, with most of the enamel missing, was rusty. There was no toilet paper in the bathroom, and there was only one face towel.

"I'll go down and get you some more towels and toilet paper," Hoke said, "but until this room cools off, you'd better come down to our suite."

Hoke left them in his suite to get acquainted, took the elevator downstairs again, and returned with two bath towels, two rolls of toilet paper, and a dozen small bars of soap. He dropped these off in Ellita's room and returned to his suite. Ellita was showing the girls her .38 pistol—although she had taken the precaution of removing the rounds before letting them handle it.

"Look," Hoke said, "I've got to go out this afternoon. There's not much to do around the hotel, so why don't you take the girls over to the Fifth Street Gym, Ellita, and watch the boxers work out? Tony Otero, the Puerto Rican lightweight, is preparing for a fight later this month, and he's a pretty good boy. You can walk over there and kill the rest of the afternoon. Then this evening, when I come back, I'll take you all out to dinner."

"I thought you said we're not supposed to go out alone," Aileen said.

Hoke pointed to Ellita, who was sitting in the Victorian chair and reloading her pistol. "You won't be alone. Ellita's with you, and she's armed. You'll be safe with her, and besides, nobody'll bother you in the daytime. I was going to suggest going to the beach, but I know Ellita hasn't got her suit with her. It'll rain later this afternoon anyway."

"The sun's out now," Sue Ellen said. "How can you tell?"

"Because in July it always rains in the afternoon."

"Don't worry about us, Hoke," Ellita said. "We'll find something to do. If you have somewhere to go, go ahead."

"I'm out of cigarettes," Sue Ellen said, "and the machine in the lobby takes six quarters for a pack. Can I have some change for cigarettes?"

"No." Hoke took two Kools out of his pack and handed them to her. "Better make these two last. If you can't support your habit on the allowance I gave you, you'll just have to stop smoking till I can find you a job somewhere."

Sue Ellen poked out her lower lip. "I don't like the menthol kind."

Hoke snatched the two Kools back from her and returned them to his pack.

"When will you be back?" Ellita asked.

"I don't know exactly, but I'll be back before dark. I've got to go to Coral Gables, and then, if Bill's back from the Metrozoo, I want to talk to him about something."

Ellita nodded and started for the bathroom. As Hoke was

on his way out, to his surprise the two girls each kissed him on the cheek.

Hoke parked on the second level of the bus station in Coral Gables, put his police placard in place instead of feeding the meter, and walked over to Miracle Mile, a block away. The Bouquetique was a narrow shop between a luggage store and a Cuban *joyería*. The flower arrangements in the window were artificial for the most part, and there was no FTD logo, but there were signs for Visa and MasterCard on the glass door. If Loretta Hickey wasn't a member of FTD, Hoke thought, and had to depend on walk-in customers only, she would be hard-pressed to pay the high rents charged on Miracle Mile. During the last two years the street had been upgraded and tile sidewalks had been added. The Mile merchants had all been assessed accordingly for the beautification.

A short Oriental woman was behind the counter. Behind her a tall, lighted refrigerator held flower arrangements and a huge vase of red roses. It was cool in the shop, and there was a pleasant odor of freshly cut flowers and ferns. In a glass-topped case beside the counter were the so-called smart things Loretta Hickey sold as well as flowers. There were silver bracelets, turquoise rings, earrings and necklaces, and a half-dozen glass paperweights.

"Yes, sir?" the Asian woman said, in a high tiny voice. She was the woman Hoke had talked to on the phone and had thought was a child. She stepped back two paces as Hoke moved to the counter, and Hoke wondered why Mrs. Hickey would hire such a shy woman as a salesperson. He decided it was because Loretta could probably get her for the minimum wage.

"Tell Mrs. Hickey I want to see her."

"She's designing in the back. I can help you?"

"No. Just tell her Sergeant Moseley is here."

The woman pushed through the bamboo curtains that

145

separated the front from the back workroom. It was almost three minutes before Loretta Hickey came through the curtains. Her lipstick was freshly applied, and Hoke figured she had redone the rest of her makeup as well.

"I meant to come earlier," he said, "but I was delayed." He opened the envelope and removed the receipt Loretta had already signed. "You'd better count it."

"I trust you." She smiled.

"But cut the cards."

Loretta counted the money, replaced it in the envelope, and then put the envelope into the wide front pocket of her blue cotton smock. Her honey-colored hair was in two braids down her back, and her face was flushed slightly.

"I was going to ask you out to dinner tonight," Hoke said, "but a few other things have come up."

"I thought you were coming to my place for dinner. I've still got all that ham, and—"

"Ham'll keep. But I won't be free till Monday night. And I'd prefer to take you out to dinner. Then, if we don't get enough to eat, we can always go back to your house and snack on the ham."

"All right. But most restaurants in the Gables are closed Monday nights."

"We don't have to eat in the Gables. I know a nice place on Calle Ocho. You like Spanish food? I don't mean Cuban, I mean Spanish."

"They use so much garlic . . ."

"Okay. Seafood it is, then."

"I'm not picky. It's just that even when you tell them no garlic they put it in anyway."

"I know a good seafood place. Incidentally, I talked to Mr. Hickey, your ex, and he's going to have Jerry cremated."

"Oh? Have they released the body?"

"Not yet. On Thursday, as I recall, there were about twenty-five P.M.s ahead of him. They only do six or seven a day, unless there's an emergency, and then they hire extra help. As you know, if you looked at the paper, there was a fire at the Descanso Hotel last week, and they've got about six charred bodies to identify, too, so—''

"I'm sure Harold'll call me when the cremation takes place. Did he say anything to you about me?''

"What do you mean?''

"About Jerry and me. Harold had this ridiculous idea that Jerry and I—well, it was just crazy. There's no way in the world I could ever get interested in a kid like Jerry.''

"No, he didn't say anything to me. But I went through a divorce myself, Loretta, and it always changes people. In fact, my wife accused me of having an affair with a young woman in the Grove. At the time of our divorce I was putting in fourteen-hour days, so I wouldn't've had time for anything like that. Even if I'd had the money it takes for motel rooms.''

"I often work twelve-hour days myself. Right now, I'm making a funeral wreath. I wish I could get more funerals.'' She blushed. "I didn't mean what you think.''

"I know what you meant, and I hope you get more funerals, too. Anyway, Minrow's Funeral Home will be taking care of Jerry's cremation. So if you want to add anything to the announcement in the papers, or if you want to invite some of Jerry's friends, you should call Minrow.''

"Jerry didn't have any friends that I know of. I tried to make a list for you, and couldn't think of anyone. But I'll call Mr. Minrow. There should be some flowers, even at a cremation.''

"Okay, then, Loretta. I'll pick you up at your house Monday night about eight-thirty, depending on the traffic.''

"All right.'' Loretta reached across the counter to shake hands. Hoke held her hand with both of his, pulled her toward him, and kissed her on the lips before he released her hand.

He turned toward the door when he heard the high-pitched girlish giggle from behind the bamboo curtain.

Hoke stopped at a Greek restaurant on his way back to his car and ate a Greek salad for a late lunch. It wasn't enough, and he was still hungry, but he decided to let it do until dinner. He showed the cashier his badge and asked her if he could use the phone. He dialed Henderson at home, and Bill answered.

"I'm glad I caught you. I didn't think you'd be back from the zoo yet, and just took a chance."

"We didn't go. Marie took the kids to Bloomingdale's instead. They hadn't seen the new store yet, and she just got her Bloomie's card in the mail."

"You should've intercepted it, Bill, and cut it into little pieces."

Bill laughed. "It's in her name, not mine. And Marie's flush right now. She just sold the same house she sold three months ago, and picked up an identical four thousand in commissions. The same house, at the same price."

"I don't get it. How'd she sell the same house twice?"

"Marie says the house sells itself. The entire interior, every damned room, is paneled in cypress, and the wood's waxed and polished. People flip when they see the paneling. Then when they buy it and move in, the wood's so damned dark they have to keep the lights on all the time, even at high noon. If they painted the paneling, the house would be ordinary, so they can't do that, you see. But a woman, spending her days in a dark house like that every day, gets depressed after a couple of weeks. So they sell it again, and move. Marie says she'll probably sell the house again before the end of the year."

"At any rate, you won't get stuck for her Bloomie's bills."

"No way. So what's up, Hoke?"

148

"I'd like to talk to you. Can you meet me at The Shamrock for a beer?"

"I guess so. But I want to look at some Toros this afternoon."

"Toros?"

"The mowers. I've been thinking about buying me a riding mower, and Toro's supposed to be the best. If I had a Toro riding mower, I could probably get my son to mow the lawn. Kids love to ride these things. In fact, if I had a mower, I wouldn't mind doing the lawn myself."

"Why not tell Jimmy that he can't use the Toro until he takes a shower after P.E.?"

Henderson laughed. "Because that would probably work, and then I'd never get to ride it."

"I need to talk to you for a while, Bill, but I don't want to interfere with your afternoon."

"I'll meet you at The Shamrock in a half-hour, Hoke. There's no hurry about the Toro. It was just something I was going to do, that's all."

"Thanks, Bill. In a half-hour then."

Hoke hung up the phone, thanked the cashier, and walked back to the bus station to retrieve his car.

Hoke was pleased with himself, by his boldness. He hadn't known in advance that he was going to kiss Loretta, but she had leaned right into it. If that fucking Asian woman hadn't been there, the kiss would have lasted a lot longer. For a moment, he had forgotten all about Ellita and the girls; he had almost changed the date from Monday to tonight. He drove to The Shamrock, parked in the dirt lot in the back, and went into the bar.

14

The lighted clock in The Shamrock said two-thirty. Henderson was already there, sitting at the bar with a light Coors draft in front of him. Two men in three-piece suits were at the end of the bar talking about cars. They looked like used-car salesmen, but Hoke knew that they were both detectives with the Metro Police Department. Prince was on the jukebox, singing "Head." The two elderly men who had played the song—one was an investigator for the D.E.A.; Hoke didn't know the other one—were listening to the lyrics, frowning with concentration.

Hoke ordered a draft Michelob for himself, and then he and Henderson moved to a table in the corner by the front window.

Hoke told Henderson about the arrival of his daughters, and then told him about Ellita's pregnancy and about checking her into the Eldorado. Henderson's fixed smile didn't change, but he listened attentively, and he didn't touch his beer while Hoke was explaining.

"Right now," Hoke finished, "they're over at the Fifth Street Gym watching Tony Otero work out. So far, I haven't had enough time to think everything out, and I don't know what to do about Ellita. That's why I wanted to talk to you about it."

"The situation's newer to me than it is to you, Hoke." Henderson sipped his beer. "Ellita'll be okay, I think. In the long run she'll be in a healthier situation. No one in her thirties should still be living at home. A few years back, she'd've been fired for getting pregnant, but not now. She can work till she starts showing, and then she can get an authorized maternity leave, married or not. Then, once the baby's born, she can be back to work within a month or two."

"I don't know what to tell Willie Brownley, or whether I should tell him or not."

"It's not your problem, Hoke. Our new assignment's only for two months, and if Ellita's only seven weeks pregnant, she's not going to show anything for another two or three months. Besides, it's up to her to talk to Willie, not you. Her being pregnant sure as hell won't interfere with our assignment. There's no danger involved, and if it ever looks like there might be, we can always leave her in the office. Or something."

"Ellita won't ask for any favors, Bill. She may not be a libber like your wife, but we can't patronize her just because she's knocked up. She wouldn't stand for it."

"In that case"—Henderson widened his metal-studded smile—"we'll have to be subtle."

"You're about as subtle as a hurricane."

"What about you? You've already given her the weekly

151

reports to do, and you had her type Morrow's confession. I could've done that, you know.''

"Ellita types without looking, and you and I both have to look. There's another thing she told me. The battery went dead on the tape recorder when we were talking to Morrow, and she saved our ass by getting the battery changed out in the hall.''

"Jesus, I didn't know that. I just thought it was a bad time to take a piss.''

"I didn't know either, till she told me last night.''

"Don't tell Brownley anything about the pregnancy. We've got to hang onto Ellita, Hoke.'' Henderson shook his head. "Do you really think she was a virgin, and got knocked up her first time out?''

"I'd like to believe it, Bill, but I can't. She's thirty-two years old. I don't see how she could live in Miami for twenty years and stay a virgin. I don't doubt that this Bruce guy she picked up was a one-night stand, but she must've experimented at least a few times before she met him. Hell, she went to Shenandoah Junior High, Southwest High, and Miami-Dade.''

"Think about what you just said for a minute, Hoke.''

"What do you mean?''

"You've got two teenage girls now, that's what I mean. Fourteen and sixteen, right? Have you talked to them about sex yet? If you don't talk to them soon and get them on the pill, you could have three pregnant girls on your hands before school starts.''

"I hate to think about anything like that.''

"You have to, Hoke. You're a father now, and you don't know what Patsy told them, or if she told them anything. Over on Miami Beach there's teenage boys running around with perpetual hard-ons, and they can talk a couple of provincial girls from Vero Beach into doing damned near anything.''

"Okay, I'll talk to them. You want another brew?''

152

"I'll get 'em."

Henderson went over to the bar to order. Hoke had wanted some advice, but not the kind he was getting. Henderson came back with two frosted mugs of beer.

"You ever talked to your kids about sex, Bill?"

"That's Marie's department. I might talk to Jimmy a little later and give him the standard lecture. I've warned them about drugs. Cripes, even the kids in elementary school are smoking pot already."

"I've got to find a decent place to live, Bill. That's my first priority."

"Why don't you borrow some money from the credit union?"

"I owe 'em too much already. I'm still paying for last year's vacation and for the new engine in my car. But I'll be a little better off now, because I won't have to send Patsy any more paychecks."

"Do you want to bring Ellita and the girls over to the house for dinner tomorrow? I can barbecue some burgers in the back yard, and we can drink a few beers. It'll get Ellita's mind off her troubles."

"I'll take a raincheck, Bill. I'm gonna spend the day looking for a house, or maybe a two-bedroom apartment."

The afternoon rain began, and the temperature in the air-conditioned bar dropped immediately. The bartender switched off the overhead fans. Hoke looked through the window. The rain came down so hard and the sky was so dark, it was difficult to see across Red Road.

"I haven't been much help, have I?" Bill said.

"Sure you have, Bill. Sometimes just talking about things is enough. The problem is I've got girls instead of boys. If they were boys, I could give 'em ten bucks apiece, tell 'em to hitchhike out to the West Coast for the rest of the summer. Then, by the time they came back, I'd have everything straightened out."

"Would you do that?"

"Why not? That's what my old man did for me when I was sixteen. When I got out to Santa Monica, I worked on a live-bait boat and saved enough money to ride the Greyhound back to Riviera Beach. I had a great summer out there in California, even though the ocean was too damned cold to swim in. But you can't do something like that with girls. I'll get them jobs next week, though. If they're working all day, they won't get into any trouble."

"I might be able to help you there, Hoke. Marie knows a lot of people. Sue Ellen can get a work permit. But Aileen, all you can get for her is maybe a baby-sitting job. You have to be sixteen to get a work permit."

"I'll worry about that next week. But if you can find something for Sue Ellen, I'd appreciate it."

"I'll talk to Marie."

"You want another beer, Bill?"

"I don't think so. To tell you the truth, I feel a little guilty about taking the day off. Teddy Gonzalez called me at home last night. He's stuck on the triple murder in Liberty City, and Slater's no help at all. These three guys— all of them black—were tied hand and foot with copper wire, and then machine-gunned from the doorway. We know the killer was in the doorway because of the way the empty cartridges were scattered, and because there were no powder burns on the victims. Two were dead when the patrol car got there, and the third guy died before the ambulance arrived."

"It sounds like a professional hit."

"More like a semi-professional hit, Hoke. The guy said 'Leroy' before he died. A pro would've made sure they were all dead before leaving."

"Just 'Leroy'? Nothing else?"

"That's all. There was no evidence of drugs in the house. The neighbors said these three guys had been living there about a week. We got an ID on all of them, but none of them was a Leroy."

154

"Christ, Bill, there must be ten thousand men named Leroy in Liberty City."

"It could've been worse. He could've said 'Tyrone.' Anyway, Slater told Teddy Gonzalez to check out everyone in the neighborhood named Leroy. In the first place, no one wants to talk to a white cop down there, especially a Latin cop, and Teddy's been running into problems without a partner. That's why he called me, and I didn't know what to tell him."

"What about Leroy's floating crap game?" Hoke said, taking a sip of beer. "I don't know if it's still in business, but Leroy's game used to move around the neighborhood in the vicinity of Northside, and that might be what the guy was talking about, or trying to say. Tell Teddy to check out the game. If it's still around, that might be a lead."

"I never worked in Liberty City. Where was the game?"

"Tell Teddy to check the files. Leroy's game was busted a few times, and he moved it around a lot, but the game was always in the vicinity of the Northside Shopping Center, because that was where the gamblers had to park. They had to walk to the game from there. Tell him to check with some of the patrol cars in the area."

"I don't know, Hoke. But it's a better lead than trying to check ten thousand Leroys who won't open the door. I'll give Teddy a ring when I get home."

"Sure you don't want another beer?"

"I don't think so. I didn't really want this one. It's still early; I think I'll drive over and look at the Toros." Henderson got up, slapped Hoke on the shoulder, and pushed through the swinging doors into the rain.

The Clash was playing "London Calling" on the jukebox. Hoke strained to listen, trying to make out the lyrics, but could only understand every third or fourth word. The whole song made no sense to him. He finished his beer and the rest of Henderson's.

155

Hoke drove back to Miami Beach in the pelting rain. He drove slowly. He was in no hurry to get back to the hotel. His little suite was no longer a sanctuary; it was full of females with unresolved problems.

15

After Hoke parked in his space at the Eldorado, he circled the hotel to check the bay side. Some of the residents had been dumping their trash into the sand of the filled-in swimming pool again, and the garbage pickup people had left a lot of litter scattered around the dumpster. Hoke entered the hotel from the rear entrance and wrote out his report at the manager's desk, reminding Mr. Bennett to call the exterminators again. Hoke wondered sometimes whether Mr. Bennett ever read his reports. The conditions rarely changed, but that was the manager's problem, not his—although Hoke hadn't considered the Norway rat invasion as one of his reporting duties when he had agreed to take on the unpaid security position at the hotel.

The girls were in Ellita's room. The three of them had been shopping, and Ellita had made curtains from red crepe paper and tacked them above the window with thumbtacks. The girls had arranged two large crepe paper bows, and these bows had been thumbtacked to the gray walls. Ellita had bought takeout food from a Cuban restaurant, together with red plastic plates and tableware. The girls had brought up one of the card tables from the lobby. There was enough red crepe paper left over for a tablecloth, and the table was set for four. A small pot of African violets had been brought from Hoke's suite as a centerpiece. A styrofoam cooler filled with iced Cokes and beer was next to the card table.

"What's all this?" Hoke said. "A party?"

"I hope you don't mind, Hoke," Ellita said, "but we decided to eat in instead of going out tonight. The girls said they never had any Cuban food before, and we wanted to surprise you."

"I'm surprised. But there's only one chair. If you move the table by the bed, I can sit on the bed. I'll get a couple of more chairs."

Hoke walked down the hall, opened an empty room with his master key, and brought back two straight chairs.

"Where'd you get all this stuff, anyway?" Hoke said, arranging the chairs around the table.

"The food's from El Gaitero's, but the rest of the stuff's from Eckerd's and the 7/Eleven."

"We met Tony Otero, Daddy," Aileen said, smiling behind her hand, "and Sue Ellen asked him if she could feel his muscle."

"Shut up, Aileen," Sue Ellen said, punching her sister on the arm.

"Did he let you feel it?" Hoke asked.

Sue Ellen nodded and blushed. "Aileen felt it too."

"How about you, Ellita?" Hoke said. "Did you feel Tony's muscle, too?"

Ellita laughed, showing her white teeth. "He's just a

little fellow, Hoke. He only weighs a hundred and thirty-four pounds.''

"I didn't ask you how much he weighed." Hoke grinned. "I asked you if you felt his muscle."

"Of course." Ellita laughed again and began to open the cartons.

There were fried pork chunks, black beans and rice, yucca, and fried plantains, all packed in separate cartons with tight foil-topped cardboard lids. There were two loaves of buttered Cuban bread, sliced lengthwise.

The girls didn't like the yucca and refused to eat it. Aileen pushed the chunks of pork around on her plate, and Hoke asked her why she wasn't eating the best part of the dinner.

"They hurt my teeth and gums, Daddy. My teeth hurt all the time anyway, and I can't chew anything hard. I was supposed to see the orthodontist last Wednesday, but Mom was too busy to take me and said you'd make an appointment with someone down here."

"Do you like those ugly braces?" Hoke said. "They look like hell, to tell the truth."

"They're too tight. I told Dr. Osmond that, but he said they're supposed to feel too tight."

"I'll take 'em off for you when we finish eating. You got any Valium in your purse, Ellita?."

"I should have," Ellita said. She got up from the table and looked into her purse for her pillbox. "I've got Valium, Tylenol-3, and some Midol."

"Give her a half Valium now, and one T-3. By the time we're through eating, they should be working a little."

Aileen took the Tylenol-3 and the half Valium with a sip of Coke.

"Do you know how to take off braces, Daddy?" Aileen asked.

"Sure. I was a dental assistant for a while when I was in the army. I learned how to do everything, including

159

extractions. They never taught me how to make false teeth though. If they had, I'd make a better set than the ones I've got now."

"I think I feel a little dizzy already," Aileen said, putting the back of her hand to her forehead dramatically.

"Are you all through eating?"

Aileen nodded. "I'm not hungry."

"There's flan for dessert," Ellita said, "but I'll save yours for you."

"Flan?"

"It's a caramelized custard. You can eat it without chewing."

"I don't think I want it. Not now, anyway."

"In that case," Hoke said, "go back to the suite and sit in the armchair. I'll be down in a few minutes."

Holding the back of her hand to her forehead, and staggering slightly, Aileen left the room, closing the door behind her.

Hoke grinned. "She's pretty good, isn't she?"

"I never knew you studied dentistry, Hoke," Ellita said.

"Neither did I. But you want the girl to have a little confidence in me, don't you?"

Sue Ellen giggled. Hoke poked Sue Ellen in the ribs with a forefinger, and she giggled again.

"And don't *you* tell her any different." Hoke finished the rest of his dinner. He then ate the pork chunks on Aileen's plate, and opened another can of beer.

"Are you ready for your flan?" Ellita said, opening another carton.

"I'll skip dessert. I'm trying to cut down on sweets. What I'll do, Ellita, I'll clip those braces off with my toenail cutters. I've got a good pair, made in Germany, and they'll cut damned near anything. You can hold her head still. Here, go down to the suite now and give her the other half Valium, and take her Coke along."

It took Hoke more than a half-hour to clip off the rubber

bands and the tiny bolts that held Aileen's braces together. The tight rubber bands were more difficult to snip away than the tiny bolts. There was a narrow gold strip glued to her lower teeth, however, and he couldn't get it off. There was no way that he could get a purchase on it with the clippers.

"I think," Ellita said, "you'll need some kind of solvent to remove that."

"Does the lower band hurt, Aileen?" Hoke said.

"I don't know. My whole mouth hurts now, so I can't tell."

"I'll leave the lower band on, then. I've got to go to the morgue on Monday or Tuesday, and I'll ask Doc Evans about it. He's probably got some kind of solvent he can lend me. But right now, you'd better lie down. Give her another T-3, Ellita."

Ellita took the girl into the bedroom. Hoke told Sue Ellen to gather up all the garbage in Ellita's room and take it downstairs to the dumpster. "But don't throw away the plastic silverware or plates. Wash that in Ellita's bathroom, and put it away in her dresser."

Hoke lit a cigarette and turned on the TV. Ellita came out of the bedroom and closed the door just as the phone rang. She picked it up.

"Put him on," she said into the phone. "Yes, sir, he's here. Me? We were just going over our plans for Monday, that's all. Yes, sir. Just a second."

She covered the mouthpiece. "It's Major Brownley."

"Shit," Hoke said. "You shouldn't've answered the phone." He took the phone from her.

"Sergeant Moseley."

"What's Ellita doing in your room, Hoke?" Brownley was pissed.

"We're trying to get a handle on what to do Monday, that's all. In fact, I met with Bill Henderson earlier this afternoon. We're all enthusiastic about the assignment,

Willie, but there's so much to do it's hard to tell what to do first.''

"That shouldn't be a problem if you saw my flag."

"What flag?"

"The red flag I attached to the Mary Rollins file. I put the Rollins file on the top of the stack so you'd get to it first.''

"I didn't see it. What I did, you see, was to divide the piles into three batches. So either Bill or Ellita must've got that one. Hold on a minute.'' Hoke put his hand over the mouthpiece. "Did you look at the Mary Rollins file? Do you remember?"

Ellita nodded. "I had it, and then put it into my reject pile. It isn't even a definite homicide, it's a missing person.''

"Ellita saw it, Major Brownley,'' Hoke said into the phone, "but I didn't. I told them we'd read all the cases first before we decided which case to work on.''

"Consider that number one, then,'' Brownley said. "I just had another irate call from Mrs. Rollins, Mary's mother. I've had one or two calls a month from this woman for the last three years. I want this woman off my back. Anyway, I told Mrs. Rollins that you were working on this case personally, so from now on you'll get all her angry phone calls. Then you'll see what I mean.''

"I'll look at it first thing Monday, Willie.''

"That's all I had to tell you, Hoke. That, and that it was an unpleasant surprise to have Sanchez answer the phone in your hotel room on a Saturday evening. You know how I feel about things like that.''

"I explained that. We were just—''

But Brownley had hung up.

Hoke hung up, turned, and grinned at Ellita. "Willie suspects a little hanky-panky. When you get up enough nerve to tell him you're pregnant, he'll put two and two together, come up with five, and tell you that Bruce, your detail man, is another Coconut Grove myth.''

"I didn't plan to tell him about Bruce. The major's entitled to know I'm pregnant, but there's no hurry about telling him. But you're right, Hoke, I shouldn't have answered your phone.''

"Fuck him." Hoke shrugged. "Let Willie think what he likes. He will anyway. Tell me something about this Rollins case.''

"It goes back about three years. Mary Rollins disappeared, but they found her car. They also found her shorts— they called 'em hot pants then—in a pole-bean field off Kendall Drive. Her bloody T-shirt was with the hot pants. They both had Type-O bloodstains, and Mary had Type-O blood. That's about it. There was no body. Her friends at work were interviewed, but no one saw her after she left work to go home on a Friday afternoon. She didn't have any boyfriends, apparently. Because of the bloody clothing, it was listed at first as a possible homicide, but was changed later to a missing person case. I remember it from yesterday because I had to look up a word in MacGellicot's notebook. He talked to a woman in Boca Raton, and then he wrote in his notes, 'Hostile to males. Nugatory results. Maybe female investigator should talk to her.' ''

"You mean 'negatory.' ''

"No. 'Nugatory.' I looked it up. It means having no worth or meaning. It's about the same as negatory, but what MacGellicot meant, I think, was that the woman was stalling him because he was a man, and she didn't like men.''

"Why didn't he say 'lying' then? Why use a dumb word like 'nugatory'?''

"We could ask him.''

"He left the department two years ago. Mac had a degree in sociology from the University of Chicago, and he got a police chief's job in some small town in Ohio. We lose a lot of good detectives that way. These little towns that advertise for a chief in the journal always flip when a Miami homicide cop applies for the job. But they usually want a new chief to have a degree besides. It's not a bad life compared with the things we have to do. Six cops, one patrol car, and a sign hidden behind a tree to make a little speed-trap money. The only crime you have to worry about is teenage drinkers pissing on the gravel in front of the town's only gas station.''

"We can call MacGellicot on Monday, can't we?''

"No, we'll just look at the file. See what else it says. Maybe you can drive up to Boca and talk to the woman, if she's still there. We'll have to do something, now that Willie called. Funny you didn't notice the red flag.''

"A bunch of the files are flagged, Hoke. You haven't got to yours yet, maybe.''

"That's what pisses me off. I don't mind doing the job, but I hate to be told how to do it. I don't like being called at home either, just to get some woman off Brownley's back.''

Hoke finished his beer.

"Tomorrow I'm going to see Ms. Westphal at the house-sitting service again. She's got an efficiency available for three weeks in the black Grove, starting next Friday. She also pays the sitter five bucks a day for living in it. If you don't mind living in the ghetto, Ellita, I can talk her into letting you have it. Three weeks'll give you a base, and you can then look around for a decent place to live. Or maybe, after three weeks, you can move back home.''

"I'm not going back home again, Hoke. If I did, I'd get the silent treatment from my father. It's time I left anyway. I would like to get a place in the same neighborhood though. That way, my mother could come over and help me with the baby.''

"You've got months to go before you have to worry about a baby-sitter.''

"I know, but I've thought about it."

"How do you feel? Physically?"

"I feel fine. I like your girls, Hoke. Not only are they well-behaved, they adore you."

"How could they? They don't even know me, for Christ's sake. And I don't know what to do with them either. You've helped me a lot."

"Did you call their mother yet? To let her know that they're all right?"

"Except for a few letters, I haven't talked to Patsy in ten years. If she wants to know how they are, she can call me."

"Maybe she's tried, Hoke? It's hard to get you at the hotel."

"I'll tell you what. Get her phone number from Sue Ellen, and you can call her. Reverse the charges, and if she won't accept the call, the hell with it."

"Sure you don't want to talk to her?"

"Positive."

"I'll call her then. If I were their mother, I'd want to know that they got here okay." Ellita cracked the door to the bedroom, then closed it softly. "Aileen's sleeping like a baby. That was awfully kind of you, Hoke, taking her braces off."

"What the hell." Hoke shrugged. "She was in pain. I'm her father, for Christ's sake."

Ellita started to cry. Hoke looked at her for a moment, then picked up his leisure jacket, left the suite, and took the elevator down to the lobby. He didn't know why he felt so lousy, so useless.

He got into his car, switched on the engine, and tried to think of somewhere to go. He didn't have anywhere to go, so he drove to the police station in Miami. He looked for the Mary Rollins file, and read through it. He leafed through two more cases—hopeless, hopeless, both of them—and then locked his office. He went down to the cafeteria for a cup of coffee and sat down alone at a table to drink it.

Lieutenant Fred Slater came in, and Hoke watched him as he got a carton of milk and a glass, and paid the cashier. Slater was grinning. He looked around the room, spotted Hoke, and came over to the table. Slater's thin lips split his pockmarked face into two ugly parts. He opened the milk carton and filled his glass.

"I just heard a good one, Hoke," he said. "How do you know when you're sleeping with a fag?" He took a sip of milk and wiped off the milk mustache with a paper napkin. "How? His dick tastes like shit!" Slater laughed and took another sip of milk.

Hoke didn't laugh. "Let me tell you something, Slater, and I want you to get it straight. You ever tell my girls a joke like that, and exec officer or no exec officer, I'll kick the living shit out of you."

"I don't know what you're talking about. It's just a joke, for Christ's sake. All I was . . . ."

But Slater was talking to Hoke's back as he walked out of the cafeteria.

16

On Sunday morning Hoke awoke at six, as usual, dressed, and drove to the 7/Eleven. He bought a dozen bagels, a quart of milk, a package of cream cheese, and three large cans of Dinty Moore stew. He also picked out a large Spanish onion, which he planned to dice and add to the canned stew for extra flavor. Back in the suite, he heated water on the hot plate for instant coffee, and when it boiled he woke the girls for breakfast. Then he walked down the hall and knocked on Ellita's door, telling her to join them in his suite for bagels and coffee.

Ellita wasn't wearing pantyhose with her skirt when she joined Hoke a few minutes later, and when she sat down and crossed her legs, he caught a glimpse of the inner side of her thighs. Her soft thighs were as white as ivory, which

167

surprised Hoke so much he stared a little longer than he had intended. Hoke had always assumed that Ellita was the same golden tan all over—like her exposed face, neck, and arms. Hoke knew that most Cubans thought of themselves as white, but he had always considered them as Third Worlders—an island mixture of Spanish, Caribe Indian, and black—and as being brown all over. For that reason, he had never objected to the department Affirmative Action program, which gave preference to minorities, both in hiring practices and on promotion lists. In Miami, however, although the majority of the population was Latin, they were still counted as a minority group. If Ellita was white as well as Cuban, Hoke figured, maybe she hadn't really deserved a promotion to a detective's slot in the Homicide Division. Ellita's white thighs were a revelation to him, opening up a whole line of new thoughts. One of these days, he'd have to talk to Bill Henderson about this as something that should be discussed at the P.B.A. On the other hand, even though Ellita had been given preference, as a Cuban, over several WASP policemen who also deserved to be detectives, she had paid her dues after working all those years as a police dispatcher. So what difference did it make? None at all. It was just nice to know that Ellita was a white woman, after all—even if she was a Cuban. Henderson liked her, and so did he, and they could hardly blame her for taking advantage of the program to get out of a boring, dead-end job.

The girls were still in the bedroom, and taking turns in the bathroom. Ellita stirred her coffee and sat back a little in the desk chair.

"I called Patsy last night, Hoke," Ellita said. "Collect. Sue Ellen also talked to her for a few minutes. She said she'd send a check to the girls to make up the difference between what you gave them as an allowance and what she usually gave them. Sue Ellen told her you were giving them a dollar a week, so she said she'd send them each a check for forty-six dollars every month."

"What else did she say?"

"She wanted to know who I was, so I told her I was your partner. But then, when Sue Ellen talked to her and told her we were all living here together, she probably got the wrong idea."

"Does it bother you?"

"What a woman who deserts her children thinks of me is not worth bothering about." Ellita added more Sweet 'n' Low to her coffee.

"She's probably relieved that there's a woman around to look after the girls, but I'm sorry she got the wrong idea about you."

The girls emerged sleepily from the bedroom and mixed their coffee in the red plastic cups Ellita had brought from her room.

"I don't see why we have to get up so early on a Sunday," Sue Ellen said.

"There're bagels and cream cheese in the sack," Hoke explained. "This evening I'll cook some beef stew, and we'll still have enough bagels to go with it. Do you think, Sue Ellen, that your mother'll send you allowance checks, like she said?"

"I know she will."

"In that case, I'll lend both of you girls five dollars, and you can pay me back when you get your checks. That way, if you want, you can buy some cigarettes." Hoke gave them five dollars apiece. Aileen put her money into her pocket, then soaked her bagel in her coffee to soften it.

"How're your teeth this morning?" Hoke asked.

"Fine, Daddy. But I slept awful hard. I don't think I moved all night."

"Good. But if they start to hurt again, and they might, ask Ellita for another T-3."

Aileen nodded.

"How about you, Ellita?" Hoke said. "Did you call your mother too?"

"Three times, but each time my father answered, so I hung up. Then I called my cousin Louisa and asked her to tell my mother I was staying here, and that I'd call her Monday."

Hoke opened his notebook and tore out a page. "I went to the office last night and took a look at the Mary Rollins file. Here's the address of that woman up in Boca Raton. Her name is Wanda Fridley, Mrs. Fridley. If you don't have anything else planned today, why not take the girls and drive up there and talk to her? Mrs. Fridley's the woman who called the department and said she saw Mary Rollins in Delray Beach. Then when MacGellicot drove up and talked to her about it, she changed her story and said she wasn't sure. His notes, that she probably didn't like him because he was a man, may or may not be valid. But maybe she'll talk to you. I was going to send you up there tomorrow, but it might be best to get this interview out of the way today, so we can work on our other cases tomorrow. This way, we can at least tell Brownley we're working on the Rollins case. I'll drive out to the site where they found her shorts and T-shirt and look around the area. I know I won't find anything out there now, but it'll be something else to add to the report. But if you don't want to go today, that's all right, too. You can buy a bathing suit, and you girls can spend the day on the beach."

"That's no choice at all." Ellita laughed. "You couldn't pay me enough money to wear a bathing suit!"

"Why not?"

Ellitta patted the top of her leg. "Fat thighs. Cellulite. I don't wear a bikini, and I don't go to the beach."

"I know you can swim. You had to pass the swimming test at the academy."

"I did. But then I sat on my ass for seven years developing cellulite. I don't mind driving up to Boca. We should

170

be back by noon or a little later, and the girls can still go to the beach. I'll go with them and watch them from a chickee.''

"Okay, that's settled. I'm going to check on that apartment in the Grove for you, and then see if I can run down Jerry Hickey's former landlady. I got the address you left on my desk last night."

"What can she tell you?"

"I don't know. I just wonder where he got the money and the white lady, that's all. There's something weird about this case, and I'm not ready to close the file on it yet. Don't you think it's a little unusual for a white boy to take a room in a black woman's house in the black Grove?''

Ellita smiled. "Not for a junkie. Besides, aren't you trying to get me a garage apartment in the black Grove?''

"But you'll be paid for living there. It isn't the same thing." Hoke recalled his reflections of a moment before, about Ellita's color, but decided to keep his counsel.

"Maybe Jerry was paid to live there, too," Ellita said.

"That's another question I could ask, I suppose. Well, look, I'll be back this afternoon, and if I'm not back, I'll call the desk and give Eddie a number where you can call me. Then tonight we'll fix the stew and all have dinner, the way we did last night. I enjoyed that.''

Hoke turned to Sue Ellen and Aileen. "Remember, Ellita's going to be on police business. So you do whatever she tells you, understand?''

Hoke's daughters assured him that they did.

Hoke parked in front of the Coconut Grove Library, the only attractive public building in the Grove. With its fieldstone facade, curving wooden walkway, and the shady branches overhanging the weathered steps, the building looked as though it had grown out of the ground. A police officer was sitting in his squad car reading *Penthouse*. The officer, still in his early twenties, was so absorbed

171

by the magazine he didn't look up until Hoke tapped him on the shoulder.

"Open the back door." Hoke showed the officer his shield. "I'm Sergeant Moseley. Homicide."

The officer clicked up the door lock, and Hoke slid into the back seat. The officer picked his cap up from the seat, slapped it on his head, and shoved his magazine under the front seat.

"What's up, Sarge?"

Hoke looked across the street to Peacock Park. A women's softball game was in progress. The harbor was filled with anchored Hobie Cats and other small sailboats with furled sails. Two bearded, shirtless men holding their shirts in their laps, their faces raised to the sun, sat on the stone wall that bordered the park. Hoke looked back at the officer. "How long you been assigned to the Grove?"

"About six weeks now. I like it better'n Liberty City. I got hit with a rock during a fracas at Northside Shopping Center." The patrolman pointed to a jagged red scar on his chin. "Fourteen stitches. After that, my squad leader thought I might be a little prejudiced, so he had me transferred to the Grove. Best thing that ever happened to me. I been working days, and things've been pretty quiet compared to Liberty City. Some chain and purse snatching, a little loitering, that's about it. On Friday nights there's been a kind of teenage invasion from all over, but I haven't been on nights yet."

"Did you know a kid named Jerry Hickey?"

"Uh-uh, but my partner might. He's been in the Grove for 'most three years."

"Where is he?"

"Up at Lum's." The officer pointed up the sloping street. "He's getting himself a Lumberjack burger. At first, we used to eat together, but now, when we take a break for a sandwich or coffee, we take turns. That way, Red said, somebody's always with the radio."

"In other words, you two don't get along."

"I didn't say that, Sergeant. We get along fine. I've learned a lot from old Red."

"Okay. You go up to Lum's and get old Red and tell him I want to talk to him. Then you can stay in Lum's and get your own Lumberjack burger."

"I was plannin' on a tuna fish."

The officer started up the mild incline, and Hoke wondered how this incredibly stupid young officer had managed to get through the police academy. But perhaps he expected too much; the kid wasn't so much dumb as he was young, that was all.

The police car was nosed into the curb, so Hoke recognized "old" Red as he limped down the street from Lum's. Red Halstead was thirty-nine, and he had been shot in the foot by a woman he had tried to disarm before she could pump her last bullet into her husband's inert body. As a consequence, Halstead had worked in Property for more than a year. The woman's husband had died, and she had been given ten years' probation by a sympathetic judge. But Halstead, after narrowly missing out on a disability discharge, had endured the necessary therapy and the boring job in the Property office and had finally regained his old job on the street. The widow had married a man a lot wealthier than her dead husband. Now she lived in a condo in Bal Harbour.

Hoke got out of the car and shook hands with Halstead. "Hoke Moseley, Red. I remember you from Property. How's the foot?"

"Fine, Sergeant, 'cept when it gets cold, but I haven't had to worry much about cold weather lately. It's eighty-eight already, and it's only ten A.M."

"Sorry to interrupt your break."

"That's okay. I was finished anyway. Who's dead?"

"A kid named Jerry Hickey. He died from an overdose

at home. But he used to hang out around Peacock Park. I thought you might know him, or know someone who did.''

Halstead nodded. ''I knew him. He had an allowance of some kind from his father, the drug lawyer. Some of the kids around here would hit him up for small change once in a while. He also sold weed, but I never caught him with any, and I must've shook him down three or four times. He was also a junkie, and he hung out sometimes with Harry Jordan. Jordan used to be a Hare Krishna, but was kicked out of the cult for skimming off the top, or something like that. But he kept his yellow robes, and now he's in business for himself. Instead of just skimming, he keeps everything he begs now.'' Halstead laughed. ''They should've kept him on and just let him take his percentage. But Jordan's straight—I mean he's not into dope. I don't think he even drinks. He's something of a guru around the Grove. He lives on Peralta, over in the black section.''

''1309 Peralta?''

''I don't know if that's the number, but I know where he lives on Peralta. He lives in a garage out back.''

''A garage apartment?''

''No.'' Halstead shook his head and grinned. ''A garage. What's going down?''

''Not much of anything. I'm doing a little backtracking, that's all.''

''You just want to talk to somebody who knew Hickey, right?''

''That's it.''

''Well, Harry Jordan knew him as well as anybody. He used to crash at Harry's, but I think he had a room somewhere here in the Grove besides. I could tell you how to get to Harry's, but the easiest way would be to just drive by. You could follow me. When I pass the house I'll flash my turn signal once and keep going. The garage'll be around to the back. I won't stop, because if I did, everyone in the neighborhood would know you were a cop.''

"Okay. And thanks, Red."

Hoke trailed two hundred yards behind the police car and followed it down Main Highway, parallel with Grand Avenue. Halstead signaled and made a right turn into the black Grove. After two more blocks, Halstead slowed, flashed his signal, and then accelerated. Hoke made a sharp turn into a dirt driveway beside a pink two-bedroom house and parked in the backyard.

A girl, sixteen or seventeen, was sitting in a webbed beach chair, nursing a baby. Her heavy bare breasts seemed disproportionately large for her slender body. Her acorn-brown hair reached almost to her waist, and she wore a soiled eggshell-colored skirt down to her ankles. Her dirty, slender feet were bare. A blue T-shirt was draped over the arm of the chair. As Hoke got out of his car, she looked at him incuriously with sienna eyes and drummed on the baby's bare back with the tips of her fingers. Her left eye was black and swollen, and there were mottled black-and-blue marks on her puffy left cheek.

The fenced-in backyard also contained a redwood table and two benches, a drooping clothesline hung with drying diapers, and several rows of vegetables—carrots, green peppers, and plum tomatoes. The garage at the end of the dirt driveway was being used as a residence. The wide garage door was missing, and the unpainted front of the small building, except for a normal door-sized entrance covered by a dusty blue velvet curtain, was composed of plywood and other odd-sized pieces of scrap lumber. The garage had an unpainted corrugated-iron roof that looked new.

A monk came through the blue velvet curtain. He was wearing a clean saffron robe and leather sandals without socks. He was about thirty, and his head, except for a short tuft of blond hair at the crown, was shaved. Despite his shaven head, he was noticeably balding. He looked at Hoke with narrowed blue eyes.

175

"Get in the house, Moira," he said.

The girl, carrying her baby and the blue T-shirt, got up from the chair and sidled through the curtain.

"How old's the girl, Harry?"

"Old enough to have a baby."

"Does her mother know she's here?"

"No. If she did, she'd send someone like you to take her home again. And then it would take Moira another month or so to escape like she had to do the last time. Why don't you people quit hassling us?"

"Moira's mother didn't send me here. It's just that I've got a daughter about that age." Hoke took out his cigarettes, and then returned them to his pocket. "What I want is some information about Jerry Hickey. I'm a police officer."

"I think he left Miami, probably Florida."

"What makes you think that?"

"A couple of guys came around and searched his old room." Jordan pointed to the pink house. "Then they talked to me. He was supposed to deliver a package or something to a Holiday Inn in North Miami, but apparently he never got there. They didn't say what was in the package, but they searched my place, too, which I didn't appreciate."

"Were they police officers?"

Jordan smiled, and wiped his mouth. "Hardly. They were both Latins in silk suits. I hadn't seen Jerry for two days, not since—did you get a look at Moira's face?

"It's quite a shiner—"

"Worse than that. Jerry chipped a piece of bone from her cheek, and she's in a lot of pain. I don't understand it, any of it. I felt sorry for Jerry because I thought he needed a place to be, you know. But when I was out, he tried to jump Moira. When she resisted, he hit her."

"He tried to rape the girl? That doesn't sound like junkie

176

behavior. Could be, now that Jerry's dead, you're blaming him for something you did yourself.''

"I didn't know Jerry was dead." Jordan's face became a solemn mask. Jordan held his hands out, palms up, and showed Hoke his forearms. They were covered with tiny red welts. "Ant bites, Mr. Policeman, from my garden. But I won't kill those ants, or any of God's creatures. And I wouldn't hit my wife.''

"You're married, then?''

"In the eyes of God, yes. Moira could also tell you I didn't hit her, but you probably wouldn't believe her either. But I didn't know Jerry was dead. I'll pray for him now, and for you, too, whether you want me to or not. Did those men kill him?''

"No. It was an overdose. Heroin.''

"May God rest his troubled soul." Incongruously, Jordan crossed himself.

"Can you show me Jerry's room?''

"That's up to Mrs. Fallon. I rent the garage from her, and Jerry had a room in her house up till about a month ago. She caught him shooting up, and she kicked him out. Then I took him in." Jordan shrugged. "He needed a place to be, and I still think I did the right thing, but I'm finding it hard to forgive him. I'm still working on that, but it'll be easier now, now that I know he's dead, I mean. Mrs. Fallon's a member of the Primitive Baptist Church, and they're down on junkies, but she'll probably let you look at his old room. I know she hasn't rented it out again.''

Hoke took out his wallet and gave Jordan a dollar bill. "Here. Better get some Tylenol for Moira.''

The dollar bill disappeared inside Jordan's robes. "God bless you, sir." Jordan bowed from the waist, turned, and went into the garage through the curtain, colliding with Moira, who had been standing right behind it.

Hoke knocked at the back door of the pink house. The door opened immediately because Mrs. Fallon, a large black woman in a shapeless gray housecoat, had been watching Hoke through the kitchen window as he talked to Jordan. Hoke had seen her sullen face when she pulled the white curtain to one side. Hoke showed her his shield and ID.

"I'm a police officer, Mrs. Fallon, and I'd like to take a look at Jerry's old room."

"You got a warrant?"

"No. But I have reason to believe that you're holding Mr. Hickey's dog a prisoner in your house. And dognapping's a serious crime.

"I don't know nothin' 'bout no dog. Jerry didn't have no dog, and he's been out of the house 'most a month now, livin' with the reverend."

"Who'd you sell the dog to? I know there's been a dog here because of that digging around the bush over there—over there"—Hoke pointed—"by those oleanders."

"I done that diggin' myself, weedin'."

"Did you know oleanders were poison? If you burn oleander bushes and breathe in the smoke, you can poison yourself and a dog, too."

"There's never been no dog here!"

"I'd like to see for myself. I'd also like to see your landlord's license for renting out rooms. You've got one, haven't you?"

"I don't need no license. Jerry was staying here, but I just let him stay as a favor, that's all."

"Did you charge him rent for the favor?"

"Jerry didn't have no room—not exactly. I just let him sleep in the utility room. I don't run no roomin' house. I told the other two mens that, who pushed their way in here."

"I'd like to see where he slept."

"I reckon I can show you where he slept. But you got no right to look in the rest of my house."

"That's all I want to see. Just where he slept."

Mrs. Fallon stepped back, and Hoke came into the kitchen. She opened the door to the utility room, off the kitchen. There was a canvas cot, a three-legged wooden stool, and some nails on the wall where clothes could be hung, but the spotlessly clean room was bare otherwise. There was no window. A single 40-watt bulb dangled on a cord from the ceiling. A long piece of brown twine was attached to the light chain. It would be possible for someone to lie in bed and turn the light on and off without sitting up.

"Did Jerry have kitchen privileges?"

"No, sir. He didn't eat much, but I fed him sometimes. I always got somethin' or other on the stove."

"You didn't let him keep things in your refrigerator then?"

"No, but he never ast."

"At least he was a clean housekeeper."

"I cleaned up after he left. And you can see there ain't no dog in here."

"The two men who searched his room—what did they look like?"

"They was white mens, but they spoke Spanish to each other. They was driving a green Eldorado with the top down. They didn't stay long. I was gonna call the police after they left, but I didn't want to get involved. I had a little cardboard box packed up with some of Jerry's clothes he left here, but they took that along. It was just some underwear and socks and a blue work shirt. I always did Jerry's laundry with mine, and it was in the wash when he left. He was staying with Reverend Jordan after that, but I wasn't going to carry it down to him. He knew it was here, and he could've come and got it."

"Did those men take Jerry's dog, too?"

"Jerry didn't have no dog! I done tol' you that ten times!"

"All right. Thank you, Mrs. Fallon. But if those two

men come back, or if Jerry's dog comes back, call me at this number." Hoke gave her one of his cards. "And thank you for your cooperation."

As Hoke drove out of the yard, Mrs. Fallon started to walk toward the garage. She'll pump Harry Jordan, Hoke thought. Jordan will tell her that Jerry's dead, and then she'll pray for Jerry, too. Mrs. Fallon's Christian prayers, Hoke decided, would help Jerry just about as much as Harry Jordan's.

17

A wire fence separated the Bajan sculptor's garage apartment and yard from the Robert E. Lee housing project. At least thirty black kids were playing some kind of grab-ass on the other side of the fence. They came over to the fence to stare at Hoke while he pulled into the narrow backyard and parked. There was a huge sculpture of a bird-like creature in the yard, blocking the way to the closed door of the garage. The wings were fashioned from automobile fenders, and the body was formed with welded auto parts. The "bird" had been painted with red rustproofing primer, and its eyes were red glass taillights. The eyes were unlighted, and Hoke wondered for a moment if the sculptor would wire them for electricity when he was finished with the sculpture. He then realized that he didn't

181

give a shit what the sculptor decided to do, because he would never have to look at it again.

Ellita, if she moved into the small apartment above the garage, would be an object of curiosity, and she would be harassed by the kids in the project. Nor could he take the place himself; there was no way that he could leave his girls alone all day in this neighborhood. Without getting out of his car, he backed out of the yard. Before his back wheels reached Tangerine Lane, a rock hit the windshield on the passenger's side, but it didn't crack the glass. The kids on the other side of the fence, squealing, ran off in a dozen directions.

Hoke turned east to South Dixie Highway and then drove south to North Kendall Drive. He took Kendall west to 136th Avenue, and turned into a Kendall Lakes shopping mall. He parked in the lot, and then paced off the approximate distance to where Mary Rollins's hot pants and T-shirt were discovered. The location was now a chain sandwich shop, featuring roast beef sandwiches. The "Sunday Special" was a roast beef sandwich with a free Coke for $2.99. Hoke went inside, ordered the special, and doused his sandwich with the chain's special horseradish sauce. The teenagers behind the counter wore oversized red muslin tams and little red jackets that didn't meet in front. Their white muslin shirts had balloon sleeves. They wore their own blue jeans, however, which diluted by about five hundred years the medieval effect intended by the management. The tables and benches were bolted to the floor, and the benches were set too far back from the table for comfortable seating. Three years ago, this shopping center had been a U-pick pole-bean field. Now it held fifty different shops, anchored by a Publix supermarket and a K-Mart. The mall was filled with Sunday shoppers, most of them wearing Izod alligator shirts and shorts, or running togs. There were a great many small children. Every one of them was eating some thing or other as the parents walked aimlessly around the mall.

Perhaps, Hoke thought, this cold-case idea of Brownley's was not such a good one after all. West Kendall was the fastest-growing area in the county, and there were hundreds of condos filled already, with more under construction. Not only did Miami have hundreds of new permanent residents moving in every day, there was also a daily tourist influx of at least thirty thousand strangers staying from one day to two months or more on vacations. A colder case than 'Mary Rollins—missing only, with no body—would be hard to imagine. It was perfectly possible that her body was buried somewhere under the thirty acres of asphalt parking lot.

Of course, Hoke hadn't expected to find anything out here anyway, but it had been more than two years since he had been this far out on Kendall Drive, and he hadn't realized how much the area had boomed. Hoke finished his sandwich and Coke, then showed the kid behind the counter his badge.

The phone was in the small back storeroom, and the kid stood uneasily beside Hoke as he dialed.

"This is police business, sonny. Get out and close the door." The boy left reluctantly but didn't argue.

Eddie Cohen answered on the twelfth ring.

"This is Sergeant Moseley, Eddie. Did Ms. Sanchez phone and leave a number for me to call?"

"Just a second. I got it written down."

Hoke waited, and then Eddie gave him a number in Delray Beach. "It's a pay phone, she said, and she'll either wait there, or be there at exactly two o'clock. If you don't call by two, don't call at all, and she'll drive back to the hotel."

Hoke looked at his Timex. It was 12:30.

"All right, Eddie. If she calls again, tell her I'm on my way to the station, and I'll call her at two from there."

183

"I'll tell her. Anything else?"

"Yeah. Don't pull the plug on the air conditioning in my suite or in Ms. Sanchez's room."

"I already did. Mr. Bennett told me—"

"I don't care what he said. You plug 'em in again right now, understand?"

"I'll see if I can find Emilio."

"Never mind Emilio. You do it yourself. Now."

"If you say so."

"I say so." Hoke replaced the receiver.

Before leaving the sandwich shop, Hoke bought an eightounce bottle of the special horseradish sauce from the boy behind the counter and thanked him for letting him use the phone.

When Hoke got to his office and turned on the desk light, two detectives on Sunday duty wandered over. They stood in the doorway, not quite coming into the small room, waiting for an invitation they didn't get. They both wore tattered jeans, ragged running shoes, and filthy sport shirts. They both had scruffy beards and long hair. Quevedo was a few years older than Donovan, but they had both been in the Homicide Division for more than three years. They looked like the bums who hung out in Bayfront Park and the Miamarina, because that was where they were working. In the last month, two sleeping bums had been doused with gasoline and set on fire, and they were trying to get a lead on the killer(s).

"I hear," Donovan said, "you're on a special assignment."

"You hear a lot of things around here," Hoke said.

Quevedo pointed to the stack of files. "Looks like a lot of cases to have out at the same time."

"It is indeed." Hoke said. "What's new on the torchings?"

"We got some leads."

"Well, don't let me keep you. I've got some reading to do and some phone calls to make." Hoke belched, and got a second, searing taste of the horseradish sauce. His stomach burned.

"We're going downstairs for coffee," Quevedo said. "Want me to bring you a cup?"

"No thanks." Hoke took the bottle of horseradish sauce out of his jacket pocket. "Here, Quevedo. You like hot stuff. This horseradish sauce is *muy sabroso*."

"You don't want it?" Quevedo said, taking the bottle.

"I've got another bottle in my car. Keep it. It goes great on hamburgers."

"Thanks. Thanks a lot."

The two detectives left. Hoke got up and shut the door. He sat at his desk again, watching the detectives as they crossed to the elevator.

The word was out already, Hoke realized. Quevedo and Donovan already knew about the cold-case assignment and were fishing around for confirmation. That meant his problems would soon multiply. Someone would notify the press, and then when the state attorney arraigned Captain Midnight, there would be reporters coming around to the division looking for details.

And what could he tell them? That the Captain Morrow collar had been merely a lucky break? That they hadn't even read through the old cases yet? It was impossible to keep anything secret in Miami; despite its huge population, Miami was like a small town where everybody knew everyone else's business. And there was too much business in the Homicide Division.

The phone rang. It was Ellita, calling from Delray Beach.

"I called Mr. Cohen again, Hoke, and he said you were going to the office. I called early because the girls are getting restless hanging around the mall here. Besides, the news is good for a change. I found Mary Rollins. She's alive and working as a waitress in Delray Beach."

"Are you sure?"

"Positive. It was fairly simple, although I had to talk to Mrs. Fridley for a long time before she would tell me where Rollins worked. It's a long story, but now that I've found Rollins—which we didn't expect—I don't know the next step. Wanda Fridley and Mary Rollins both went to Miami High together. In the same class. Mrs. Fridley married a pre-development salesman in Boca, and she's been living in Boca ever since. She just happened to run into Mary by accident at the Delray Beach café where Mary works. Mary told her not to tell anyone she was there. Apparently, Mary staged her own disappearance as a way to escape from her mother. Mary worked at an S and L in Miami, and lived at home. She had to turn over her paycheck each week to her mother, and she was a virtual prisoner. Then she met a guy in the S and L one day, and dated him. He's a married man with three children, and he lives here in Delray Beach. Mary got a raise at the S and L, but didn't tell her mother about it. She started saving her extra raise money, telling her mother the company was paying in cash now each week instead of by check. That way, her mother wouldn't know about the extra money—"

"Can you shorten this a little?"

"Not very well. Then, when Mary had two hundred dollars saved, she planted her bloody shorts and T-shirt in the pole-bean field out in Kendall, and caught a bus to Delray Beach. She thought if her mother figured she was dead, she wouldn't look for her."

"Where did the blood come from?" Hoke said.

"Most of it came from a bloody nose. When she gets excited, she said, her nose bleeds. The rest was from a cut finger. She already had a suitcase with some other clothes and things in it stashed away at the bus station in a locker. She rented a room here in Delray, got a job as a waitress, and she's been up here ever since. Her affair with the married man is still ongoing, as they say, and she gets to see him

186

once a week—sometimes twice a week. This is the story she told Mrs. Fridley, and the same one she told me. Mrs. Fridley would've kept the secret, she said, but Mary borrowed fifty dollars from her, promising to pay her back the following week. Then, when she didn't pay it back, Mrs. Fridley got mad and called Homicide and said she'd seen Mary Rollins. By the time we finally got around to sending MacGellicot up to Boca, Mary had already seen Mrs. Fridley again and paid her ten dollars on account. She was short, and could only pay her back at ten dollars a week. So then, when MacGellicot talked to Mrs. Fridley, she'd decided not to turn in her old school friend and she stalled MacGellicot. She was ashamed, she told me, for not trusting Mary to pay her back the fifty bucks. Mary lives in a ratty little room here in Delray, and she only spends an occasional afternoon in a motel with her boyfriend.

"Actually," Ellita chuckled, "Mrs. Fridley was dying to tell someone the story. Once she got started talking, it all tumbled out.

"Anyway, I drove up to Delray and found Mary. She's working at the Spotlight Café, so I got her address from the manager. I talked to her then, and I believe her. She knew, she said, that her mother was using her for support, and that she'd never have a life of her own unless she ran away. I feel sorry for her, Hoke. She's not too bright, and for a thin girl she's not bad-looking, either. But she doesn't seem to realize that this guy's using her just as much as her mother did. Eventually, she believes, after her boyfriend's children are grown, he'll divorce his wife and marry her, you see."

"But did you get a positive ID?"

"Of course. Driver's license and birth certificate. She showed me both of them. Do you want me to pick her up and bring her back down with me, or what? I hate to turn this young woman over to her mother again, although—"

Hoke laughed. "Sure. Bring her in! And then, after we

return Mary to her mother, I'll drive you home and return you to *your* mother and father.''

After a five-second silence, Ellita said, ''I guess I wasn't thinking.''

''No, you weren't. Just borrow Rollins's license and birth certificate, and we'll make Xeroxes down here and mail them back to her. Major Brownley can then call Mrs. Rollins and tell her that Mary's alive and well. That'll be the end of it. We don't have to tell Mrs. Rollins where her daughter lives. Twenty-six years old, she can live anywhere she wants. We don't have to tell her mother shit. But before you come back down here, reassure Mary that we won't give her address to her mother. Otherwise, she might stage another fake disappearance and take off again.''

''She's really afraid of the mother, Hoke. Do you want to talk to her?''

''Hell, no. Just get her address and place of employment so I can write a memo on it to Brownley. We'll attach the Xeroxes to it, and the case is closed.''

''I can give you the address now.''

Hoke wrote the information Ellita gave him on a yellow legal pad.

''You did a good job, Ellita. You know I can't give you any overtime, but if you put in a voucher for mileage up there and back, I'll sign it. Did you have lunch yet?''

''We ate at the Spotlight Café, where Mary works.''

''Okay. Add your lunch receipt to the mileage, and I'll reimburse you for lunch on the voucher, too. See you back at the hotel.''

Hoke chopped up the onion and added it to the three cans of beef stew simmering in the pot on his hot plate. He set the switch to Low-Low and sniffed the aroma. This was one of Hoke's favorite meals. The girls would enjoy it.

Ellita and the girls didn't ask for seconds, however, when they ate dinner. Hoke told them they could reheat the stew for lunch the next day. While they ate, Ellita retold the story about Mary Rollins and showed Hoke the birth certificate and driver's license.

"Has she got a new license under a new name?"

"She doesn't have a car, and she didn't change her last name. She just calls herself Candi now, with an *i* and no *e*. She's got a little nameplate on her uniform. She was pretty happy when I told her—convinced her, rather—that we wouldn't tell her mother where she was living. She showed me a photo of her boyfriend. He's about fifty, and he's got a gut out to here." Ellita made a circle with her hands to demonstrate and burst into tears.

"What's the matter, Ellita?" Sue Ellen said.

"Nothing." Ellita wiped her eyes with the back of her hand. "I've got to wash my hair." As she got up from the table to go to her room, Hoke's phone rang.

Hoke picked it up and gestured for Sue Ellen and Aileen to stay seated and not follow Ellita to her room.

"Tony Otero's down here, Sergeant Moseley." It was Eddie Cohen. "He wants to talk to your daughter Sue Ellen. Shall I send him up, or does she want to come down here?"

"Tell him to wait at the desk. I'll be right down."

Hoke hung up the phone. He told the girls to clear the card table, fold it up again, and put things away. "I'll be back in a few minutes, and then we'll have a little talk."

Tony Otero, wearing a white linen suit, white shoes, and a red silk necktie, smiled at Hoke and shook hands with him when Hoke met him in the lobby. When Tony smiled, Hoke noticed a dark line above Tony's four upper front teeth. He realized that the little boxer was wearing an upper plate. He hadn't noticed it when Bill Henderson had introduced him to the lightweight a few weeks ago.

"Let's sit over here, Tony." Hoke gripped the boxer's elbow with a thumb and two fingers and led him over to a tattered divan in the lobby, away from the desk. The divan was well separated from the old ladies watching the TV set on the wall.

Tony was looking past Hoke's shoulder, toward the elevators.

"Sue Ellen won't be coming down, Tony. What gave you the idea you could talk to my daughter?"

"I was going to ask her out to dinner. Take her out for a steak maybe."

Hoke shook his head. "How old are you, Tony?"

"Twenty-four."

"D'you know how old Sue Ellen is?"

"Seventeen, she told me."

"She's *six*teen. Just barely sixteen, hardly going on seventeen."

"Sixteen? Seventeen?" Tony shrugged. "What's the difference? I was just going to ask her out to dinner, no shit."

"Why?"

"She's a pretty girl, and I got nothing else to do tonight. I just thought that—oh, I see! You think I—" Tony laughed. "No, Sergeant, I'm not wanting to screw the girl, no shit. I'm in training, you know. I won't be able to do nothin' like that till after the fight next month. My mana-ger'd kill me, no shit."

"But after the fight you'd make your move, right?"

"After the fight, I go back to Cleveland."

"Do you know what 'propinquity' means, Tony?"

"Pro—propinquity? Sure, I'm a pro. I been fightin' five years now, man. I'm number twenty-two in *Ring* magazine, no shit. Number twenty-two."

"Not pro. Propinquity. It's a word. And what it means is close together. Two people, in propinquity, eventually get married, you see. If there's no propinquity, there's no marriage. So if you only have propinquity with someone you'd be willing to marry, you'll never make a bad marriage."

"I don't want to get married, man. I *been* married, but not married now, no shit."

"I know you don't want to get married again, Tony. That's why I can't allow any propinquity between you and Sue Ellen. Sue Ellen's only allowed to go out with a man who'd be a suitable husband for her, and no one else. Because, you see, without propinquity there can be no marriage. So inasmuch as you don't want to marry Sue Ellen, and she doesn't want to marry you, you can't take her out to dinner. Or talk to her down in the lobby here, or ever see her again. Get my meaning?"

"Well, I don't want to get married, no shit. I got a Jaguar out in the lot, man. I can always find a girl to take to dinner, no shit. Just tell her I stopped by to say hello."

Tony got to his feet, and so did Hoke.

"No, I won't tell her that, either. If I did, she might get the wrong idea, that you were trying to develop some propinquity. The best thing for you to do is to get into your Jaguar, drive away, and forget all about Sue Ellen."

Tony threw his shoulders back and looked around the shabby lobby. "This place is a dump, Sergeant Moseley, no shit. I got to get going."

"Good luck on the fight."

"I don't need no luck, no shit. I'll put that Filipino away in the third round."

Hoke held out his hand. Tony Otero ignored it and walked stiff-backed to the double doors without looking back.

Hoke took Sue Ellen and Aileen up to the roof. He took three webbed chairs off the stack and arranged them on the duckboards so that he could face the girls as he talked with them. Hoke had the view across the bay to the city, and the girls, looking past him, saw the steel elevator door. It was hot on the roof, but a damp wind from the Atlantic, gusting occasionally, made it bearable. The girls had changed back into their shorts and T-shirts. They had never been out of Florida, and they paid no attention to the heat, but Hoke was perspiring beneath the arms of his clean sport

191

shirt. His face was oily with sweat, and he cleared the perspiration off his forehead with a sweeping forefinger.

A Chalk's Airline amphibian, coming in for a landing on the water, was almost level with the roof of the hotel. As the three of them turned to watch the plane, it honked its horn three times.

"Did you hear the goose honk?" Hoke said.

The girls nodded. "I thought I did," Aileen said.

"The pilot always does that to alert the ground crew on Watson Island that it's coming in for a landing. The last time I came in from Bimini there was a nervous guy aboard. When it honked three times, he said, 'Why'd it do that?' I told him that the pilot was honking for the bridge tender to open the bridge, and the guy almost crapped his pants."

The girls giggled. "That's for boats," Sue Ellen said. "They have to blow a horn three times to get the bridges lifted."

"I guess he knew that much," Hoke said. "That's why he believed the amphibian had to do the same thing."

"Will you take us over to Bimini sometime?" Aileen said.

"Sure, but there's nothing there. It's only sixty miles and twenty minutes away by Chalk, and it's a nice place to take girls for a weekend. Just don't try to pin me down to any definite time. You know by now we have a cash-flow problem. This is all family talk, understand, just between the three of us. I don't tell my partner everything, and you're not to say anything to Ellita, either."

"What's the matter with her, Daddy?" Sue Ellen said. "Why was she crying?"

"She's got a few problems of her own, but I can't discuss Ellita's personal problems with you, either. If she wants to tell you, she will. All I can say is that she's been living at home, and now she's left home and she's going to get a place of her own somewhere. She's never lived alone before, and I guess she misses her mother." Hoke smiled, and patted Sue Ellen's left knee. "I suppose you girls miss your mother, too?"

The girls looked at each other.

"Not me," Sue Ellen said, lighting a cigarette with her disposable lighter.

"Me neither," Aileen said. "I thought I would at first, but I haven't so far."

"Maybe it hasn't caught up with you yet. Besides, Cubans aren't like us. What's that you're smoking, Sue Ellen?"

"It's a generic cigarette. That's the only kind the machine downstairs carries, and they don't taste like much of anything."

"I should've warned you about that. That's Mr. Bennett's personal machine. He stocks his own machine, you see, and at a buck and a half a pack he makes a bigger profit on generics than he would on real cigarettes. From now on, buy your cigarettes at the supermarket, you'll save fifty cents a pack."

"I've never seen Mr. Bennett, or Emilio either," Aileen said. "Everybody's always looking for Emilio, but no one ever finds him."

"Mr. Bennett gets the kind of help he pays for. But Emilio's around. You can see the evidence of his work. Didn't you notice how neatly the gravel driveway was raked this morning? That's Emilio. But Mr. Bennett only comes around late at night, when he comes around at all. Otherwise he'd be bothered by the residents complaining to him all the time. But it works out. Any time an old lady gripes to me or Mr. Cohen, we refer her to Mr. Bennett. But that's not what I wanted to talk to you about. Your mother's house in Vero Beach. What's she going to do with it? Will she sell it or rent it out?"

"She'll never sell it," Sue Ellen said. "She and Curly'll live in it when the Dodgers come back for spring training next year. She could probably rent it, but I can't see her doing that, not with all her nice things and all.''

"It was just a passing thought," Hoke said. "If Patsy would give me the house, I could try for a job on the police force up in Vero, and—"

"No, Daddy." Sue Ellen shook her curls. "Momma wouldn't give you anything. You might not believe it, but Momma doesn't like you very much. Isn't that right, Aileen?''

"She hates your guts, Daddy," Aileen said, nodding in agreement. "That's a fact.''

"I've often suspected that," Hoke said, "especially when her lawyer calls me. But it was just a thought. I'd hate to live in Vero anyway. But we're going to have to be practical. Tomorrow morning, when I go to the station, Sue Ellen, I'll take you with me. Then you can start looking for work at all the places of business closest to the police station. The cafés, shops, drugstores, dry cleaners, whatever. Go to each place in turn, but the closer to the police station you find work, the easier it'll be for both of us. That way, when you get a job, I can drop you off each morning on the way to work, and then bring you back here, or wherever we move to next Friday, when my shift is over.''

"I've never had a job before. What do I say?''

"First, you have to look nice. Wear a dress and pantyhose, and some shoes with heels—not those running shoes. Fix your hair and put on some lipstick. Then, you walk in and say, 'I'm looking for a job.' The guy or the woman who runs the place will then say, 'We don't need anybody.' What you do then is point out that they do need someone. Show them how dirty their windows are, and that they need washing. Point out the dust, and other dirty things. Then tell them that you'll clean the place up for three dollars an hour. About every third place, especially the smaller shops, is always crummy. So you'll get some work all right. A cleanup person for only three bucks an

194

hour's a bargain, so they'll hire you instead of doing it themselves. Do you have any problems with that?''

Sue Ellen frowned. "What about stuff to clean with? Should I buy some—"

"No. At only three bucks an hour, they'll have to furnish the equipment and cleaners and whatnot. All these places have brooms and rags and soap, but they're too lazy to use it. Concentrate on shoe stores. Did you girls ever use a restroom in a shoe store?''

"I asked once," Aileen said, "but they said it was for employees only.''

"You know why they said that? It's because the rest rooms in shoe stores are the dirtiest johns in the entire United States. Shoe salesmen, wearing suits and ties, think they're too good to clean up their john, so they let it go to hell. You can get two hours' work, or six bucks, for every shoe-shop john you clean. They're filthy.''

"What about me, Daddy?" Aileen said.

"Until you're sixteen, you can't get a work permit, but you can go into private enterprise. There's a good way to make some money. When I was a kid up in Riviera, I washed dogs one summer, and you can do the same. I used to get two dollars a dog, but times have changed with inflation. You can charge five bucks a dog now, and they'll pay up without a word, because people hate to wash their own dogs. We'll get you a bucket and some laundry soap from the utility room, a dozen towels or so, and you can hit up the dog owners in the apartment houses around here. No dogs are allowed in the hotel, but a lot of these old people in the apartment houses have them. So you can wash their dog, dry it off with towels, and pick up five bucks a dog. If you wash four in the morning, and four more in the afternoon, you'll make forty dollars a day.''

"If it's so easy to make forty dollars a day, why doesn't Emilio do it?" Aileen said. "You told us he worked in the hotel for nothing except his room and tips. These old people around here aren't going to tip him much—they can't even find him."

"It's hard to explain, honey"—Hoke took a breath—"but Emilio's a Cuban refugee who was raised as a Communist in Cuba. The Communists don't understand the American way of life. They don't allow free enterprise in Cuba, and their government finds everybody jobs, jobs they have to take whether they want them or not. When there are no jobs, they give them free food and a place to stay anyway. Besides, Emilio gets a check for eighty-five bucks a month from some Cuban refugee organization here in Miami Beach, just because he's a Marielito. If he started to make any money on his own, they'd stop giving him the check. He wouldn't jeopardize losing that check for anything. He was brought up to think that way in Cuba, you see. If he wanted to work and make a lot of money, he'd leave Miami and make fifteen or twenty bucks an hour in the East Texas oilfields. But you girls are WASPS, and you've got to realize that you've got to make your own way in the world. As girls, you've got two choices. Either you work, or you marry some guy who'll support you."

"I don't want to get married," Aileen said. "Ever!"

"Okay, then. You can wash dogs. Don't be disappointed at first, when you get turned down a lot. You may not get a single dog to wash. But when someone does see you washing a dog out in the yard, they'll bring theirs over to you, too. People are like that. They don't want to be the first one, you see. Later on, when we get settled in Miami, you'll get repeat business, too, a regular route. Then you can go around and wash the same dogs every month or so. But for the rest of the week, you can practice here on South Beach, and get some experience."

"What about dog bites? A lot of dogs don't like strangers."

"I used to have a muzzle I put on them first. So just wash small dogs at first. Then, after you get your first five bucks, pick up a muzzle at a pet shop. Don't wash any pit bulls, Dobermans, or Chows. Do you know what these dogs look like?"

Aileen nodded. "Curly Peterson's got two Dobermans. Twins."

"That figures. Okay, now, everything's settled. Except now I have to tell you about sex. First, though, what did your mother tell you about sex?"

"She already told us everything, Daddy," Sue Ellen said, looking at her fingernails. "You don't have to talk about sex."

"She tell you about the clap, syphilis, AIDS, herpes, shit chancres?"

"Not about AIDS," Sue Ellen admitted.

"AIDS you don't have to worry about. That comes from anal sex. If you avoid anal sex, you won't get AIDS, but the point is, I want you girls to avoid sex altogether. There'll be a lot of pressure on you down here. Miami isn't Vero Beach, you know."

"There was pressure in Vero, too," Sue Ellen said.

"I know, I know, but the young guys running around down here are different. They'll tell you anything. They'll start by asking you to feel their dong. Then the next thing you know, they'll ask you to jerk it a few times. First thing you know they'll talk you into giving them a blow job. Bang! You've got herpes or gonorrhea of the throat. So, no sex, period. Any guy who gets laid won't ask you to marry him, either. That's something else to remember. But I'm not unreasonable, Sue Ellen. If some guy wants to marry you, bring him around and I'll talk to him. You're sixteen, so you can get married with my consent, but I'll have to check the guy out first."

"How do you mean, check him out?"

"His father. I can check his father's credit rating in Dun and Bradstreet. I can check the boy's school records and find out what kind of I.Q. he has. You wouldn't want to marry a moron, would you?''

Sue Ellen giggled.

"Then there's his family. I'd have to see his family, find out if there's a dwarf or something in his family. You wouldn't want to have a baby dwarf, would you?''

"No!" Sue Ellen laughed.

"It isn't funny, Sue Ellen. Some of these guys have rap sheets, and I can check that out. Or else the guy might be married already, and be lying to you. That's why you shouldn't have sex until after you're married, you see. Because once he gets it, he won't marry you. Meanwhile, I know you girls are normal, and you'll have normal urges. That's natural. But to relieve your urges, just go into the bathroom, lock the door, and masturbate. But remember this, masturbation is a private matter. Do it alone, and not to each other, and don't ever talk about it.''

"Not even to Ellita?" Sue Ellen asked.

"Especially not to Ellita. Jesus. She's a Cuban and a Catholic. She'd be shocked if you told her about any of this stuff I'm telling you. But VD is the worst. A dose of clap'll make an old man out of you before you're thirty.''

Both girls laughed.

Hoke grinned. "That's what my old first sergeant used to tell us every payday, when I was in the army. So it won't make an old man out of you girls, but clap's harder on a woman than it is on a man because it can make you sterile. Got any questions?''

The girls looked at each other. Aileen smiled; Sue Ellen studied the tip of her cigarette. "Can I let the hair grow under my arms? Like Ellita?''

"Not yet. Wait until you're eighteen. Okay? And any questions you have, ask me, and if I don't know the answer, I'll find out for you. If you can't trust your father to give you the straight goods about sex, who else have you got? Okay, run along now. I'm going to stay up here for a while.''

198

The girls kissed him and took the elevator down. Hoke lit a cigarette and walked to the parapet. The sun was down, but the entire western sky was still a watercolor wash of red, purple, and orange. Low on the horizon, there were darker, slanting shafts of blue-black, indicating the rain that was passing through the Everglades.

All in all, Hoke thought, his little talk had gone fairly well, but he was glad it was over. He had left out a lot, but there were some things the girls weren't ready for, even though they were brighter than he had thought they were. They had made it easy for him, too, by not asking a lot of dumb questions. But he still didn't know what he was going to do about finding a decent place to live.

18

Hoke let Sue Ellen off near the county courthouse in downtown Miami and told her to meet him across the street at the Government Center Metrorail station at 5 P.M.

Ellita had left the hotel earlier that morning, and she had dropped a note on Hoke's desk at the station, explaining that she was meeting her mother at her cousin's house. Her mother had two boxes of clothing and some other things for her to pick up. She intended to be back at the station by eight-thirty, if not before. Before leaving the station, Ellita had taken all of the files to the interrogation room and aligned the three piles on the deal table. She had left the Mary Rollins file and the Xerox copies of Rollins's birth certificate and driver's license on Hoke's desk.

Hoke typed a short report about finding Rollins, made a Xerox copy of the report for Lieutenant Slater, and then took the closed file into Major Brownley's office. Brownley looked up and frowned when Hoke entered without knocking.

"The Rollins girl's alive, Willie, and living in Delray Beach. Sanchez found her yesterday. But she also promised Rollins that she wouldn't tell her mother where she was living. So now you can call Mrs. Rollins and tell her that her daughter's alive and well."

"Are you positive?"

"It's all in the report. If you don't want to call Mrs. Rollins, I'll do it."

Brownley was reading the report, and he didn't lift his head. "No, I'll call her, Hoke. It'll be a pleasure to withhold the girl's address. The mother really bugged me about her daughter."

Hoke left Brownley's office, put the Xerox copy of the report in Slater's in-box, and went down to join Bill Henderson in the interrogation room. He told Bill about Sanchez's finding Rollins. They both read silently for a half-hour. Then Ellita came in at a quarter to nine, bringing them some coffee and doughnuts she had picked up in the cafeteria.

"Everything go all right?" Hoke said.

"Much better than I expected. My mother's on my side now, and she even agreed with me that it was time I found a place of my own. Meanwhile, my furniture and the rest of my things will just have to stay there till I find an apartment. But I feel a lot better after talking to my mom."

"If you're looking for a house to rent," Henderson volunteered, "I can ask Marie to find you something. She handles a lot of rental properties in Little Havana."

"Thanks, Sergeant Henderson." Ellita shook her head. "That was my original plan, to find a place near my parents, but I think a one-bedroom apartment in a different area would be better. I don't even want to be in the same neighborhood now, and I don't want to live in Little Havana either. Talking to Mary Rollins taught me a lot about my own feelings. I know they didn't do it consciously, but my parents were taking advantage of me." She smiled at Hoke and sat at her place at the table. "What did Major Brownley say about Mary Rollins, Hoke?"

"He said he'd call her mother."

"Is that all?"

"He won't kiss you, Ellita. Willie isn't much for patting people on the head. But he's happy about it. Now that we've arrested Captain Midnight and cleared the Rollins file, he'll probably get together with Slater and give the media the info on our cold-case assignment. I've decided that none of us will talk to reporters. No matter what you tell these people, it's never enough. They'll be after us every day for progress reports. We can't say what we're working on, because it might alert someone we're checking on. So let's just say nothing at all. I'll talk to Brownley about this later and tell him that he'll have to be the spokesman—he or Slater. Slater loves to talk to reporters, as if you didn't know, and I've already told him I'll send him the same progress reports we send the major."

"So we just say 'No comment,' right?" Henderson said.

"No, not 'No comment,' just refer reporters, either on the phone or in person, to Slater."

A few minutes later Major Brownley came into the room. He puffed on his pipe, then pulled his jacket down in the back.

"Seeing as to how yesterday was Sunday, Sanchez," he said, "I don't mind authorizing four hours of overtime pay." He placed a hand on Hoke's shoulder. "Add Sunday's overtime to the voucher, Hoke, when you send it through." He left the room and closed the door.

Bill Henderson grinned at Ellita. "That's about as

close to ecstasy as Willie ever gets, Ellita. Congratulations.''

''I didn't ask for overtime,'' Ellita said.

''Don't reject it,'' Henderson said. ''You may never get it again. On this assignment, we aren't even entitled to comp time—are we, Hoke?''

''It's just us three,'' Hoke said, ''so we'll adjust our hours to what we have to do, that's all. I've got to take some time off this week for house hunting, and so does Ellita. Any time you need a few hours off, Bill, just tell me.''

Henderson tapped the file he was reading. ''I haven't run into a promising case yet. All this shit is just too old, Hoke. I really should be out there on the street with Teddy Gonzalez, working on the triple murder.''

''We haven't winnowed 'em all out yet, Bill. Out of fifty, we should get four or five—''

''We've solved two already,'' Ellita said.

''That doesn't help us,'' Henderson said. ''With two out of the way already, Brownley's gonna expect miracles now, and we may not resolve another case in the next two months.''

''In that event,'' Hoke smiled, ''consider the assignment a vacation. Slater's running Teddy around in circles out there.''

''I know.'' Henderson shook his head. ''The poor bastard. But he was happy as hell when I told him about Leroy's crap game.''

At ten-thirty, Hoke went into his office to check the distribution. He skipped through the junk, looking for the lab report on Jerry Hickey. There was no lab report, so he took the elevator to the forensic lab.

Dan Jessup, the chief technician, was lighting a cigar with a Bunsen burner. His long left arm was covered by the sleeve of a dark blue cardigan, but the right arm of the sweater dangled. The rest of the sweater was bunched up and pinned to the back of his shirt. He looked like he was either taking the sweater off or putting it on, but Hoke knew that Jessup always wore it that way because his arthritic left arm was always cold. Jessup was a bald, wiry man in his late thirties. The corners of his short mouth pointed down; it gave him a petulant expression.

"I didn't get the lab report on Hickey, Gerald," Hoke said.

"No shit."

"It was promised for today."

"Today isn't over. You'll get it through normal distribution."

"It isn't in this morning's distribution."

"Should be. I remember initialing it." Jessup went to his desk and searched through three file boxes. One was marked NOW, the second NEVER, and the third, SOME DAY. The Hickey report, together with a half-dozen others, was in the NOW box. Jessup put his glasses on and read it.

"That was good shit the kid had, Hoke. About as close to pure heroin as you'll ever see. It was only five percent procaine and thirty percent mannitol. The rest was almost pure H, with a few impurities."

"Mannitol? That's the baby laxative, isn't it?"

"You might say mannitol's also used as a baby laxative. The dealers probably use more mannitol to cut coke and heroin nowadays than they ever used for babies. Anyway, if Hickey wasn't used to shit this strong, it could've been an accidental OD."

"Dan. You know an overdose can't be proved either way."

"I know that. I'm just saying that an accidental OD was possible. I know what you can prove and what you can't. I've spent ten fucking years in this freezing lab. Did Hickey have piles?"

"I don't know. They haven't done the P.M. yet. He could have, but I don't know."

"Well," Jessup said, "if he had 'em, he had 'em bad, because the blue tinfoil wrappers you sent came from Nembutal suppositories. To get Nembutal suppositories, you need a doctor's prescription."

"Can't you buy them on the street?"

"You can buy anything on the street, Hoke. But I never heard of anyone selling hemorrhoid suppositories on the street. Have you? You can't get high on 'em. They just relieve your pain and put you to sleep, that's all."

"There are people in Miami who'd pay damned near anything for a good night's sleep."

Jessup smiled. "I wish they had 'em for arthritis. I could slip one under my arm at night. That's all I can tell you, Hoke." Jessup handed Hoke the typed report. "It don't make no never-mind anyway. If Hickey had piles, they don't bother him now."

Hoke nodded, folding the typed sheets in half. "Thanks, Dan." Hoke hesitated at the door. "You know, Dan, I can remember when we used to go out to lunch once in a while."

"Me, too, and it's my fault. It's just that I've been so damned busy lately. Why don't you call me some time? I still have to eat, and we can have lunch anywhere you want except the cafeteria."

"Okay. I'll call you. Not this week, but maybe next week."

"Good. And another thing, Hoke. A lot of my old records have been sent into storage at the warehouse on Miami Avenue. So if you're going to need any old lab reports from four or five years back, you'd better send me a memo on it soon and give me a little lead time."

"What do you mean?"

"I mean if you need any old lab reports for those cold cases you're working on."

"Sure, Dan, I'll let you know. But there's nothing I need right now."

205

Hoke left the lab and returned to the interrogation room. If Dan Jessup knows about the cold cases, he thought, everybody in the damned building must know about it by now. How, Hoke wondered, did the word get out so fast! The Morrow case, that was it. The detectives in the division had talked among themselves about that old case and put two and two together.

At eleven-thirty, Bill Henderson was called away from the interrogation room to answer a phone call. Sue Ellen came into the room a few minutes later with her thin lips compressed. She clutched her banana-shaped purse so hard her knuckles whitened.

"What's the matter, honey?" Hoke said, getting up from his chair. Ellita rose, then sat down again.

"I couldn't do it, Daddy." Sue Ellen shook her head. "I just couldn't do it. It was hard to go into any stores, and when I did they were always speaking Spanish and all, and I couldn't ask for a job. I knew I wouldn't get one anyway, and I was too scared to ask. All I did was fill in an application at the Burger King across from the downtown campus of Miami-Dade, but the manager there said he usually just employed college students part-time. He let me fill in the application, but I know he won't hire me."

"Did you eat lunch yet?"

"I'm not hungry. Are you mad at me, Daddy?"

"Of course not." Hoke patted her shoulder. "Now, didn't you take Spanish in school?"

Sue Ellen shook her head and bit her lower lip. "You couldn't take a language at my high school unless you passed an aptitude test, and I didn't pass it. Instead of a language, they gave me civics."

"It doesn't matter. Maybe it'll be better if you just help your sister wash dogs this week. We'll get you a job later, after we move next Friday."

"I'll drive Sue Ellen back to the hotel, Hoke," Ellita offered. "She can help me unload the stuff from my car. Then I'll see that the girls both have lunch before I come back."

"If you don't mind."

Bill Henderson came back to the room, and Hoke introduced him to Sue Ellen. Bill bent over and shook hands with the girl. "You've certainly got your father's eyes, but you're a lot prettier."

"Thank you," Sue Ellen said. She looked down at the floor, still on the verge of tears, and edged away.

Ellita got her purse and opened the door.

"When you get back, Ellita," Hoke said, "type up the overtime and mileage voucher and leave it on my desk. It'll take five working days to get your money, so we'd better send it in today."

Sue Ellen kissed Hoke good-bye. Hoke hugged her. "Cheer up, baby. Don't worry about it." She and Ellita left together.

"She's not a bad-looking girl, Hoke, but she shouldn't be running around downtown by herself."

"She's been looking for a job. But she's a little shy."

"School's been out for a while, Hoke. Most of the part-time jobs've been grabbed off already. That's what Marie told me."

"It won't hurt her to look. I'll find her a job later, after we move back to the city."

"I just had a call from the Dade County Stockade. Louis Dyer. He's a corrections officer now, but he used to be a Metro policeman when I knew him. Have you run across the Buford homicide in your pile? A black guy, a drifter and can collector, killed under the Overtown bypass."

Hoke shook his head as he glanced at his list. He looked at Ellita's pad. She had crossed out a Tyrone Buford; the accordion file on Buford was in her reject pile.

"Here it is." Hoke read the summary sheet on top,

frowning. "I would've rejected this one myself. Buford was a wino, and he was found on a strip of cardboard under the overpass. A dozen or more bums sleep in that area every night, and he could've been killed by anybody. Those guys fight each other every night just to have something to do. I don't see why Brownley picked this one in the first place. It isn't even a possibility."

"Probably because he was black, Hoke. He couldn't very well pick all white cases." Bill read the summary sheet, then leafed through the notes in the file. "I remember this Buford. He was an obnoxious sonofabitch. There were several complaints about him, but no arrests. He collected aluminum cans, and I remember seeing him in the old Jordan Marsh lot, before they built the parking garage at Omni. He usually worked parking lots, and he would stomp on the cans before he put them in his Hefty bag. He would tell people, when they walked through the lot, that stomping the cans gave him a headache. Then he would hit 'em up for three dollars and forty-nine cents to buy a bottle of Excedrin. When he was turned down, he cursed them out. Some people complained, but there was no point picking him up for panhandling, and no one ever swore out a complaint."

Hoke grinned. "Brownley probably liked the man's style, asking for three dollars and forty-nine cents. Some people, especially young women, would dig a rap like that and give him a dollar or so. Some of these secretaries downtown'll believe anything."

"But somebody killed him, Hoke. And Dyer said on the phone he's got a prisoner over in the stockade who wants to see a Homicide detective about Buford."

"Okay, let's go over and talk to him. We can't solve any cases sitting around here on our ass."

"I already told Dyer we'd be coming over," Henderson said, slipping into his seersucker jacket. "If Dyer didn't

208

think it was an important lead, he wouldn't have called me.

Henderson drove his car, and they decided to stop for lunch before driving to the stockade. They ate at the Tres Cubanos Café on Seventh Street, both ordering the $3.95 *Especial*, which included *café con leche* and *flan* with the *arroz con pollo* main dish.

At the Dade County Stockade they identified themselves, asked for Louis Dyer, and put their pistols and handcuffs into a metal-bound wooden box. The jailer locked the box with a padlock and took them down the hallway to a small, pastel-green interrogation room with a door of heavy wire mesh. There was a folding table, a pair of straight chairs and a coffee-can lid on the table. The brown linoleum floor was freshly waxed.

Louis Dyer, a stocky, serious man in his late forties, joined them a few minutes later. He shook hands with Henderson, who introduced him to Hoke. Dyer then handed Henderson the stockade file on an inmate named Ray Vince.

"I don't know if there's anything to this or not," Dyer said. "The guys in here are always looking for an angle, trying to make some kind of deal. Vince is pulling a single for assault, with six months suspended. But the chances are good now that he won't get the six-months suspension. He broke his wife's jaw, and her parents filed the charges when she was in the hospital. When his wife could talk again, she begged the judge to let him out. She needs the paycheck, you know. But before the judge decided what to do, Vince made another inmate eat a towel, so I don't think the judge'll release him now. He'll probably have to do the full twelve months."

"How can a man eat a towel?" Hoke said.

"He didn't eat all of it, he only ate part of it. Then when he started to choke to death, another inmate pulled the towel out and tore about half the guy's vocal cords out at the same time. He's still in the locked ward at Jackson Hospital. If he ever talks again, he'll be lucky if he can whisper.''

"What was it?" Henderson asked. "A face towel or a bath towel?"

"Bath. This guy stole Vince's towel, you see, and when Vince found out who took it, he told the guy if he wanted it so bad, he could eat it. Then he made him eat it.''

"So now Vince wants out," Hoke said, "and wants to make a deal?" Hoke opened the stockade file and read the first page.

"It's all in the file," Dyer said, "the kinda prick Vince is. If it was me, I wouldn't trust him at all. But then, it ain't up to me, is it? I guess it won't hurt to talk to him, if you're working on old cases, Bill.''

"Who told you we were working on old cases?"

"When I called Homicide and mentioned Buford, the duty officer said you were on the cold cases, and I told him I knew you, that's all. So he called you. Why, is it some kind of a secret?"

"Not anymore," Henderson said.

"We'll talk to him," Hoke said. "This case is four years old, and there're no leads at all.''

Dyer let himself out and returned a few minutes later with Ray Vince. Dyer opened the door and then locked Vince in with the two detectives. Hoke closed Vince's file and handed it to Henderson.

"Just holler when you're through." Dyer walked away.

Ray Vince was heavy set, with a soft white paunch that drooped in folds over his jail denims. His white T-shirt was immaculate, but it didn't cover his pasty, hairy midriff. His russet hair was long, combed straight back. His nose had been broken at one time and reset poorly. He stared at the detectives with flat blue eyes.

Hoke, who had glanced hurriedly through the file, had

learned that Vince was a truck driver who had made two round trips a week to Key West from Miami. He had earned about eight hundred dollars a week. No wonder his wife wanted him back. There was one previous arrest in addition to the current assault charge and conviction, though that case hadn't gone to trial. Vince had broken a hitchhiker's arm with a tire iron, but there were no witnesses, and Vince claimed that the man was trying to break into his truck. The man who had his arm broken claimed that he had merely asked Vince if he could get a ride back to Miami with him.

Hoke lit a Kool, then offered the pack to Ray Vince.

Vince shook his head. "I don't smoke."

"We're from Homicide, Vince," Henderson said. "What do you have to tell us?"

"I want outa here. I was supposed to get out next month, and now it looks like I'll have to spend six more in here. I want to make a deal of some kind."

"You shouldn't've fed the man the towel," Hoke said.

"What was I supposed to do? He shouldn't've stole it. If the guy had asked to use my towel in a nice way, I might've loaned it to him. But he stole it."

"I don't think you'd've let him use it, no matter how nicely he asked," Henderson said.

"Maybe not, but the sonofabitch stole it. Can I sit down? I was playing volleyball, and I'm a little pooped."

"Grab a chair," Hoke said. "What kind of deal do you have in mind?"

"Just tell the judge that I'm cooperative, and to give me a little consideration, that's all. My wife wants me out, and so does my boss. So I shouldn't have to pull another six months in the stockade because some sonofabitch in here's a thief. It ain't fair."

"We can't promise you anything," Henderson said. "You'll just have to tell us what you've got."

"It may not be anything, and I'll admit that. But I'm trying to be cooperative with the law. I've had some domestic problems, just like any married man, but I'm a good citizen."

"So talk," Henderson said.

"Well, the other night some guys were in the latrine drinking bang-bang, and they were all bragging to each other about how tough they were. Usually it don't mean nothing, they're just mouthing off, you know."

"Were you drinking bang-bang with 'em?" Henderson asked.

"No, I don't drink that stuff. It makes you crazy. I was just in there takin' a shit. Then this one guy, Wetzel's his name, bragged about killing a nigger in Overtown a few years back."

"What was his name, the black man's name he said he killed?"

"Wetzel was slurring his words, being pretty drunk, but it was either Burford or Buford, something like that."

"Was it the man's first name, or last name?"

"I don't know. He didn't say, but people in here ain't much on first names. They usually call a guy by his last name."

"Did he say how he killed him?" Hoke said.

"He torched him. That's what he said, but he said he took eighty dollars off him first. He might've been lyin', but Wetzel's an arson suspect, and he's in here now for carryin' a can of kerosene. He's been over in the city jail, but he was transferred over here last week because of the overcrowding order. So I figgered it all adds up. He's a firebug, he had a can of kerosene, so maybe he did torch himself a nigger a few years back."

"Thanks," Henderson said. He crossed to the wire-mesh door and called out to Dyer. "We're ready to go, Mr. Dyer."

"Is that all?" Vince said. "What about our deal? Will

you talk to the judge for me? I cooperated with you guys, didn't I?''

"Sure you did, Vince," Hoke said. "Are you sure you'll get your old job back when you get out?"

"I'd better!" Vince thrust out his jaw.

"We can't help you, Vince," Hoke said. "But there are two other Homicide detectives who can—Detectives Quevedo and Donovan. They'll be over to talk to you a little later. Just tell them what you told us, and try to remember any details. They'll take care of you. In the meantime, see what else you can find out about Wetzel. Detective Quevedo is very interested in firebugs."

"Can't you guys say something nice about me, too?"

Bill laughed. "It's hard to say something nice about a guy like you, Vince, but we'll put a note in your file."

Dyer unlocked the door. He took Vince down to the end of the corridor and turned him over to another corrections officer, who would escort him back to the yard.

Dyer rejoined Henderson and Hoke, and Hoke returned Vince's stockade file.

"He wasn't much help to us, Louis," Henderson said. "But there'll be two more Homicide detectives coming over to see him later. Quevedo and Donovan. Vince told us our man was torched to death, but Buford was killed with an icepick through the ear. The handle was still in his ear when they found him, and he wasn't burnt. But Quevedo and Donovan are looking for a firebug."

"Quevedo?" Dyer said, frowning. "I know him. He was the guy who fell in love with a painting, wasn't he?"

"That's the rumor," Bill said, "but he got over it. If I was you, I wouldn't mention it to him, though."

Bill and Hoke retrieved their pistols and handcuffs, and headed back to the station.

When they got back to the interrogation room and the files,

Hoke sent Henderson out to the bullpen to fill Quevedo and Donovan in on the information Vince had given them about Wetzel. Hoke then called the morgue from his office and asked the secretary if he could talk to Doc Evans.

"He can't come to the phone now, Sergeant Moseley," the woman told him. "He's doing a P.M. and can't be interrupted. But I can give him a message."

"Do you know if you've done the autopsy on Hickey, Gerald?"

"Let me check . . ." Hoke waited for almost two minutes before she came on the line again. "No, not yet. But they might get to him tonight. Evans is supposed to get a part-time pathologist in tonight to help out with the Descanso Hotel victims. We've been pretty busy around here."

"Okay, but just ask him to check—when he does the P.M. on Hickey—and see if the man had piles. And if so, what kind of suppositories he was using."

"You mean like Preparation H?"

"That, or whatever. Whether he had piles or not, I mean hemorrhoids."

"I've made a note. Where should he call you?"

"I don't know where I'll be yet, but tell Doc I'll call him back about this later on."

"You spell 'Moseley' with an *e*, don't you?"

"That's right. Most people leave out the second *e*. And thanks a lot."

Hoke looked at his Timex. It was only 3 P.M., but he couldn't face the idea of reading files for another hour and a half. There were times, he knew, when he could no longer look at the outside world from inside the asshole. This was one of those times. He left his office and returned to the interrogation room.

Sanchez looked up from her file and frowned. "Bill told me you'd been over to the Dade County Stockade. You should've left me a note. I didn't know where you were."

"You don't need to know everything, and we weren't gone long."

"I know that. But if someone wanted to know where you were, and I couldn't tell them, it would make you look bad. How could I cover for you?"

"All right. Next time I'll leave you a message. What else?" Jesus, Hoke thought, she's already practicing to be a mother.

"Did you sign my voucher?"

"I didn't see it."

"I put it in your in-box."

"I didn't look in my in-box. I'll sign it now, and then I'm going back to the hotel. You can put the files away, and tell Bill to go home, too. He can fill you in on what we found out at the stockade. Okay?"

"It's only a little after three." Ellita glanced at her gold watch.

"I know what time it is. I've got to go out tonight, and I don't know what to do about the girls."

"Go ahead. I'll take them out to dinner, and maybe we'll go to a movie."

"That would be very kind of you."

"Not really. That hotel depresses me as much as it does the girls. Maybe instead of a movie I should look for an apartment. I've circled some classifieds in the *Miami News*."

"Hold off on that for a while, Ellita. I've got an idea I want to talk to you about later. All right?"

Ellita shrugged. "There's no great hurry, I guess."

"Just put the stuff away and go back to the hotel, Ellita. As far as I'm concerned, it's quitting time."

Hoke signed Sanchez's voucher, placed it in Lieutenant Slater's in-box, and left the station. Hoke would need Ellita to help him with the girls, but this wasn't the right time to suggest that they share a house together.

* * *

215

Sue Ellen and Aileen were waiting for Hoke in the lobby of the Eldorado. Aileen ran to meet him when he came through the double doors, hugged him, and stood on tiptoe to kiss him on the cheek when he pulled back. She handed him seven one-dollar bills.

"I washed two dogs, Daddy," she said, looking down at the floor, "a dachshund and a little toy poodle. The lady who owned the dachshund paid me five dollars, but the man who had the poodle only gave me two. He said the job wasn't worth more than two."

"Did you tell him in advance that you charged five?"

"Yes, I did. But he only gave me two."

Hoke returned the seven dollars. "Here, put it in your purse. You earned it, and it's your money. Do you remember where this guy lives?"

"The Alton Arms." She nodded and pointed. "On Third Street."

"What's his name?"

"Mr. Lewis."

"Okay, we'll go over and talk to him."

"Can I go too?" Sue Ellen said.

"No. Ellita'll be here in a few minutes, and you can tell her we'll be back soon. Otherwise she'd worry about where you were."

Hoke and Aileen walked the three blocks to the Alton Arms, a fading pistachio-colored apartment house two stories high with a pink Spanish tile roof. There was a veranda in front, and a half-dozen residents—four old ladies and two old men—were sitting on plastic-webbed chairs and looking across the street. Their view was another two-story apartment house, with four old people sitting on webbed chairs looking back at them.

"Is that Mr. Lewis, honey?" Hoke asked. "The man with the poodle in his lap?"

"That's him. He's holding Thor. That's the dog's name."

Hoke and Aileen climbed the porch. Hoke took out his badge and ID case and showed it to the old man. Mr. Lewis, who had gray hair and a gray face, turned pink, and his arms and legs trembled.

"Police Department, Mr. Lewis," Hoke said. "I understand that you owe this little girl three dollars."

Mr. Lewis got to his feet and handed the miniature poodle to the old lady in the next chair. The tiny dog snarled at Aileen and began to bark. Mr. Lewis took out his wallet, removed three dollars, and held them out to Hoke. His fingers were trembling, and he worked his mouth in and out. Hoke shook his head and inclined it toward Aileen.

"Give it to the girl."

Mr. Lewis gave Aileen the three dollars. "I was planning to eat on that money this week," he said. "I hope you're satisfied."

"Bullshit," Hoke said. "If you can pay a hundred a week to live at the Alton, you can pay for getting your dog washed. You can also apologize to the little girl."

"I'm sorry," Mr. Lewis said. He put his wallet back into his hip pocket and retrieved Thor from the old lady. The dog stopped yapping immediately. Mr. Lewis walked to the doorway that led into the apartment house foyer. He opened the door and turned. "I'm *not* sorry! I'm *not* sorry!" he said in a high reedy voice. He then stepped swiftly through the door and into the foyer, pulling the door closed behind him.

On their way back to the Eldorado, Aileen said, "If Mr. Lewis needed that money to eat on, Daddy, I'd rather not take it. But he never told me that this morning."

"He's a liar, Aileen. Don't feel sorry for him. A miniature poodle like the one he had, if he's got the papers on it, sells for two or three hundred bucks. If he gets hungry enough, he can always sell the goddamned dog. At any rate, you've washed your last dog over here. Some of these people over here on South Beach are crazy as shithouse rats. You and Sue Ellen put on your bathing suits and we'll all go over to the beach for a swim. If we're lucky, maybe we can get an hour or so on the beach before the rain starts.''

19

H oke only had one credit card, a Visa card from an obscure bank in Chicago. He had applied for it in person when he had taken a prisoner to Chicago, and the bank never checked his abysmal credit rating. He called two different seafood restaurants before he made a reservation; he wanted to make certain that his Chicago card would be honored. The card itself was good because Hoke always paid the ten-dollar minimum charge every month. He knew it was the only credit card he was ever likely to have.

La Pescador Habañero's maître d' assured Hoke over the phone that his Visa card was acceptable. Jackets were required at La Pescador, but if Hoke didn't have a jacket, there was a suitable selection in the cloakroom, and he would be furnished with a jacket at no extra charge. Ties, of course, were not required, but if the visitor from Chicago found the evening too humid, he could have a corner table in the courtyard, where the absence of a jacket would not be noticed by the other patrons.

"Never mind," Hoke said. "We prefer the dining room, where it's air-conditioned. And I'll be wearing a leisure suit."

"Excellent!" the maître d' said. "As I understand it, leisure suits are coming back into style again."

"And I'll want a bottle of wine. Bordeaux, if you have it—"

"Any particular vintage?"

"I don't care. Just have it uncorked and breathing on the table when we get there."

That'll cost me, Hoke thought, but what the hell? He hadn't been laid in a long time . . .

Hoke had mixed feelings about having dinner with Loretta. He was horny, but he was far from confident that he would end up in Loretta's bed. Was she interested in him as a lover, or did she take him up on his invitation just because she wanted an expensive dinner? In a way, Hoke knew he was indirectly trying to buy a piece of ass, but a man could spend a lot of money on a woman and end up without so much as a good-night kiss.

This woman was sexy as hell, and physically attractive, but Hoke knew how *he* looked. He had no idea how Loretta felt about him. One thing Hoke knew for sure: Some women liked to fuck cops just because they were cops, and he hoped that Loretta was one of them. This was something he and Henderson had talked about and taken advantage of often enough in their police careers.

Women were attracted to power and money—not just to a man's looks. They were interested in a man's personality, his occupation, especially interesting occupations. How a man *looked* was way down there, about seventh on the list.

As Henderson had put it once, "Every woman wants to fuck her daddy, Hoke. A cop's got a badge and a gun, so he's an authority figure. She can't screw her daddy, so a cop's the next best thing."

Henderson's opinion was oversimplified perhaps. Still, look at Harold Hickey. He had power and confidence, *plus* good looks, or Loretta wouldn't have married him. Hickey had been on the verge of big fees when she had married him, and she had known he would make it. That's why Hoke hadn't believed Hickey when he said Loretta had been sleeping with Jerry. She was too smart to jeopardize her marriage by sleeping with a skinny, run-down junkie. It didn't make sense—unless there was something going on Hoke didn't know about.

On the other hand, Hickey took himself so seriously that he didn't recognize sarcasm when he heard it. What did the kid say when Hickey had charged the boy with screwing Loretta? "I didn't think you'd mind, Mr. Hickey." If that wasn't sarcasm, what was it? And if the fat next-door neighbor had really told Hickey about the so-called affair, how had she found out? Did she peep through the windows? She was purportedly a friend of Loretta's, but it didn't seem likely that Loretta would confide that kind of information to anyone. More likely, Ellen Koontz had merely suspected it, then reported her suspicions to Hickey as fact. And he had bought her story.

Loretta was attracted to power all right. Otherwise she wouldn't want to own her own shop—a business she could run her own way—instead of working as a designer for someone else who would have all of the problems. The problem was, Hoke didn't know Loretta well enough to make any educated guesses about her. The best thing to do, Hoke decided, was to get Loretta to talk about herself. Once he got to know her a little better, everything would work out fine.

Before Hoke left the hotel, he shifted his holstered pistol

from the small of his back, where he usually carried it, to the front. When they got to the restaurant, he would un-button his jacket so Loretta could see the butt of his revolver showing above the waistband. As Henderson once said, "Showing a woman your pistol is just like showing her your cock." Maybe so, and maybe not, Hoke thought, half-amused at Henderson's ready theories; but with a face like mine, I need every advantage I can get.

The dinner went very well, Hoke thought. The bottle of wine was only twenty-eight dollars and the bouillabaisse for two, as recommended by their waiter, only thirty. A green salad and a rice pudding with raisins were included with the dinner, and they finished their meal with two dollar-fifty espressos.

Loretta Hickey, in a low-cut white chiffon dress, looked lovely to Hoke. She was wearing a lavender orchid (Hoke had ordered it and charged it to the Eldorado's telephone) pinned to her narrow waist. Hoke had told the Vietnamese girl at the Bouquetique to hand the orchid to Mrs. Hickey when she left the shop, figuring that if he was going to order a corsage, he might as well give Loretta's shop the business. Loretta was delighted with her orchid.

"You may not believe it, Hoke," she'd said when he picked her up at her house in Green Lakes, "but it's been years and years since I've been given any flowers. People think that because I have my own shop, I can get all I want free. That may be true, but I do love flowers, and I certainly didn't expect such a lovely orchid. Even if I did pick it out myself."

"On the phone I told the girl to pick it, and to hand it to you when you left."

"Oh, no, Dotty wouldn't dare risk her taste against mine. She's a Vietnamese refugee, you know, and she's practically helpless around the shop. But she's all I can afford at the moment. What I really need is a good designer. Because I'm usually working in the back, I miss a lot of gift sales in front. Dotty Chen couldn't sell a Cuban a cup of coffee.''

Hoke grinned. ''And they drink ten cups a day.''

Three strolling guitar players came to their table in the dining room and played and sang a song. Although Hoke's Spanish was limited, he got the drift that the three singers wanted to die in combat in Cuba with their faces turned up toward the sun. He gave the player nearest him a dollar bill and they strolled off, singing lugubriously, to another table.

''The only thing worse than three Spanish guitars,'' Hoke said, ''is one violin.''

''That's right. Three are okay, but one violin sounds screechy.''

''How's business, Loretta?''

''Not all that good, lately. It should be good, but it isn't. There're too many street people on corners selling old cheap flowers, and the prices I have to pay are ridiculous. I have to sell roses for five dollars apiece, and people just won't pay that much for roses. I'll be glad when summer's over and the season starts.''

''I guess you have to borrow money before holidays?''

Loretta nodded. ''At sixteen percent. And it's always a guessing game. For Mother's Day I bought too many carnations. For some reason, no one wanted any this year, so even though I was busy for three days, I had to eat the carnations. I just barely broke even. If I could find a buyer, I sometimes think I'd sell the shop.''

''Then what would you do? It might be hard to work for someone else after you've owned your own business.''

''But I wouldn't have the headaches. A good designer, and I'm a good one, can work anywhere in the country. And people in the business know me, too. I put on design demonstrations at the last two floral conventions in Miami Beach. And I'm not so crazy about Miami that I want to stay here forever. If I wanted to, I could go to Atlanta like that!'' Loretta tried to snap her fingers, but they wouldn't.

"Why don't you, then?''

"What?'' Loretta laughed. Her face was flushed from the wine and the food. "And give up my own shop? I'd be crazy to give up my shop in Coral Gables to work in Atlanta. At least we can still walk down the street in the daytime. The last time I was in Atlanta, I was afraid to walk down Peachtree by myself at high noon.''

"Do you want an after-dinner drink, a post-prandial? A short Presidente brandy maybe?''

"We can have a drink back at the house. I've got beer and a bottle of bourbon at home.''

Hoke grinned. "Sure you don't want to go out to a disco first?''

"Please!''

Although Hoke had to pay another dollar for valet parking, and the attendant had stolen his toll change from the ashtray, he thought he got off lightly for the evening. The wine had been good, but Hoke had poured most of it for Loretta. She was feeling the effects of it, too. On the drive to her house, Loretta gripped his arm with both hands and once in a while rubbed her face against his shoulder.

When they got into the house, Hoke took off his jacket and tossed it on the couch. Loretta went into the kitchen and came back with an unopened bottle of Jack Daniel's. Black label.

"I usually don't buy bourbon,'' she said, "because no one ever drinks it. I've had a few parties here, but most people want Scotch or vodka. Miami's mostly a vodka town, isn't it?''

"Or a pot town, a coke town, and a 'lude town.''

"Do you want some pot? Being you're a policeman and all, I thought—''

"No, no pot. I'll just have a short Jack Daniel's with a little water. If I have too many drinks, I can't perform, and

224

I can feel the wine a little. I'm mostly a beer drinker, but what I want most right now is you." Hoke pulled Loretta into his arms and kissed her. She tasted like wine, and she forced her hard, hot tongue between his dentures.

Hoke unbuttoned his shirt and tossed it on top of his jacket on the couch. He unbuckled his belt in front and unclipped his holstered pistol.

Loretta looked at the picture window and the opened draperies, and laughed. "The neighbors across the street can see you. Maybe you'd better undress in the bedroom."

"I understand." Hoke grinned. "You want the neighbors to think you're after me for my money."

Loretta, carrying the bottle, led the way to the bedroom, and Hoke followed her.

Loretta switched on the bedside lamp. The unmade bed was a mess. While Hoke undressed, she swept the long-legged dolls to the floor, removed the crumpled quilt and top sheet, and pulled the flowered bottom sheet tight. Hoke plumped up the pillows, stretched out on the round bed, and clasped his hands behind his head.

Hoke's erection throbbed with anticipation. Loretta went into the bathroom; Hoke listened to the water run in the sink and thought he could hear his heartbeat above the sound of the running water. He sat on the edge of the bed and picked up the bottle of Jack Daniel's from the bedside table. He unscrewed the cap, took a mouthful of whiskey, and swished it around for a moment before he swallowed it. He took another, shorter drink and recapped the bottle. He felt fine now. Because of his dentures, he always worried a little about his breath. A man never knows for sure whether he will get laid or not, Hoke thought, even if he's married. Especially if he's married. The woman, finally, always selects the man, the time, and even the place.

Once, when Hoke had thought he had a sure thing, he had driven the woman home, locked his car, and walked to the front door, expecting to spend the night. She had unlocked her door, stepped inside, said goodnight and slammed the door right in his face. He had been astonished. The next time he took her out—and he had called her again—everything had worked out well. He asked her why she had slammed the door on their first date.

"You locked your car," she said. "And when you locked your car, so damned confident and macho, I said to myself, the hell with you, boy."

Women, sometimes, were hard to understand.

Loretta had scrubbed the makeup off her face, removed the barrettes from her hair, and brushed it out. Her thick hair was fluffy around her shining face. Her breasts were fuller than he had thought they would be, with prominent pink nipples. The triangle of pubic hair was darker than her long blonde mane.

"Should I switch off the lamp?"

"No. I like to see what I'm doing. And you've got a damned nice figure."

"Lay back," Loretta said, "the way you were before, with your hands behind your head."

Hoke stretched out again, clasping his hands behind his head. Loretta, on her knees, crawled between his spread legs and sat back slightly. She reached beneath Hoke's balls, searching for his anus with a greased forefinger. She found it and shoved her finger in.

"Don't!" Hoke said. "I don't like that."

"It got you hard, didn't it?"

"Hell, I was already hard. I've been hard all day."

Hoke reached for Loretta, but she ducked below his hands and buried her face in the hair on his stomach. She bit into it, sucked up some skin, hard, very hard, and made slobbery sounds. This is what she did to Jerry Hickey, Hoke thought. She put those hickeys on his neck the night he died.

Hoke's erection collapsed suddenly and, he thought, irrevocably.

"That'll do," Hoke said.

"What's the matter?" Loretta laughed. "Don't you like love bites? You can give me one if you want."

"Turn over."

"What?"

"I said, turn over. On your stomach."

"Why?"

"I want to put it up your ass, that's why."

"Oh, no you won't! I'll do anything else you want, but not that—"

"Why not? Haven't you ever had an anal orgasm?"

"No, and I don't want one, either. Why don't you just let me suck you off? I'm very good at it, I really am." She licked her lips and smiled. "I'll give you an around the world—"

"You can blow me next time, after I've put it up your ass.

"I can't, Hoke," she said. "I've got hemorrhoids; it would hurt too much. Hemorrhoids go with floral designing. I'm on my feet all day, every day, and I've sure got them. If you don't believe me—"

"That's okay. I believe you."

Hoke got off the bed, put on his shorts, and started toward the bathroom.

"Where're you going?"

"To the bathroom. I'll just be a minute."

Hoke closed the bathroom door and slid open the mirrored door to the medicine cabinet. There was a bottle of Dexedrine, some Bufferin, a half-dozen bars of bath-size Camay soap, dental floss, four packets of tomato-flavored Kato (potassium chloride for oral solution), a bottle of peroxide, a four-ounce bottle of iodine, seven unused Bic razors, a half-tube of family-sized, mint-flavored Close-up toothpaste, and an empty plastic bottle that had once contained Breck shampoo. On the tank top of the toilet there was an opened tube of K-Y jelly, a box of tampons, and a small leather kit of tools for taking care of finger and toenails.

Hoke rummaged around in the small plastic wastebasket beside the toilet. There were used Kleenex tissues, some honey-colored hairballs, a cardboard tube from a used toilet paper roll, and at the bottom of the basket, a tiny ball of blue tinfoil.

Hoke was perspiring heavily. The smell of Pine-Sol cleaner was strong in the room. He washed his face and hands, dried them on a dinky, delicately embroidered guest towel and concealed the ball of tinfoil in his hand as he went back into the bedroom.

"What's the matter, Hoke?" Loretta said, sitting up on the edge of the bed. "Are you sick?"

"No, I'm okay. I'm just a little nervous is all. I'll get my cigarettes from my jacket."

Hoke went into the hall, then ran to the living room. Loretta's purse was on the round coffee table in front of the couch. Hoke rummaged through the purse and found a narrow cardboard box of suppositories, each of them wrapped in blue tinfoil. There was a typed Ray's Pharmacy label on the cardboard box.

282 454 Dr. Grossman
One at bedtime. Mrs. L. Hickey.
Nembutal 200 mg. Sups/
(Renewable, but dr must be called)

Hoke put the suppositories back in the purse and took out Loretta's checkbook. He glanced at the total in the bank, and then tore a blank deposit slip from the back of the checkbook. He put the deposit slip and the ball of tinfoil into his leisure jacket pocket, then started back down the hall. He ran into Loretta at the bedroom door. She had slipped into a robe. He hoped she hadn't seen him come out of the living room.

"Are you sure you're all right, Hoke?"

"Yeah, but I could use a beer."

"Lie down. I'll get you one."

Loretta went into the kitchen, and Hoke went into her bedroom. He lit a cigarette. His hands were shaking. He pulled on his socks and was putting on his pants, when she came back into the bedroom with a red can of Tecate beer. She handed it to him.

"Look, Hoke, it's no big deal. So you lost your hard-on, and now you're embarrassed. You were too anxious, that's all."

Hoke opened the can and took a sip of beer. "This has happened to me before, Loretta, but this time I've also got a knot in my stomach. I've . . . I've had a hard week and I'm keyed up. I should've taken a nap or something this afternoon."

"Don't get dressed. Lie down. Take a nap now. In an hour or so, you'll be fine." Loretta sat on the edge of the bed and let her robe fall open. "Come on, baby. Lie down, and let me hold you. You'll fall asleep in no time."

Hoke took another sip of beer, then dropped the butt of his cigarette into the can. "No, not tonight. I just don't feel right. I'll call you tomorrow."

Hoke sat on the chaise longue and laced his shoes.

"Don't brood about this, Hoke. These things happen to men once in a while, but it doesn't mean anything. We should've taken our time and necked a little in the living room before rushing into bed. All you've got is an anxiety attack."

"I know. Next time it'll be different. But the best thing for me to do now is to go home."

Loretta went with him as he retrieved his pistol in the living room. He knew he had to kiss her good-bye at the doorway, and he managed to do it, but it was the hardest thing he had ever done. He wasn't positive—not yet—and he still couldn't prove it, but he knew in his heart that after Loretta Hickey had fucked her stepson, she had killed him herself.

He just didn't know why.

Hoke unlocked the door to his suite at 12:40 A.M. He looked in on his daughters, and they were both asleep. The girls wore short, white cotton nightgowns, and they had kicked off the sheet. Sue Ellen, sleeping with her mouth open, was on her back. Aileen was curled into a knot, hugging an eyeless teddy bear. In their sleep they looked much younger than they did when they were up and running around. With her eyes closed, Aileen didn't look too old to be sleeping with a Teddy bear. Hoke covered the girls with the sheet and left the door open to the sitting room so they would get more cool air from the chuffing air conditioner.

Hoke took the elevator down, stopping and locking the elevator at each floor as he sniffed for cooking smells and listened for the sounds of loud talk and laughter. But the hotel after midnight was like a mausoleum.

Eddie Cohen had been asleep on a couch in the lobby when Hoke first arrived, but he was awake now, playing a game of Klondike on a burn-scarred card table. Except for a standing bridge lamp beside the table, and the fluorescent lights above the desk, the lobby was dark.

"What's the matter, Eddie? Can't you sleep?"

"I slept a little. Mrs. Feistinger's on my mind."

Eddie gave up his game and gathered his cards together. He shuffled them three times and offered them to Hoke to cut. Hoke tapped the top of the deck instead of cutting them, and Eddie laid them out for a new game.

"Mrs. Feistinger didn't pick up her paper this morning, or yesterday's either," Eddie said.

"Shit. Have you seen her around?"

Eddie shook his head, looking at his cards.

230

"Did you check her room?"

"Hell, I've got enough to do around here. But I thought I'd tell you about it when you came in, and now I have."

"Have we got another one, Eddie?"

"How the hell do I know?"

"What's her room number?"

"Four-oh-four."

"Want to come up with me?"

"I can't." Eddie shook his head and put a queen of hearts on a king of spades. "I gotta stay here and answer the switchboard."

Hoke walked to the elevators.

Mrs. Feistinger was dead, all right, and she had been dead for a day or two, but the room didn't smell so bad because the air conditioning, on high, was going full blast. She was in her eighties, and almost bald. Her blue-tinted wig, complete with ringlets and Mamie Eisenhower bangs, was on a Styrofoam head on the bedside table. She was wearing a blue flannel nightgown and was covered by a sheet and a multicolored afghan. Her pale gray eyes stared sightlessly at the cracked ceiling. Her jaw was rigid; Hoke wouldn't be able to get her false teeth into her mouth without using a lot of force, so he dropped them back into the glass of water. He put the wig on her, though, knowing that she would have wanted it that way, and would have put it on herself if she had known she was going to die in her sleep.

Hoke returned to the lobby and told Eddie to call Kaplan's, the funeral parlor the Eldorado had an arrangement with. It would be a half-hour before Mr. Kaplan arrived with his hearse. While he waited for Kaplan, Hoke looked up Mrs. Feistinger's guest card and discovered that she had listed a cousin in Denver as her next-of-kin. He wrote down the Denver address for the funeral director.

Kaplan arrived with his two grown sons and sent them

upstairs on the elevator with a folding stretcher. Hoke handed him the slip of paper with the information.

"Mr. Bennett'll check out her effects, Mr. Kaplan. If she's got an insurance policy, or some money, he'll see that you're paid."

"I understand that. There's usually something. We always work it out together. Me and Mr. Bennett go back a long way."

"But in case there isn't any insurance, she's wearing a diamond ring. Don't mention it to the cousin, and if she doesn't come up with the funeral expenses, the ring will more than cover it."

"Don't worry, Mr. Moseley. I take care of everything. I notify Social Security, I get the necessary six death certificates—everything. I've had this arrangement with Mr. Bennett for several years now."

After the hearse left, Eddie brought out a bottle of Israeli slivovitz and two glasses. They drank at the desk, then Eddie poured two more shots before locking the bottle in a cabinet behind the counter.

"We saved a full day," Eddie said, "and this time no one saw the hearse. Some of them around here get very upset when someone dies. I wish everybody subscribed to the morning paper. It was almost a week that time when Arnie Weisman passed away. Nobody checked his room because somebody said he was visiting his son in Fort Lauderdale. It turned out he didn't have no son in Lauderdale or anywhere else. I still remember how his room smelled. That's why I didn't want to go up there with you tonight, Sergeant Moseley." Eddie looked down at his shot of slivovitz. "I wasn't really worried about the switchboard."

Hoke grinned. "I thought as much. I also suspect that you knew she was dead because you didn't pull the plug on her air conditioner the last couple of days. But it makes no difference to me, Eddie. Mrs. Feistinger had a long life."

"She was eighty-four, she told me once. But she probably took off a few years. Either that, or she added on a few. Sometimes the old ladies like to add on a few so you'll say they don't look that old."

"You've seen your share come and go, Eddie."

"I've seen a few all right. I'll type up a little notice and put it on the bulletin board tomorrow."

"Cheers, Eddie. For Mrs. Feistinger."

"For Mrs. Feistinger."

Hoke went into the manager's office and typed his report for Mr. Bennett, adding that he had told Mr. Kaplan to keep the old lady's ring for the funeral expenses. There were two or three deaths a month at the retirement hotel, and Mr. Bennett and Kaplan always took care of the paperwork. Deaths weren't Hoke's responsibility, but he kept a carbon of his report to cover himself.

It was after 3 A.M. before Hoke could fall asleep. On the other hand, he had thought, when he first went to bed, that he wouldn't be able to sleep at all.

20

oke awoke groggily at 6 A.M., heated water on the hot plate for instant coffee, put his teeth in, and shaved in the bathroom. He had learned already that if he didn't get to the bathroom first in the morning, the girls spent an unconscionable length of time in there. They also managed, somehow, to use every dry towel, and they consumed an unfathomable amount of toilet paper.

When Hoke was dressed, he filled two cups with strong instant coffee and walked down the corridor to Ellita's room. He banged the door twice with his knee and called out to her. Ellita, wearing her nightgown and a pink quilted robe, opened the door. She had on her large silver circle earrings; she actually does sleep in them, he thought.

"Sorry to wake you so early, but I wanted to talk to you.

"I was awake, but I didn't want to get out of bed yet." She lifted the cup in a toast. "This is exactly what I needed. Come on in."

Hoke sat in the straight chair, and Ellita sat on the edge of her unmade bed. She had turned off the air conditioner, and the odor of her Shalimar and musk was strong in the small room, but not unpleasantly so; maybe he was getting used to it.

"No use dragging it out," Hoke said, "so I'll get right to the point. We've both got a problem, but I think we can work it out together. I've been through some of this before, and you haven't, but in the next few months some strange things will happen to you. You'll start getting sick in the mornings, and later on, when the baby starts growing inside you, it'll take over your entire body. You'll get these periods of extreme lassitude, and your ti—your breasts, I mean, will hurt. You'll still be able to work okay, right up until the eighth month, but there'll be days when you'll have to force yourself to do anything. You'll also have to see a doctor at least twice a month. You'll have to give up spicy foods, and coffee, too. Then, when the baby comes, you'll either have to take an extended leave without pay, or else have someone take care of it when you go back to work."

"I know all this, Hoke. And I'm sure that my mother will—"

"Your mother'll help some, yes. But with your father's attitude, her help will be limited at best. So let me finish. What I thought was this: When I get a house in Miami, it'll be easier to get a three-bedroom than a two-bedroom, so why don't you move in with me and the girls?"

"I still have to pay the rent for my parents' house, Hoke—"

235

"I know. You told me that already. But money won't be a problem, or not so big a problem as it is now. I'll have my entire pay, now that I don't have to pay half of it for child support. And what I'm gonna do, I'm going to go to one of these credit places where they consolidate all your debts and then you pay it off at so much a month with just one payment. In a few months, we'll be in good shape financially. Sue Ellen'll be working, and you can just pay a small portion of the expenses if you want—say half the Florida Power bill, or something like that."

"I've got quite a bit of money saved, Hoke."

"You won't have to touch your savings. You'll need your money for the baby. We can drive to work together, and if we need another car during the day, we'll get one from the motor pool."

"It takes an hour to get a pool car, sometimes longer than that."

"We're partners, and we'll be together anyway. So we'll still be able to use one car most of the time. The point is, I need you as much as you need me. The girls like you, and you can help me out with them. I know you've never lived alone before, and you shouldn't be all alone while you're pregnant. And certainly not after the baby's born. The girls can watch the baby, and it'll be good for them to learn what it's like."

"It doesn't seem right to move in on you, Hoke. I love the girls, but—"

"They love you, too, Ellita. You're a role model for them. We're scheduled to go to the range next month, and I thought maybe we'd take the girls along and you could teach 'em how to shoot a pistol. I'm too impatient to teach 'em, I know."

"I don't have to move in on you to teach them how to shoot—"

"Don't say move in *on*, Ellita, say move in *with* us. We'll be like a kind of family. You can have the big bedroom, the master bedroom, all to yourself. We'll get your bedroom furniture, and that way there'll plenty of room for you and the baby when it comes."

"When *he* comes." Ellita smiled.

Hoke grinned. "He or she, it doesn't make any difference. Girls are all right, too. My girls have been spoiled by their mother, but they'll get straightened around gradually. Right now, they're still confused about things. But once they start working, they'll change their attitudes in a hurry."

"The girls are fine now, Hoke." Ellita finished her coffee. "I'm touched, Hoke, I really am. And I guess you can see how half-hearted my protests are. Last night I was just sitting here in this crummy little room, and it got to me. I kept thinking, this is the way it's gonna be from now on. Alone every night, and on long weekends, too. I'm pretty tough, you know that by now, but I'm not ready to live by myself. Not yet, anyway, even if I had a nice furnished apartment. So I don't have to think about it, Hoke. I'm ready to move when you are." Ellita got up, and Hoke hugged her awkwardly. He kissed her on the cheek, then took her cup.

"I'm glad, Ellita. We move on Friday. The girls will stay in the hotel today, and I'll give 'em lunch money. After you're dressed, come down for more coffee. There're still a few bagels left, too."

Hoke opened the door. "I'll let you tell the girls you're going to live with us. They'll be as pleased as I am."

Hoke, Bill and Ellita read their files and took notes with very little small talk until nine-thirty. Hoke was called to the phone by the duty officer. There were six cardboard boxes to be picked up at the Greyhound baggage office.

"How late are you open?" Hoke asked the clerk.

"Till six."

These boxes were the things Patsy had shipped to the girls from Vero Beach. Hoke had forgotten all about them, but he was glad they had arrived at the station. Now he had a legitimate excuse to get out of the office. Of course, he didn't need to have a reason to come and go as he pleased (after all, he was in charge), but Henderson would rather do almost anything than paperwork and usually wanted to come along.

When Hoke returned to the interrogation room, Armando Quevedo was talking to Henderson and Ellita. Quevedo had shaved off his beard and was in a light-gray polyester suit, a white shirt, and a dark-blue necktie imprinted with silver pistols. He hadn't cut his long hair, but he had tamed it with some kind of hair oil. He reminded Hoke of an M.C. at a wet T-shirt contest. For a moment, Hoke hardly recognized his fellow detective.

Quevedo flashed his teeth in a smile. "I gotta go to court today, Hoke. That's why I'm in disguise. I was just telling Sergeant Henderson here that the lead you guys gave us on Wetzel didn't pan out. As it turned out, we couldn't hold him for anything. We had to let the bastard go, and he was the only suspect we had on the torchings and the Descanso Hotel fire. He was picked up downtown by a patrolman right after the hotel fire because he was carrying a can of kerosene. But you can't charge a man with anything just because he's got a can of kerosene. Wetzel stuck to his dumb story, and he wouldn't change it."

"Did he live at the Descanso?" Hoke asked.

"No. He usually lives under a tree in Bayfront Park. Wetzel claimed he bought the can of kerosene to fill his Zippo lighter. He had a Zippo filled with kerosene, so we were stuck with his story and so was he."

"But what about Buford? Did Wetzel say anything about that?"

"When Buford was killed three years ago, Wetzel was in jail in Detroit. That checked out, so we released him.

But then we drove him up to Fort Lauderdale and dumped him in Broward Country. I think we managed to scare him enough to keep him out of Dade County, anyway. But on the hotel fire and the other torchings, we're back to square one."

"What did you think of our boy Ray Vince?" Henderson said, broadening his metal-studded smile.

"That sonofabitch is scary, isn't he? He probably heard something, or he wouldn't've come up with Buford's name. But when those guys get high on bang-bang, they're liable to say anything. A lot of squeals come out of the stockade, but this one didn't pan out, that's all."

"What exactly is bang-bang?" Ellita asked.

"It's a drink the inmates make in the stockade under the barracks. They save potato peelings from the kitchen, the syrup from canned pineapple, raisins from the canteen, and then they get some yeast and brew it up in any kind of container they can get. When it ferments there's a high alcoholic content, but I wouldn't drink it for a million bucks. You can go blind from drinking shit like that. Pardon me, Ellita."

"*Claro*, Armando! I wouldn't drink shit like that either." She smiled at Quevedo.

"Maybe you and I can go out for a drink sometime—"

Ellita shook her head. "I'll take a raincheck, Armando. I've got to lose some weight."

"I thought you said you had to go to court," Hoke said.

"You're right." Quevedo looked at his watch. "I gotta get to court."

After Quevedo left, Hoke told them that he had to pick up his daughters' baggage at the bus station and see a real-estate woman about a house.

"You want me to help you with the stuff, Hoke?" Bill said, getting up from his chair.

"No, it's just a few cardboard boxes. You'd better

stay here and take a look at the distribution. By tomorrow sometime, I'd like to have a short list of cases we can get started on—even if it's only one case we can all agree on.''

"I'm ready to start on Bill's pile now," Ellita said.

"Okay. Bill can start on yours when he's finished. I'll just have to get back to mine later."

Hoke put on his jacket and left. He drove to the Fina station a block away from the police department where he always traded and used the phone in the office while the manager filled his tank and checked under the hood. Hoke called the morgue and asked for Doc Evans.

"What made you think the Hickey kid had piles, Hoke?" Doc Evans said when he answered the phone.

"The lab report. There were some tinfoil balls in the ashtray by his bed, and they checked out as Nembutal suppositories. Nembutal can kill a man, can't it?''

"If you take enough of it, yes. But Hickey only had one, or maybe two, gobs up his ass. There was enough to put him to sleep, but it didn't kill him. He died from too much heroin, Hoke."

"Did he have piles?"

"No. He had diverticulitis, but no piles. He was a little young to have diverticulitis already, but it wasn't bad enough to bother him. About forty percent of us over forty have got diverticulitis, but most of us don't even know it. I've got it myself, but it doesn't bother me because I don't eat tomatoes, cucumbers, or anything with little seeds. You avoid little seeds, you won't have a problem."

"If Hickey didn't have piles, why would he use Nembutal suppositories?"

Doc Evans laughed. "Maybe he wanted to get high and have a good night's sleep at the same time. Nobody knows how a junkie's mind works, Hoke, but they'll try damned near anything. I can remember, a few years back, when they were all smoking banana skins. They'd bake the skins

240

in the oven, scrape off the inside, and roll cigarettes. There was no dope in the bananas at all, but they got high anyway.

"I remember that."

"If you want a nice sleepy high, Hoke, mix paregoric with some pot. Then when it dries, you've got a smoke that'll make you high and sleepy at the same time. It's a lot cheaper than heroin and Nembutal. I don't know what else to tell you, Hoke. Do you need the autopsy report right away?"

"No. Not right away."

"In that case, you'll have to wait three or four days before we can get it typed. We're a little swamped over here right now."

"That's okay. I can wait."

"Fine. Why don't we have lunch?"

"I can't today, but I'll call you. In the meantime I just have one more question, Doc. My daughter's got a strip of gold glued to her bottom teeth. The orthodonist put it on too tight, and I can't get it off. Is there some kind of solvent I can get to remove it?"

"Jesus Christ, Hoke! A solvent strong enough to dissolve gold would burn holes in her gums. When we have lunch, just bring your daughter by the morgue, and I'll take it off for you. After twenty years in pathology, I could make a fortune by repairing the iatrogenic work done here in Miami."

"What kind of work?"

"I'm busy, Hoke. Remind me, when we go to lunch, and I'll tell you more than you want to know. It's one of my pet peeves."

"Thanks, Doc. I'll call you soon."

"See that you do, or I'll call you." Doc Evans hung up.

Hoke drove to the Greyhound station, identified himself,

and picked up six cardboard boxes that he loaded into the back seat of his car. The boxes were sealed with gray plastic tape and were heavier than he had expected. Possessions. The six boxes containing his daughters' worldly possessions dissolved any lingering doubts, if he had ever had any, that their move was only temporary. There was no disputing it; Sue Ellen would be with him for two more years, and Aileen for four. At least when they were eighteen he could send them out into the world legally and get them off his hands. But in the next two and four years it was still his responsibility to prepare them in some way to earn their livings. He had never really thought about it before, but the responsibilities of fatherhood were mind-boggling or, to use the current term, seismic.

When he got to Coral Gables, Hoke found an unmetered parking space on Murcia and walked to the International Bank of Coral Gables. He showed his shield to the uniformed bank guard, a frail, white-haired man who had a long-barreled .357 magnum in a low-slung leather holster. Hoke told the old man he would like to talk to the bank officer who handled old accounts and made loans.

"That could be either Mr. Waterman or Mr. Llhosa-Garcia."

"I think I'd rather talk to Llhosa-Garcia."

"That's him back there." The guard pointed.

"Thanks. If you got a lighter gun, old-timer, your kidneys wouldn't hurt you so much at night."

"I know, I know!" The old man cackled and slapped his holster.

There were several desks behind a mahogany rail in the back of the lofty, cavernous room. There were four desks in a column of twos in front of each officer's larger desk. Four busy young women occupied the desks in front of Mr. Llhosa-Garcia's, and the loan officer was talking into a beige telephone, the same color as the blotter in his leather desk pad. The banker had thick, curly gray hair surrounding a mottled bald spot, and a narrow, carefully trimmed black mustache. His round face was sallow, and there were dark half-circles beneath his brown eyes. He was wearing a vest over his shirt and tie, but when he noticed Hoke approaching his desk, he got to his feet, took the suit jacket from the back of his chair, and slipped into it with an easy practiced motion. He indicated the customer's seat with a courteous gesture and sat down again in his well-upholstered leather chair.

"Yes, sir."

Hoke placed his badge and ID case on the blotter. Llhosa-Garcia read the ID card first and then examined the badge.

"Homicide? I've never seen one of these badges before. Is it solid gold?"

"Gold-plated. Maybe at one time, when gold was thirty-five bucks an ounce, they were solid gold, but if so it was a long time ago. I've never checked into it."

The banker nodded. "How may I help you, Sergeant Moseley?" There was no trace of accent in his voice, which surprised Hoke a little. This guy, apparently, had been in the United States a long time.

"I've got an irregular request. I want to get some information on one of your accounts." Hoke opened his wallet and took out the blank deposit slip he had removed from Loretta Hickey's checkbook. He smoothed it out and passed it across to the banker. Llhosa-Garcia read the name and address printed on the slip, frowned, and then placed the slip on the blotter so Hoke could easily pick it up again.

"I'm afraid I don't understand . . ."

"There's not much to understand. Mrs. Hickey has an account here. She's a businesswoman in the Gables, and she has been for several years. What I'm interested in are

243

any and all transactions she's made during the past few days—say, the last week.''

Llhosa-Garcia shook his head and smiled. "We don't give out information like that about our clients.''

"You do if there's a court order. I'm conducting a homicide investigation, and this information may or may not prove to be important. But I need it anyway. Sometimes, to save taxpayers' money, and in the cause of justice, we cut a few corners to expedite matters. For example, you, as a banker, have to report all cash deposits of ten thousand dollars or more to the federal government. Isn't that right?''

Llhosa-Garcia nodded. "In most cases, yes, although there are certain transfers and revolving accounts that—''

"But you don't have to report any deposits of nine thousand, nine hundred, and ninety-nine. Isn't that also correct?''

Llhosa-Garcia laughed. He sat back and clasped his hands behind his head. "Who told you that, Sergeant? This is a venerable bank. One of the founders was William Jennings Bryan, and he ran for the Presidency three times.''

"And he lost three times. You know, things have changed a good deal since Bryan hyped real estate in Coral Gables. I want—I need—to know what kind of transactions Mrs. Hickey made in the last few days. Any information you give me will be confidential, just between the two of us, and I won't contact my friend in the DEA no matter what I discover.''

"What's this homicide investigation of yours got to do with the Drug Enforcement Agency?''

"Absolutely nothing. But there's a DEA agent I know, a guy I used to ride patrol with a few years back, who would also like to know what's in Mrs. Hickey's account. That is, he would if he knew what I know about Mrs.

Hickey. But he doesn't know what I know, and I'm promising you I won't tell him. Any information you give me will be strictly between us, and no matter what comes up later, your name'll never be mentioned." Hoke pushed the deposit slip back toward the banker.

Llhosa-Garcia got up, went to the desk in front of his, and said something quietly to the young woman sitting there. She nodded and left her desk. Llhosa-Garcia sat at her desk, and Hoke came up behind him to look over his shoulder. The banker rubbed his fingers on the lapels of his suit coat for a moment and then started to key some numbers into the desktop computer terminal. Hoke had his notebook out, but green numbers appeared and disappeared on the screen so quickly there was no time to make any notes. Llhosa-Garcia logged out, the screen went blank, and they returned to the banker's desk.

"I'm not giving you anything in writing. Understand?"

Hoke nodded. "Of course not. It isn't necessary."

"She's got four hundred and eighty-two dollars in her checking account."

"That much I know is true."

"She owes the bank eighteen thousand dollars, and she hasn't paid the last two installments on her loan. But that doesn't mean anything to us, because she's been late before." He shrugged. "That's the flower business, Sergeant. It's feast or famine. But over the years, Mrs. Hickey's been a good customer, and her credit's good with us. She also rented a safe-deposit box last Wednesday, a Class C box at thirty dollars a year. There are also a few outstanding checks, but the names don't matter. If you want to look into her safe-deposit box, come back with your court order. We don't know, or care, what people put in their boxes, except in the case of the lady last year who put a bluefish in her box because she didn't like us. We had a hell of a time finding where the smell was coming from."

"Thank you. I appreciate your cooperation, Mr. Llhosa-Garcia," Hoke said.

"Don't patronize me, you slimy sonofabitch," the banker said hoarsely, lowering his voice. "I didn't tell you a fucking thing."

"Maybe not. But I've got a hunch that Mrs. Hickey will pay her overdue installments in a few days. And maybe the entire loan."

"I don't give a shit whether she pays it off or not. My salary doesn't go up or down on a little business loan like hers."

"You speak English very well, Mr. Llhosa-Garcia."

"That's because I was born in Evanston, Illinois—not Cuba, where you think. My surname helped me get this job, but it also makes me vulnerable to pricks like you, and you took advantage of me. If you told your DEA friend you suspected a Latin banker of laundering, he'd be down here interrupting our work, even though we have nothing to hide. But if you'd gone to Bruce Waterman with this crap instead of coming to me, he'd've called the Coral Gables chief of police."

"We've got a Latin quota in the Miami Police Department, too."

Hoke stood up and extended his hand. Llhosa-Garcia got to his feet to remove his jacket and draped it over the back of his chair. He ignored Hoke's hand and sat down again, without looking up, to remove some papers from his in-tray. Hoke picked up the deposit slip, put it back in his wallet, and walked out of the bank.

Two doors down from the bank, Hoke went into a shoe store. There was only one customer, a heavyset Latin woman who was trying on a pair of gold-satin pumps. The clerk who was helping her had a dozen shoe boxes scattered around him on the floor. The other clerk was sorting sales slips behind the cash register.

"I'd like to use your phone," Hoke said, showing the clerk his badge.

"Right there. On the counter."

Hoke looked up the number in his notebook and then dialed the Bouquetique. Loretta Hickey answered.

"This is Hoke, Loretta. I want to take you to lunch."

"Oh? Just like that? After the way you acted?"

"Yeah. I had a lot on my mind. The thing is, I want to talk to you, and I can't talk to you privately in your shop, not with customers coming in. Besides, you have to eat lunch anyway, and so do I."

"I don't know that I want to see you again."

"Yes, you do. But whether you want to see me again or not is irrelevant. I want to see you. Have you got your car?"

"How do you think I got to work?"

"You have your car, then."

"Of course."

"Do you know where Captain Billy's Raw Bar is, in Coconut Grove?"

"Off Bayshore Drive?"

"That's it, about two blocks north of City Hall, on the bay. Meet me there at one o'clock. I'll get there a little earlier and find us a table on the outside patio."

"What's this all about, Hoke?"

"You, me, Jerry, a cold beer, and lunch." Hoke hung up the phone.

"Thanks," Hoke said to the clerk.

The clerk, who had been listening to the call, said, "That didn't sound like police business to me."

"No shit. When was the last time you cleaned your rest room? It's filthy in there."

"What makes you say that? We got a woman comes in every Friday night."

"In that case, I'll send an inspector over next Thursday to take a look at it."

Hoke left the shop as the clerk headed for the back of the store.

21

oke parked in the Coconut Grove marina lot near the boat launch ramp and walked the block back to Captain Billy's Raw Bar. Captain Billy's had been owned and lost by eight different owners during the last ten years, but the neon sign that flashed CAPTAIN BILLY's off and on had never been changed. The sign had cost the original proprietor a good deal of money, so the name of the restaurant didn't change when the owners did. The current owner had finally made a success out of the place by enlarging the patio and having Seminole Indians construct palm-thatched chickees over more than half of the outside tables. Some patrons still preferred to sit at tables in the sun instead of beneath the roofed chickees, because they were afraid that a lizard might fall from the fronds into their conch chowder. The patio was popular with a younger crowd in the evenings. There was a small raised stage in the center of the patio, and at night a bluegrass group played until 2 A.M. At lunchtime, however, rock music was played over outside speakers, so Hoke got a table by the edge of the pier, as far away from a speaker as he could get.

Hoke sat with his back to the bay under the shade of a chickee. He was only about ten feet away from the restaurant's tame pelican, which sat on a post at the base of the short wooden pier. This pelican had squatted on this same post for more than three years, and he had lost his ability to fish because restaurant patrons fed him chunks of their leftover fish sandwiches. In the beginning of his residence, the pelican had eaten pieces of fish with the breading still on them, but now he wouldn't accept any fish unless the breading was removed. Every time Hoke came to Captain Billy's, he looked for the pelican. He was always glad to see that the bird was still there.

The short luncheon menu was printed in black ink on a polished empty coconut. Hoke's teenage waiter, wearing a T-shirt that read I EAT IT RAW AT CAPTAIN BILLY'S, sauntered over to Hoke's table.

"For now," Hoke said, "just bring me a pitcher of Michelob draft. I'm waiting for a friend, and we'll order later."

Hoke took out his notebook, glanced through it, and then listed on a blank page the points he wanted to make with Loretta Hickey. The possibility that she might not show up never entered his mind, although he had finished four of the six glasses of beer the pitcher held before she arrived at one-thirty.

Loretta was wearing a lemon-colored silk blouse and a green linen suit skirt. She carried the matching jacket over her left arm. Her dark green lizard purse matched her pumps. The purplish eye shadow she was wearing made her cornflower blue eyes seem paler, and her bare arms were very white and lightly freckled. Hoke waved to her when she came through the gate, and she crossed the gravel patio slowly, teetering slightly in her high heels.

The wooden benches to the hatch-cover tables were affixed permanently to posts driven into the ground, so Hoke just got to his feet and nodded when she reached the table.

"It's hot out here, isn't it?" she said, as she sat across from Hoke.

"A breeze comes and goes, and a beer helps."

"I'd rather have a drink, I think."

"They just serve wine and beer here."

"A white wine spritzer then."

Hoke handed her the coconut shell menu and signaled the waiter.

"What're you going to eat, Hoke?"

"The fried clam sandwich is always good, but I'm going to have a dozen oysters on the half-shell."

"Bring me a cup of the conch chowder," Loretta told the waiter.

"And bring the lady a white wine spritzer and another pitcher of beer for me."

The waiter left, and Loretta took a package of Virginia Slims out of her purse. Hoke leaned across the table and lighted her cigarette with a paper match.

"This has been a hectic morning for me," Loretta said, watching him. "That's why I'm a little late."

"That's okay. It's been hectic for me, too. I got a court order this morning and had a temporary seal put on your new lock-box at the Coral Gables International Bank."

"You what? You had my lock-box opened?"

"No, I didn't say that. I had it sealed so that no one can open it. A temporary seal, that's all. I can get the seal removed at any time, and I won't have to open it first."

"I don't understand—"

"That's why I invited you to lunch, Loretta, so I could explain some things to you. The box is sealed temporarily, and it won't be opened until after the indictment. If I do ask for an indictment, they drill it open if you won't turn over your key, and then they'll also charge you for the drilling fee."

"What's this all about, Hoke?"

"Jerry Hickey. I don't know how much money's in your lock-box, but I think it'll either be nine thousand or twenty-four thousand bucks. But you left a thousand of it on Jerry's dresser. Not a large sum for drug dealers either way, but a big score for Jerry Hickey and a woman with a small business going down the tubes. If there was more than twenty-five thousand involved, the guys Jerry ripped off might've looked for him a little harder. And if there had been much more than that, you'd have been afraid to kill Jerry."

"Kill Jerry? Me?" A hint of dampness appeared above the lipstick on her upper lip. "Jerry died from an overdose, and you know it!"

"Let me tell you what happened, Loretta." Hoke held up his hand as the waiter approached the table. The waiter brought the conch chowder and the oysters on a tray. He also gave them silverware, wrapped in paper napkins. He placed Loretta's wine spritzer in front of her. Hoke poured the last of the beer into his glass and topped it off with a head from the fresh pitcher. The waiter put the empty pitcher on his tray.

"Anything else?"

"Bring me some freshly grated horseradish," Hoke said.

"Yes, sir. I'll be right back."

Hoke squeezed lemon juice on his oysters and shook a few drops of Tabasco sauce on each oyster. Loretta sat rigidly on her bench, with her back straight and her hands in her lap. Her cigarette, forgotten in the abalone shell ashtray, sent up a thin column of smoke. Perspiration was dotting her upper lip.

The waiter returned with a saucer of horseradish and two

packets of oyster crackers in little plastic bags. Hoke put a spoonful of horseradish on each oyster.

"I'm off on some details, Loretta, but I can give you a broad outline. The missing details will come out during the investigation. Jerry was a bag man for some dealers in town. His father probably got him the job to give him something to do, or perhaps as a favor for one of his clients. Most of his clients were dealers. Jerry ripped off the dealers. I don't know what his motivation was. For all I know, you put him up to it, or suggested it. Jerry probably didn't know himself, because junkies never make long-range plans.

"Then he came to you and asked you to hide the money for him, and maybe to hide him as well. You needed this money for your business. The whole amount, I mean. You were already two payments behind in your bank loan, and you didn't know what to do about getting any more. At any rate, when Jerry trusted you with the money, you rented a lock-box and put it away, except for a thousand bucks. Then you went home and made love to Jerry that night. Or at least you tried to. When a junkie's got his fix, he's not all that interested in sex."

Hoke forked an oyster into his mouth, chewed for a moment, and then took a long swig from his glass of beer.

"But you had another little trick to get him aroused, didn't you, Loretta? Only this time you had a different variation. You slipped a Nembutal suppository into his ass along with your finger. I think he had shot up already. Then, when Jerry fell asleep, you gave him a second shot of heroin in the same punch-mark he'd made before.

"The combination killed him. Good shit, and prescription-quality Nembutal. More than enough to kill a skinny run-down junkie like Jerry Hickey."

Hoke ate another oyster and took another swig of beer.

"That's the most preposterous story I've ever heard," Loretta said.

"But it's a hell of a story, isn't it? A weird case like this one'll make the front pages, not just the local section. Harold Hickey's name'll come into it, too, so when I take it to the state attorney's office, they'll love to pry into your ex-husband's activities. This will give them the excuse they need."

"Why are you doing this to me, Hoke? What have I ever done to you?"

"I don't have to do anything at all, Loretta. What I'd like to do is something *for* you instead."

"What do you mean?"

"A proposition. What do you pay on your mortgage at Green Lakes?"

"My house, you mean? The mortgage is one sixty-eight a month, but it goes up every year when the taxes change. What's this got to do with anything? I never did anything to Jerry, and you can't prove I did."

"I don't have to *prove* anything, Loretta. I'm a detective, an investigator. I turn in my findings, and based on my report the state attorney either makes an indictment herself or turns the information over to the grand jury. The guilt or innocence is determined by a jury of your peers, and half of that jury will be Roman Catholics with very little English. But either way, the trial will get a lot of notoriety. No matter what the jury decides, by the time the trial's over, you'll be lucky if you can get a job hawking flowers at a stoplight. No matter what happens, your career as a Coral Gables businesswoman is finished."

"I'm innocent, Hoke. I've got some money in my lockbox, I'll admit that. But this was money a man in Atlanta owed me for a long time, and—"

"What's his name and address?" Hoke said, taking out his notebook. "I'd like to talk with him."

"I can't tell you that." Loretta shook her head. "He wouldn't want his name brought into this. He's a married man . . . His wife doesn't know he paid me the money back."

"Sure." Hoke put his notebook away and ate another oyster.

"You're not going through with this, are you?"

"I don't have to, no. I've got a little plan where you and Jerry can redeem yourselves. Jerry never did anything for anyone while he was alive, and you're as selfish as he was. But I've got a proposition for you. Move to Atlanta, and take that designer's job you've been offered up there. Sell your shop in the Gables for whatever you can get for it, and clear out. Stay in Atlanta for four years. During those four years I'll live in your house in Green Lakes and pay the mortgage payments of one sixty-eight a month. At the end of this exile you can have your house back, and if you save your money in Atlanta, maybe you can open a new business down here again. I don't give a shit what you do. All I want is the use of your house for four years, and I'll maintain the place."

Loretta stubbed out the butt of her smouldering cigarette. For a long moment she stared at the brown pelican on the post. "None of this makes any sense," she said at last. "Why do you want my house? If you think I've got money hidden in the walls, or anything like that, you're crazy."

"I need a house to live in for four years. It's that simple. There's nothing crazy about it."

"You have no evidence against me. Zero. If you went to the state attorney with a wild story like that, she'd laugh at you."

"I wouldn't go today. I have a few more loose ends to tie up first. That's why I only put a temporary seal on your lock-box. But when I file my report, all the gaps will be filled. Meanwhile, it'll just say in the newspapers tomorrow that you are being investigated in the alleged homicide of your stepson, Jerry Hickey. Sex, drugs . . . your Gables customers will like that, won't they? And so will the bank, when you ask for another loan.''

"What about my furniture?"

"Take it, leave it, or put it in storage. Just be out of the house by noon Friday, and I'll drop everything. I'll come by your shop tomorrow for a few minutes and bring a written agreement for a four-year lease. Then I'll take the seal off your lock-box, you can get your money, and you're off to Atlanta. Or wherever you want to go.''

"It isn't that easy to sell a business, not that quick. Not a flower shop.''

"Move into a hotel. Get an agent to handle it. But I want that house by Friday noon. That's the deadline.''

"You're a rotten sonofabitch!''

"If you don't want your conch chowder, try one of my oysters.'' Hoke refilled his beer glass.

Loretta lit another cigarette, using her own lighter. "You're getting into something a lot deeper than you realize, Hoke. Can you wait here for a while? I want to make a phone call.''

"If you're going to call a lawyer, you'd better call your ex-husband. You might ask him how he found out you were fucking Jerry.''

"Jerry told him, and it was a lie.''

"Uh-uh. Your fat friendly neighbor, Mrs. Koontz, told him. Jerry just confirmed it, that's all.''

"Ellen? I don't believe it.''

"Ask your husband when you call him.''

"I'm not calling Harold. I want you to talk to a couple of friends of mine. Will you wait?''

"Sure.''

Loretta picked up her purse and crossed the patio to the bar. She passed something to the bartender, and he put a phone on the bar. As she talked into the phone, she gestured with her left hand, making circles in the air. Hoke had a good idea about who these two men would be, but he wasn't certain. Maybe, despite what she'd said, she was just talking to Harold Hickey. Or maybe to her own lawyer. Hoke took out his pistol, set it on his lap, and covered it with a paper napkin. Loretta came back to the table and sat down.

"I don't want to move to Atlanta, Hoke. My business is going to get a lot better now, and if I had to stay away for four years before coming back, it would mean starting all over again."

"Look at it this way. If the case goes to trial, a good attorney could probably get the charge reduced to manslaughter. At most you'd get three years, and you'd be out in one. But with a dope lawyer like Harold Hickey on the stand as your chief character witness, probation would be out of the question with the tough judges we've got down here. Believe me, Loretta, four years of living well in Atlanta will be a lot better than a year in the women's prison working in the laundry."

"None of this makes any sense, Hoke. It was only a matter of time before Jerry died of an overdose or got killed by the people he was working with—"

"Just shut up about it before I change my mind."

"My friends'll be here in a minute. I want you to talk with them first. Then, if we can't work something out, you can have my house—if that's all you want."

"That's all I want."

"I'll wait—over by the gate." Loretta got up and left the table. Hoke watched her teetering walk as she crossed the gravel to the gate in the wooden fence. He drank another glass of beer. Five minutes later, two young men came into the patio. Loretta talked to them for a moment before the three of them came over and joined Hoke at the chickee. Loretta sat down, but the two men on either side of her stayed standing. Both were in their late twenties, and they both wore linen jackets, open-collared sports shirts, and lightweight slacks. The taller of the two had a

St. Christopher medal the size of a silver dollar on a gold chain around his neck, and there was a bulge under the left armpit of his white linen jacket. They were sleek and well-fed, with the expensive sculptured haircuts of TV anchormen, but Hoke wasn't deceived by their appearance. He had seen too many like them in the courtrooms, accompanied by attorneys in three-piece suits.

"Loretta here," the tallest man said, "told us that you've got something that belongs to us."

"What's that?"

"Twenty-four thousand dollars."

"Why not say twenty-five, and round it off?"

"Because she returned a thousand already." He turned sideways and pointed to the top of a brown envelope in his jacket pocket.

"Doesn't the envelope say one thousand and seventy?"

"It says that, but there's only a thousand in it. She told us you've got the other twenty-four."

Hoke looked at Loretta. She stared back at him with a determined expression, but there was a tic in her left eyelid.

"When you lose something, and somebody finds it, the finder gets to keep it," Hoke said. "If you 'found' Loretta's thousand, that's her tough luck. But you'll never find my twenty-four. I've got it, and you've lost it." Hoke put his pistol out on the table, turned on its side. Holding onto the grip, he used his free hand to cover the weapon with a paper napkin. "Your trouble is, there's no way you can ever prove I've got it."

"We've got the serial numbers written down—"

"Did you tell Jerry Hickey you had the serial numbers written down, too?"

The man said nothing, meaning he had.

"He took it anyway, didn't he?" Hoke said. "If you were dumb enough to use a junkie like Jerry as a courier, you deserve to lose the money. Write it off to experience, and forget about it. But I'm not going to forget what you two bastards look like. From now on, any time I see you— either one of you—you're going to jail."

"On what charge?" the smaller man said, lifting his chin. "You don't even know our names."

"I could bust you right now for making a disturbance in a public place, resisting arrest without violence, and for carrying a concealed weapon. Now both of you get the hell out of here! You stay, Loretta."

The two men looked at each other for a moment. Then they backed away. They walked to the gate, stopped, and looked over at the table.

"You should've warned me, Loretta," Hoke said, forcing a grin. "I'm not as convincing a liar as you are. They'll talk to you some more, your friends over there, but if you can really convince them that I've got the money, it'll be all yours, safe in your lock-box. I don't want it. Like I said, all I want is the house."

"I'm afraid of them, Hoke."

"I'm not. But you should be. When they tell their bosses what happened, they might try for some kind of retaliation against me, but I think they'll write it off instead, or cover it out of their own pocket if they have to. To you and me, it's a lot of dough, but it isn't that much to them. So do we have a deal on the house?"

Loretta stared at him, then at the two men in the distance. "I don't have any choice. That's what you're saying."

"That's right. And if you decide to leave in the morning, leave the key in your fake rock, but put it in the back yard, near the back door so I can find it. Put all the mortgage papers and stuff on the dining room table, and when you send me your new address in Atlanta, I'll see that you get a legal lease on the house."

Loretta shook her head and stood up. "I can't figure you out, Hoke."

"It's simple, really. I need the house. And I'll take good care of it for the next four years till you come back—if you decide to come back to Miami."

"I don't know what I'm going to do. Nothing worked out the way I planned."

"Nothing ever does. You'd better go. Your friends are getting impatient. Just stick to your story, whatever it is you told them, and they'll let you go. At least I hope so, for my sake. I need the house."

Loretta started to say something else, changed her mind, and turned abruptly away. She joined the two young men at the gate and they left together, one on either side of her as they headed for the parking lot.

Hoke returned his pistol to its holster. He forked another oyster, and then put it down again. His appetite was gone. His stomach burned and his throat was constricted. He was letting the woman get away with murder—and with the money she had killed for as well. But the fact was that his case against her was weak on a number of counts and probably wouldn't make it past a grand jury, despite everything he'd just made her believe. She'd be back out in no time, and laughing at him. The two slimeballs were still in town, but they would learn the true meaning of police harassment, and he knew every trick in or out of the book. Within six weeks, or two months at the most, they would leave Miami, move to Yuba City, California, and consider their new home a paradise.

Hoke didn't like himself very much. He never had, now that he thought about it. Still, a man had to take care of his family.

At least he had the house in Green Lakes.

Ellita and the girls would love living in Green Lakes, especially after staying at the Eldorado for a few days. Later on, after they got settled, he could go down to the Humane Society and pick up a puppy for the two girls. He would make them take care of the dog, too, teach them something about responsibility.

On Thursday he would send Ellita down to the water department and Florida Power to put down their deposits and to get the name changed on the service. The phone could wait; a cop always had a little priority when it came to getting a new phone. Yes, Thursday would be plenty of time for the deposits. By that time they'd be finished reading all the cases and they could start working on a few of them that were getting colder every day.

Hoke took one of his oysters, still in the shell, over to the pelican and offered it to him. The pelican turned its bill and head away, refusing the oyster. Either he doesn't like the horseradish, Hoke thought, or he doesn't like me.

Hoke paid his tab. Then he borrowed the phone at the bar, called his lawyer, and told him he was coming over to get a lease made up for his new house.

22

When Hoke got to the station on the following Monday morning, he paused to read the bulletin board before going to his office. A new promotion list was posted. Slater had been promoted to captain; Bill Henderson had made commander; and Armando Quevedo had been promoted to Sergeant, now that Henderson's sergeancy was open.

The new rank of commander was a compromise, after the city manager vetoed the colonelcies the new chief had wanted. The rank of commander was to be higher than a sergeant but lower than a lieutenant, something like a warrant officer in the army. Each division in the department had been allotted one of them. A commander would be entitled to a salute and a "Sir" from the lower ranks, but wouldn't be in command of any men or task force. His major function would be paperwork, plus taking the responsibility for property and keeping track of it, thereby relieving captains and lieutenants of these irksome chores. This would give the latter more time for supervisory duties, and allow them to get away from their desks more often.

Major Brownley would never get that eagle for his uniform now, Hoke thought, but he was happy about Henderson's promotion.

Henderson was in the little office, glowering into a Styrofoam cup of coffee.

"Good morning, sir, Commander Henderson, sir," Hoke said, throwing Henderson a salute.

"Fuck you," Henderson said. "I don't know why they picked me. You and two other guys outrank me by date-of-rank, and I didn't take any exam or ask for this promotion."

"We'll find out when we talk to Willie Brownley at ten, I suppose. But congratulations, Bill. If anyone around here deserves a promotion, you do."

"But I'm not so sure I want it. The rank doesn't make sense. Why call a man a commander if he doesn't command anybody or anything except a desk?"

"They had to call it something, I suppose. And they couldn't use warrant officer because everybody's already an officer, including the lowliest rookie on the street."

"I don't like the insignia, either. It's a silver lozenge. When I think of a lozenge, I think of a piece of candy."

"Don't look at it that way, Bill." Hoke grinned. "Just think of the extra fifty bucks a month you'll get."

"Big deal. I could make that much in one night, wearing my uniform and watching the polka dancers at the Polish-American Club."

"You still can—"

"No I can't either. A commander has too much rank for

that. But I'm going to take it because of Marie and the kids. I just talked to Marie on the phone, and she's happy as shit.''

"I'm happy for you, too, Bill, all shitting aside."

"Thanks, Hoke. But you should've got it instead of me."

"I think Brownley wants to keep me on the cold cases. But I don't know what you'll be doing. You won't stay with me and Ellita, not as a commander."

"I know that. Where's Ellita, anyway? Didn't she come in with you?"

Hoke shook his head. "She's got a doctor's appointment at ten, so she won't be here for the meeting either."

"Are you settled in yet, in the new house, I mean?"

"We're getting there. We haven't picked up Ellita's bedroom suite, but we'll get it sometime this week. But Saturday, Sue Ellen got a job at the Green Lakes Car Wash. She started this morning."

"Doing what?"

"They trade off. Part of the time she'll be vacuuming the cars before they go through the wash, then they trade places and she dries the cars with towels after they've been through it. Vacuuming is best, she said, because if she can talk the customer into a pine spray or a new car spray, she gets a fifty-cent commission. Also, all the people pool tips, and they're divided equally at the end of the day. But otherwise, she gets minimum wage."

"That's a good job for a kid. What about the little girl?"

"I don't know. I'm going to see if I can get her an afternoon paper route in the neighborhood, delivering the *Miami News*. But I want to keep her close by, in the neighborhood. Sooner or later a route'll open up. Otherwise, everything's working out fine so far."

"What do you want me to do this morning?"

"I don't know. You might just summarize all of the cases you've read so far, what your thoughts are on them.

We've picked the first five, but you won't be working on them now, so I don't know what else to tell you."

"I've done that already, but it isn't typed."

"You don't have to type it. I'm closing out the Gerald Hickey case as a probable accidental OD this morning, and we won't start on the Dr. Raybold case until I've talked to Ellita about it. Raybold's the first one on our list."

"It's got good potential, Hoke, and I'd like to work with you on it."

"Why not? You're staying in the division, no matter what else they give you to do, and you'll still be able to help with some of these cold cases."

Teddy Gonzalez knocked on the door, which was open, and then came into the office. Gonzalez was in his early twenties, with an A.B. in History from Florida International University. He had wanted to teach history, but joined the police force instead when he couldn't find a teaching job. He wore a suit and tie, and his shoes were shined, but he had a nervous habit of biting the cuticles on his fingers.

"Congratulations, Commander Henderson," Gonzalez said, smiling.

"Thanks, Teddy," Henderson said. "What's on your mind?"

"Not much of anything, right now. I just wanted to congratulate you, that's all. I followed up on that tip you gave me about Leroy's floating crap game, and it's still in operation. Leroy Mercer, who ran it all these years, has been dead for about eight months. His son Earl runs it now, but they still call it Leroy's game. I checked around at Northside, and found out that the game was held up about a month ago by three men. And those three guys who were killed could've been the holdup men. If so, they could've been found and killed for holding up the game. That sounds reasonable, although it doesn't seem likely that they'd be

265

killed for the small amount of money they took from the game.''

"How much was in the game?"

"I don't know. But according to the snitch I talked to, there was never more than five or six thousand bucks in any of those games."

"In Liberty City," Hoke said, "five thousand bucks is a hell of a lot of money. Did you talk to Earl Mercer? Question him, find out who was playing when the game was held up. Then run down each guy, and see where he was on the night of the murders."

"Earl isn't in town, and the game isn't playing right now. My snitch said he went back to Tifton, Georgia, to stay with his mother for a vacation."

"Who's your snitch?"

"The old black man who takes tickets at the Royale Theater. All they play at the Royale is kung-fu movies, and Shaft reruns. They got a double-feature Shaft movie on now, and old Bert says he hasn't been able to get around much lately because they've been so busy. Anyway, that's where the case stands. I really don't know what to do next. You got any more suggestions, Sergeant—I mean, Commander?''

"I don't know, Teddy. It seems to me you've got reasonable cause to get the chief up in Tifton to pick up Earl Mercer. At least for questioning. Then you can go up there and talk to him. What do you think, Hoke?"

"I think that Slater should turn the case over to a black detective. Nobody in Liberty City's going to tell Teddy much of anything. And hearsay isn't enough to pick up Mercer either. What did Slater tell you, Gonzalez?"

"I haven't talked to him about the crap game yet. He won't be in today, anyway. He's lecturing at the police academy."

"We've got an appointment at ten with Major Brownley," Henderson said. "I'll suggest to him that the case go to a black detective."

"I'm not trying to get out of anything," Teddy said. He put a finger in his mouth and began to chew it.

"We know that, Teddy. But you've taken it about as far as you can. Haven't you got anything else to work on?"

"A DOA on Fifth Street, but it looks like a suicide. I won't know for sure till I see the P.M."

"Work on that, then," Henderson said, "and I'll talk to either Slater or Brownley about taking you off the triple murder. If we were still working together, Teddy, if it makes you feel any better, I'd ask to get off the case myself. If Lieutenant Slater won't take you off, he ought to at least get a black detective to work with you on it."

"*Captain* Slater," Hoke said, grinning.

"That's right." Henderson smiled. "He was insufferable before. I wonder what he'll be like now with two bars."

"The same," Hoke said. "Actually, now that he finally made captain, he might mellow out a little."

"Thanks a lot," Teddy said. "And congratulations again, Sergeant Henderson. Commander." Teddy left the office, and they watched him through the glass as he crossed the squad room toward his desk.

"What do you think of Gonzalez, Bill?"

"I don't know yet. But he's got a lot of guts. It takes nerve for a white man to go down to the Royale Theater and hang around in the men's room there for a chance to talk to an old ticket-taker. I know he's armed, and all that, but I wouldn't want to hang around in there alone for very long. Jesus, look at Armando!"

Armando Quevedo was coming toward the office from the men's room. He had a short haircut, with white sidewalls, and he was wearing a brown silk suit with an opened collar shirt, and a wide grin.

Quevedo stood in the doorway and spread his arms.

267

"Congratulations, Bill," he said. "Thanks to your promotion, I finally got my three stripes."

"And a haircut," Hoke said.

"You would've got your three stripes no matter who got the commander rank," Henderson said. "So you don't have to thank me. Besides, your score was the highest on the division list."

"I know, but thanks just the same."

"If you guys haven't got anything else to do," Hoke said, "why don't you do it somewhere else. I've got work to do, and people will be coming around all morning to congratulate you."

"Come on, Bill," Quevedo said. "I'll take you down to the cafeteria and buy you a second breakfast."

"Why not?" Henderson got up from the desk. "Can I bring you anything, Hoke? Coffee?"

"No, I don't think so. Ellita fixed a pot of Cuban coffee at home this morning."

After the two detectives left, Hoke closed the Gerald Hickey case, wrote a summary memo in longhand, and then placed the file next to the typewriter on Ellita's side of the desk. "Accidental OD." The folder, thickened now with additional papers, would go into the closed files. He wouldn't have to think about it again, Hoke thought, for at least four more years. And in four more years, he'd only have another four to go until retirement. And maybe, just maybe, Loretta Hickey wouldn't come back. After a few months, or a year, when he had saved some money, he might even be able to write to her and offer to buy the damned house in Green Lakes.

At 10 A.M., Hoke and Henderson knocked on Major Brownley's door. He beckoned them in, got to his feet, and came around the desk to shake hands with Henderson.

"Congratulations, Bill."

268

"Thank you, sir," Henderson said, towering over the major.

"Sit down, sit down," Brownley said. He went behind his desk and picked up his burning cigar from the piston ashtray. "Where's Officer Sanchez?"

"She's got a doctor's appointment," Hoke said as he sat down.

"Couldn't she make it for another time?"

"Female trouble. She had to see her gynecologist."

"Oh, that's different. Well, we don't need her anyway. You can fill her in, Hoke. You probably think I'm disappointed about the colonelcies being shot down, and I am— a little. But I knew the money wasn't in the budget in the first place. Of course, the money wasn't in the budget for the commanders either, but the city manager just didn't want that much brass in the department. When he gets fired—and no manager lasts more than two or three years in Miami—the chief may get through to the next one. Anyway, even though I left the choice of the commander promotion up to Captain Slater, I approved of it because the final decision was mine. You outrank Henderson, Hoke, and I want to clear up any resentment you might have."

"I don't have any." Hoke sat back in his chair. "I'm happy doing what I'm doing, and I don't think you could find a better candidate in the division than Bill. After all, we worked together for more than three years."

"Okay, Hoke. Henderson will be Captain Slater's assistant, and Slater felt that he could work better with Bill than he could with you. It's that simple. And I agreed with him, because I think Bill can work with almost anybody."

"Slater isn't all that easy to get along with," Henderson said. "What's my job description?"

"I'm getting to that. You'll take Slater's desk out in the bullpen, and he'll take back his old office. That means that you'll have to furnish an office in Room 3 for Hoke and Sanchez. I'm leaving them on the cold cases, as a permanent assignment. So get them some filing cabinets, a type-writer, and a typing table. You can take the big double desk in there for yourself and replace it with Slater's smaller desk. You'll need the double desk because you're getting a secretary. You'll need one, because all of the paperwork in the division will go through you before you take it to Slater.''

"Will I still report directly to you, or do I report to Captain Slater?" Hoke said.

"To me. But send copies of your weekly reports to Bill here. He'll have to know what's going on. Still, I want to give you as much leeway as possible. Another thing, Bill. When you get your secretary, make an inventory of every-thing in the division, supplies and all, because you'll have to sign for all the division property."

"Jesus Christ," Henderson said. He took out a hand-kerchief and wiped his face.

"What's the matter?" Brownley said.

"That's a lot of paperwork."

"I know. That's what the rank calls for. You'll also be responsible for shift assignments, overtime, things like that. But Captain Slater'll fill you in on the specifics. It's a desk job, Bill, and you won't have to go out into the hot sun any longer. It might sound a little tough now, but you'll work into it all right. Besides, you'll have a secretary. What would you rather have, a male or a female?"

"Female. I don't want any gay secretary."

"A male secretary isn't necessarily gay, Bill. The way unemployment is in Miami right now, I could get you a male secretary with a degree in economics. The line-item pays ten thousand a year, with COLA increments every six months."

"I'd rather have a woman."

"Okay. But when you advertise the position, remember that you can't specify that you would rather have a woman. You and Slater can work out the ad. Now we haven't got

270

a written job description for you yet, but there's no hurry. None of the divisions know exactly what to do with this new rank. But I'll work on it with Captain Slater, and you can put any suggestions you have in writing and send them to me. Okay? I guess you'd better get going. You've got a lot to do.''

"Yes, sir." Henderson got up, gave the major a half-hearted salute, and left the office. Hoke stood up, too.

"Just a minute, Hoke, I want to talk to you."

Hoke sat down again, and took out his cigarettes. He lit a Kool and put the match into the major's ashtray.

"I understand," the major said, "that Officer Sanchez is living with you now."

"She's renting a room from me in my new house in Green Lakes. But that doesn't mean she's *living* with me, if that's what you're implying. I've got my two daughters with me now, and she's been a big help to me with them."

"I didn't mean to imply anything."

"Yes you did, Major, but that's your hang-up, not mine. I know you're a deacon in your church and all, but there's no rule against us living together, even if we were. We're partners, and without any regular hours, so our arrangement will work out fine."

"Maybe I'm old-fashioned, but I don't want any criticism. People like to talk, you know."

"Not as much as you think. At any rate, you'll have to talk to Ellita about this, not me. She told me already that she wanted to talk to you."

"All right. My door is always open. Tell her to come and see me. But meanwhile. I'm leaving you two on the cold cases for an indefinite period, not just the two months I originally planned. A time limit of any kind is too restricting, and sort of defeats the idea. What are you working on now?"

"The Dr. Raybold homicide. It's four years old, but it's our best bet. He was shot in his driveway at six-fifteen in the morning. We know the approximate time because the man on the paper route discovered the body when he threw the paper on the lawn, and the body was still warm. But nobody saw the shooting. Mrs. Raybold was still asleep, and didn't hear the shots. There were two of them, one in the head, and one through the heart. There were no clues at all, but six months later Mrs. Raybold married Dr. Sorenson, who was Raybold's partner in the clinic. This was a professional hit, and whoever did it probably knew that Raybold had an operation scheduled at St. Mary's Hospital at 7 A.M.. He wasn't robbed, for example—"

"So you think Dr. Sorenson and Mrs. Raybold wrote the prescription?"

"Yeah, but there's more to it than that. If you want, I'll get the file and we'll go over it, but right now all I can say is that it's promising. There's nothing definite yet."

"Never mind. You know what you're doing. Just keep me up to date in the weekly reports. I'm not looking for any miracles. You've done a hell of a job so far, and the best thing I can do for you is stay out of your hair."

"Yes, sir." Hoke stood up. "Is there anything else, Major?"

"No—yes. You know Henderson better than I do. He didn't seem very enthusiastic about his promotion."

"He's happy enough, Willie. It's just a lot to absorb all at once, that's all. But no one would be thrilled, knowing he had to work with Captain Slater every day."

"Maybe that's it." Brownley stood up. "Thanks for coming in, Hoke."

"Yes, sir." Hoke went back out to his office and opened the drawers to his desk. Now that he had to move, he decided to clean out all the accumulated junk first and throw it away before toting the rest of his things down to the interrogation room. Henderson, with all of the work he had to do, would be needing the big desk right away . . .

The phone rang a few minutes after eleven. Ellita Sanchez was on the phone. "I called earlier, Hoke, but I guess you were still in with Major Brownley. I just left the doctor's office. I got there at nine forty-five, but I didn't get in to see the doctor till ten-thirty. But the nurse took my urine specimen at ten, so I didn't have to hold the jar in my lap."

"What did the doctor say?"

"I'm fine. No problems. I don't have to see him again for six weeks."

"Good. You can come in then, and help on the move. We're moving permanently into Room 3. Tonight we'll take the girls out to dinner and celebrate."

"Celebrate what? Moving out of the office?"

"No. Bill Henderson got promoted. He made commander, the new rank the paper mentioned yesterday. Remember?"

"Bill made it? How come he got it instead of you?"

"Dumb luck. That's why we're celebrating. It could have been me."

About the Author

Charles Willeford's novels include MIAMI BLUES, COCKFIGHTER, and THE BURNT ORANGE HERESEY. He reviews mystery and suspense novels for *The Miami Herald*. He lives in South Miami, Florida.